THE DEAD
CIRCLE

KEITH VARNEY

2nd Edition (2.1)

PAPERBACK
ISBN: 0996606416
ISBN 13: 978-0-9966064-1-7

E-BOOK
ISBN: 0996606408
ISBN 13: 978-0-966064-0-0

www.thedeadcircle.com

THE DEAD CIRCLE SERIES

To Jillian

THE DEAD CIRCLE REVIEWS

"Keith Varney had me hooked from the prologue —
I knew immediately that The Dead Circle would be a
book that I would have a hard time putting down...
the setting of post-apocalyptic Detroit city was very
well thought out and bone-chilling."

ChasingMyExtraordinary.com

"I found the story to be highly engaging. Varney
painted a truly horrifying picture of the world post-
apocalypse... As for the peculiar illness which seemed
to strike without prejudice, it was fatally horrible. It
was impossible to tear away from the image in my
mind... I can absolutely visualize this book as a movie!
Would I go see it? Definitely, but only if my husband
sat beside me holding my hand the whole time (and if
I had a blanket to cover my face during the scary
parts.)"

SavingsInSeconds.com

"Very well written, and very well told! I really felt like
I was in the story with Chris and Sarah - I found
myself rooting for them; mad at them when they
made some stupid decisions; and really loving that
through all the hard stuff, you could tell how much
they truly loved each other! I love a good love story,
and setting it right in the middle of a zombie
apocalypse takes some major talent!"

APageToTurn.net

"This story starts out so innocently. Then something happens that knocks you back on your heels. From then on, you are in Chris and Sarah's shoes. You struggle with them, you strategize with them. You run with them. Will you die with them? This is one I'd recommend to those who enjoy an apocalyptic thriller with a new spin on zombies. And to those who like suspense with a touch of horror. Like a pressure cooker, the suspense builds, the danger builds, your connection with the characters builds. "

FUOnlyKnew.com

"This book is a cross genre thriller. The survival aspect will appeal to fans of Weir's The Martian. All the while the scary themes will appeal to horror and zombie aficionados! Really this book was an instant hit for me. The only slight problem is that the second in this series isn't written yet and I have to wait!"

EmilyReadsEverything.com

"I've read many zombie books, but I've never read one quite like this!! It was amazing...What can I say to do this story justice?... It's an incredibly unique and entertaining read and one I devoured. The author grabs you from the very start and takes you on one heck of journey. The idea behind the "zombies" was brilliant. I loved that he took an old idea and made it his own! The whole plot was fast paced and gripping...I absolutely loved everything about this book...I guarantee that once you start, you won't be able to stop. It's amazing!"

BookLoversLife.com

"This was one of the most fascinating books that I have read in 2015. The author Keith Varney really keeps the reader on their toes in this one!... this book was one that delights the zombie reader or lover for sure because it knocked me off my socks... I recommend this book to those that love meaning behind a story, because this author really gives you the background of the characters which fulfills his duty as one that writes with clarity. I can only rate this FIVE STARS because it is ONE OF THE BEST available! GET WITH THIS ONE GUYS, you can NOT GO WRONG in this choice!"

OgitchidaBookBlog.com

"Wow! This is the kind of horror story that once you start reading it, you cannot stop until you get to the end. You have to know what happens to the people in it."

3PartnersinShopping.com

"Of all of the books that I've read about supernatural post-apocalyptic infestations, this book serves as the most practical guide to how my spouse and I could survive the apocalypse. And perhaps that's what makes it the most disturbing zombie selection: it could possibly be re-categorized amidst "non-fiction" or "survival guides" sometime in the future... *The Dead Circle* is gruesome, quirky, familiar, and terrifying. Don't eat while reading. That's all I'm saying. Probably avoid drinking as well."

Brennan Book Blog

CONTENTS

ACKNOWLEDGMENTS

This book would not have been possible without the support and guidance of my wife, my family and my friends who took the time to help me create this. Thanks to Julie Oliverio who first made me believe that writing a novel was possible. To Melissa Teitel, Derek Roland & West Hyler for their terrific feedback and being my greatest cheerleaders. To Scott, for helping me put just a touch of science in my science fiction. To Elise Fields and Midtown Detroit Inc for being so generous in giving me so much information on the history and the hope of the great city of Detroit. To Rachael Derello for her generosity and valuable perspective. To Karen Greco, author of the terrific Hell's Belle series, for all of her sage publishing advice. To Stephen King for teaching the world that there is great joy in writing, reading and getting the crap scared out of us.

And most importantly, to my wife Jillian who devoted an incredible amount of time and talent to edit this book. With charm, kindness and patience, she consistently pushed me to aim higher than my own expectations. If any of the writing is successful, it is so because of her wisdom and guidance. Anything that sucks is entirely mine. Thanks wife.

.

PROLOGUE

"When it bites, don't jerk too hard. You want to set the hook, but if you pull it too fast, it might rip out."

"Out of its mouth? Like through its lip?"

Adam's forehead crinkles as he thinks. There's no emotion to the question, just consideration.

Phil feels like he should enjoy watching his son parse through new ideas. To a six-year-old, everything is completely fresh and deserves to be thought through—but for Phil, watching his son's mind work has become a queasy experience.

"Wow. I bet it hurts a lot. That's awesome!"

Phil winces. There is a certain glee in Adam's voice that makes his stomach churn a little. *Uh oh*. He and Melissa had whispered about this a few times late at night after Adam fell asleep. They didn't want to put a name to it because then it would be real, or at least feel

1

more real. They told each other that "Sometimes it takes a while for a child's compassion to kick in?" or "that kids are selfish by nature and don't always think of the experiences of others." Their talks are always peppered with nervous laughter and not-so-funny jokes. They strain to keep the topic light, hypothetical. Without really noticing that they are doing it, they find themselves nervously fiddling with their glasses or tying and untying their shoelaces over and over. It's an elaborate subconscious trick to avoid eye contact. They are lying to each other and they both know it.

"Well, it's sad that the fish is in pain Adam... Even if we want to catch dinner, we don't want anything to suffer right?"

"Why not?"

Already regretting the decision to take his son fishing, Phil feels himself starting to sweat.

"Well-"

"So fishes breathe water right?"

"Yeah they do..." *Oh God where is he going with this?* "It's kind of the opposite of us. They breathe water and we breathe air."

He's not sure what Adam is getting at, but a venomous light behind the boy's eyes sends a chill down Phil's spine. *Oh Jesus no.* He is sickened by a sudden bolt of grim insight. For the first time, he realizes that what scares him about his son is not just his lack of compassion. It is much worse. He can't squelch the stomach-clenching thought that Adam takes some sort of cancerous enjoyment in the suffering of others, a perverse sort of glee. Nauseated by the idea,

Phil quickly attaches a mental question mark to the end of it, but deep down he knows the punctuation is authored by denial.

"So when a fish is in the air, it's like when we're in the water? It has to hold its breath?"

"Uhh... yeah. If we stayed under water too long, we'd run out of air and drown. In the air the fish would drown too... or I guess suffocate."

"Neat! I can't wait to catch one and see how long it takes for it to—" he sounds out the word carefully, adding it to his vocabulary "...suff-o-cate!"

Jesus. I'm literally raising Dexter.

"Adam, why would you want to do that? The fish would be in pain... It would be really scared and..." Phil didn't know what to say, especially when he remembered that going fishing was *his* idea.

"I want to experiment, Daddy." His words come out calmly, almost nonchalant. "If... if I look at the fishes' face really really closely, can I tell when it dies?"

What the fuck am I supposed to do with that? He sighs. *It's time Mel and I stop kidding ourselves. What did we do wrong?* He resolves to purchase the book on childhood psychopathy that he keeps glancing at in the bookstore but can't bring himself to pick up. *I mean, how could I even take that to the counter? What will the checkout person think? I'd rather buy porn!*

Fishing was a terrible mistake. Why didn't I think this through? I'm taking my son—who I'm afraid is a budding serial killer—to go kill things? I'm such an idiot. Maybe I was hoping that he'd find some compassion when faced with a real living creature. Keep enjoying your denial bucko. Here he is grinning like a maniac with some sort of mental murder-boner.

Phil's conversation with himself is interrupted by a rumbling sound from above. It's surprising. He's used to hearing all sorts of noises in the distance or behind him, but he very rarely hears an unexplained noise directly over his head. *A jet? Or was it the sound of another boat's engine being reflected off the water?*

He looks up.

Something is flying towards them, plummeting almost straight down. At first it's just a tiny speck, only noticeable because it's in motion, but it grows quickly, falling toward the earth at terminal velocity.

Phil's final thought is a memory of playing outfield on his high school baseball team. He remembers the image of a ball streaking out of the sky headed toward his prized leather glove. He had carefully inscribed the twelve-inch Rawlings with his jersey number. He was number 11 just like his hero, another Phil who played for the New York Giants. As a kid from Detroit, he was supposed to like the Lions, but they were terrible back then. So, Phil adopted the team from New York because he had the same name as their quarterback. It didn't matter that he played baseball, not football—or that most of his friends told him that Phil from New York sucked ass—he was number 11 and proud of it.

But the object flying toward him is no baseball. In the time taken by a single movie frame, he sees the craggy black exterior of the meteor. Even after breaking through the atmosphere and burning down to the size of a grapefruit, its surface is still uneven and rough, like volcanic rock. In that fraction of a second, Phil feels a powerful wave of searing heat preceding the meteor. It blows the baseball cap off his head. The hat never gets far–there isn't enough time for it to even begin to fall—before the meteor hits the surface.

The impact causes the small boat—and its passengers—to explode. Pieces of each fly into the air in an unnatural rainfall of debris. The heat from the meteor is so intense that the water instantaneously boils on contact, causing curtains of steam to rise from the surface. Slowing rapidly as it crashes its way through forty feet of cool water, the meteor eventually slams into the bottom of the lake with a leaden thud.

The crater created by the impact is quickly obscured by a large cloud of silt and seaweed. Bubbles fight their way out of the murky darkness on a journey to the surface. They dance with each other as they pass through sinking bits of boat and gear. They twirl through the fingers of a small solitary hand as it makes its way down to the bottom. A fishing rod, a shoe, a human leg, the bubbles don't make distinctions about what they are passing through, they have only one objective: to recombine with the air.

In the crater, muddy water frantically boils around the rock. Soon, a red liquid starts to leak from several jagged cracks. Similar to blood streaming out of a shark bite, the liquid puffs into the water like red smoke. It churns in the boiling deep, then slowly dissipates into the great lake system.

On the surface, more steam rises through the floating wreckage. It ascends over the trees ringing the shoreline and is flicked to and fro in the lazy air currents circling the lake. It eventually disperses into the clouds that hang over Lake St. Clair and the city that hugs its border.

The city of Detroit.

***

Shirley Thompson hates hipsters. She knows this is a liability as the owner of a small homemade ice cream shop on Clifford Street, but she can't help it. Most of her clientele are either office drones working in the towers or yuppie hipsters renovating lofts into Bikram Yoga studios or folk art galleries. Most of her customers assume that she is also a transplant from Los Angeles or New York taking advantage of the cheap real estate in Detroit, but she's not. She was born just a few blocks away and has stayed there her whole life. In the last ten years, her neighborhood has been beset with, as she would put it: 'entitled, put-it-all-on-Daddy's-credit-card, too-cool-for-school, pretentious douchebags.' She has to restrain herself from constantly rolling her eyes at their mustaches twisted into points with organic beeswax, and their $300 vintage sneakers. She's annoyed by their condescending belief that they are 'saving the poor pathetic city' and that the locals should be grateful for everything they do despite the fact that all they've succeeded in accomplishing is raising all of the rents and pushing the locals out of their own neighborhoods.

What really drives her insane is that they assume she is one of them because of her quirky retro style. Her shop looks like it sprung out of a Rockwell painting, with chrome barstools and red and white checkered table cloths. Despite being born in 1983, she dresses like a 1940's pinup—like her beloved grandmother had—with dark red lipstick matching her blazing red hair, usually offset by a dark green or purple pencil skirt or vintage swing dress.

Shirley believes what separates her from the hipsters—beyond the fact that they have *positive* balances in their bank accounts—is that she actually likes her sense of style. There is nothing ironic about her big earrings and thick black-rimmed glasses, she just likes how they look.

The more she interacts with the hipster transplants that seem to be infesting every corner of downtown, the more she is convinced that they actually have condescending disdain for everything. That everything they claim to enjoy—be it public knitting or vinyl records or even their politics and philosophy—they seem to be subtly mocking. To her, it feels like they have to keep one layer of ironic distance between themselves and rest of the world. It's as if they never really got over being teased in middle school for being too passionate about whatever they liked—because nothing was lamer than *caring* about stuff. Now they can't seem to commit, or admit, to actually un-ironically giving a shit about anything.

Shirley gives a shit—specifically about ice cream. When she was little, her parents were rarely home, both working multiple low-wage jobs to support Shirley and her three sisters. That left most of the parenting duties to her grandmother who lived in their tiny attic. The family didn't have money for a lot of toys or activities, but her grandmother found ways to scrape together a couple bucks at a time—usually collecting cans or selling the vegetables she grew in their backyard—to buy ingredients for homemade ice cream. Then she would collect Shirley and her sisters and they would all make it together. They put the cream, vanilla extract and sugar into a mixing bowl set in a bucket of ice and rock salt. Then they would take turns stirring it over and over for an hour until it hardened. After tasting true homemade ice cream—the kind that had four ingredients and none with more than two syllables—she was never able to eat the big brand stuff they sold at the corner store. It was magical, both for the desert and for the time she got to spend snuggled up against her grandmother's soft arms as she poured in the cream. As the years went by, one by one, her sisters found makeup, sports or boys more interesting, but Shirley never stopped making the perfect vanilla with her grandmother. When her grandmother died, Shirley knew what she wanted to do for a living. She wanted to make her grandmother's perfect four-ingredient—"five if you want chocolate or strawberry!"—ice cream in a tiny shop modeled after their little kitchen.

It took her fifteen years of working overtime at dead-end jobs to cobble together enough money to rent her little store, but she knew her grandmother would have been proud of her. She was not interested in expanding and creating an empire, or even in trying to compete with the 68 flavors at Friendly's. If she could sell one more waffle cone a day than she needed to pay her rent, she would be happy for the rest of her life.

Shirley arrives at her shop, Scoops, at five o'clock in the morning. It's a tiny space, only twelve feet wide, with a counter separating the entrance from her freezer and the three large ice cream machines she had rescued and restored from a scrap yard—she reluctantly had to give up stirring by hand. She sets them up with ingredients for the only three flavors she offers: chocolate, vanilla and strawberry. As the machines whirl behind her, she gets the toppings ready and prepares to make fresh whipped cream and homemade waffle cones.

It's a lot of work for one person, but she can't afford to pay any employees yet. When she opens the doors at eleven o'clock, just in time for the office buildings to start emptying for lunch, she's already exhausted. Shirley has just taken one last thin waffle out of the press to roll it expertly into a cone shape to cool and harden, when the door chimes and in walks the hipsterest hipster she has ever seen.

"Whoa, this place is amazeballs. It looks like my grandma's kitchen wallpaper took Molly."

"Oh, thanks! It was actually inspired by *my* grandmother."

"It's so brilliantly tacky and pathetic. It's like a John Waters set! Is this some sort of ironic pop-up restaurant?"

"Um... It's not ironic at all."

The guy is in his twenties and sports a mustache and thick glasses under a trucker hat. His corduroy pants have been cut off above the knees, perhaps to show off his orange tube socks. She watches as he ostentatiously keeps shifting a pack of American Spirit cigarettes from hand to hand. *As if to dare me to tell him they're going*

to kill him so he can point out that they are 'organic,'
she thinks.

"Do you have any dairy-free Thai basil bacon
flavor?"

"Uh... no? Sorry?"

"Oh, you totes should get some. I read about it on a
blog. It's apparently disgusting, but in an awesome
way."

*Didn't people stop saying 'totes' years ago? Or has he
already appropriated it ironically?*

"I see. What I have is-"

"How about anything with kale?"

"Well, I have vanilla, chocolate and strawberry."

The man considers this for a moment. *He is literally
twirling his mustache. Does he think he's in a movie?*

"Oh, wow. Are you sure this place isn't a joke?"

"Nope. Just selling ice cream. Do you want to try
some? It's made fresh this morning, right here in the
shop."

"The locals can't handle anything complicated huh?
Not ready for the big bright world of adult flavors? I
wonder if anybody here in the flyovers even knows
what kale is."

"I'm a local. I've lived in Detroit my whole life."

The man continues talking obliviously. "I came
over from Brooklyn. Williamsburg you know? I mean I
actually grew up in Kansas, but I didn't find my
relevancy until I hit the burg. I'm a proud 718."

"Huh?"

"Brooklynite. Obvy."

Shirley starts to feel like his whole persona is verging

on performance art. She wants to scream 'you can't be serious!,' but she can't honestly tell if he is or not.

"Uh huh."

"I moved there after I finished my doctorate in comparative poetry and contemporary mythology. My thesis was about Professor X from the X-men as an allegory for moral relativism in pre-soviet Russia."

"Interesting. How long were you in Brooklyn?"

"I occupied it for about eighteen months. Until my tyrannical one percent overlord kicked me out. I would have asked my parents for money, but they just bought me the Vespa, you know?"

He looked at her like she totally understood what he was going through. She did not.

He continued. "I can't believe my landlord wouldn't accept barter for rent. I was willing to teach him Klingon as a second language."

"Hard to imagine there are limitations to the barter system. So, do you want some ice cream?"

This has got to be some sort of elaborate joke. Right? Right? Shirley couldn't decide if he was making fun of her, society, himself, or just an idiot. *Maybe he can't tell either? Perhaps he has spent so much time swimming in sarcastic detachment that he's lost track too.*

"Oh no. Gross. I don't eat dairy. It's all just steroids and cow mucus." He scratches his mustache with his pinkie.

I wonder if he knows that in a couple of years, hipster facial hair is going to be the 21st century mullet.

"So is there anything I can get you?"

"Call me when you open a place for people with educated palates." He starts to leave.

"Yeah. Have a good day."

Trying to hide her frustration, Shirley puts her head down and cleans the already spotless counter until she hears the door close. *This is going to be one of those days huh?*

*

When she finally exits the shop at 6:15 PM, she decides to sit down on a bench in Grand Circus Park. She often jokes with her customers about the name—pointing out that it is neither grand nor has a circus—but it is a great place to stop and breathe for ten minutes before she gets on the bus to go home. She looks down at her register receipt, grimacing at the fact that she only sold forty-seven items. Most of her customers bought waffle cones for four dollars each. Her grand sales total is $193.43. It's enough to pay that day's expenses and leave her with the tidy sum of $3.56 for her efforts. She does the quick math and realizes that she made just shy of twenty-nine cents an hour.

Fall has finally started pushing summer out to pasture and she knows it will only get harder to sell ice cream when it is ten degrees outside. The only glimmer of hope is that a woman who works in the tower down the block expressed interest in Shirley providing ice cream for an office birthday party later this month. All Shirley really wants to do is scoop her own ice cream in the storefront one cone at a time, but she knows that if she wants to survive, she will need the money that comes from catering. She pulls the woman's card out of her pocket. It reads "Rebecca Anne Louis - Office Manager."

"Well Rebecca Anne Louis - Office Manager, expect a call from me tomorrow along with a free pint of each flavor delivered to your desk!"

The evening sky is overcast and a strong wind blows through the artificial canyons between the tall buildings. It's one of her favorite types of weather. The early October breeze, while blustery, still clings onto the last heat of summer, sending thick clouds blowing across the sky at twice normal speed. It will rain soon, but not yet. Shirley takes a deep breath and lets it out slowly. She tries to let the stress of her day wash off as she muses that in this particular spot, from this very specific angle, Detroit is really beautiful.

Grand Circus Park has been maintained carefully as if the city government, knowing that they are powerless to improve all the large swaths of forgotten neighborhoods and crumbling infrastructure, decided to make a few small pockets of the city really nice. The grass is mowed and trimmed and there are flowers planted in neat little rows along the sidewalks. The litter which seems to coat most of the city has been eradicated on at least this block. She imagines that from space, the park must look like a small clean spot rubbed off a filthy window with a giant thumb.

Shirley reminds herself that when it gets dark in a couple of hours, even this beautiful park won't be safe and that if she walked a single block to the west, she'd come across that strange empty space of crossing streets leading nowhere.

Her stomach grumbles. All she's had to eat today is ice cream. It's free, but does murder on her stomach. A gnawing tickle in the back of her throat reminds her that she's thirsty too. *When was the last time I had anything to drink? Coffee this morning? Did I even drink the diet coke I brought for lunch?* As the sole employee at her store, she is entirely at the mercy of customers. She can't really do anything that can't be immediately interrupted by someone walking in the door. It makes meals and bathroom breaks somewhat awkward. She would prefer her customers not see a half-eaten tuna sandwich sitting behind the counter and she definitely doesn't want them to know that the lady who is serving them ice cream just took a crap.

Being slammed with customers is stressful and exhausting. Having nobody walk in the door is also stressful and exhausting, for different reasons. She reaches into her purse for her water bottle to discover that, surprise surprise, she has forgotten it in the shop. She considers going back for it, but just shrugs.

"Hey, I've got more than three whole dollars burning a hole in my pocket. I can afford a bottle of water."

She looks around the park hoping for a hot dog cart or a newsstand. Strangely she doesn't see anyone selling anything. In fact, she doesn't see anyone at all. At 6:30 PM in the business district, people are already starting to close up shop and disappear into the suburbs. Much like many centers of struggling cities across America, by

8:00 PM downtown will be a ghost town.

With a slight grimace, Shirley notes a water fountain perched between two shrubs. It's old, surely original, as it is far more regal than anything that would be installed today. The fountain is iron and carved stone rising out of the pavement. It's an art-deco remnant of Detroit's economic glory days. A hundred years after being installed, it's covered in grime and graffiti. Half of an old bumper sticker is affixed to the side. It says 'Fire Millen.' Somewhere in the back of the useless trivia folder in her brain, she thinks this has something to do with the Lions. She's not sure if they did indeed 'Fire Millen' yet or not.

"Water is water right?" She says aloud.

She gamely walks over and takes a drink. The water tastes flat and metallic. Grimacing, she wonders if her tongue feels the tiniest bit numb, but she figures she's just imagining it. *Gross. I should have let it run longer. When was the last time someone was brave enough to drink from this fountain? How old are the water pipes? What are the chances they are made of lead? Or are filled with rat shit or tetanus?*

Shirley wipes her mouth with the back of her sleeve and walks away from the fountain digging her keys out of her purse. Her mother always told her that women should have their keys in their hands before they get to a parking lot in case there is trouble. Reluctantly, she admits that this might actually be decent advice, especially at this hour.

Shirley's keys drop out of her hand. She doesn't fumble them, she just opens her palm and they fall to the pavement with a jingling noise. She does not stop to pick them up. Rather, she continues walking, making no sign she even noticed they were gone.

A few steps later, her purse hits the pavement. She doesn't call herself a klutz and retrieve it like she did the day before. Today, she does not seem to care. It's as if she simply doesn't need it anymore. Her steps become slower, less assertive, but she's still walking west.

Her right elbow twitches. It twitches again, more strongly. Her left arm flies out violently in an abrupt isolated movement that looks like something between a muscle spasm and a modern dance move. The body that Shirley used to inhabit steps out of one of her bright red pumps and continues walking barefoot.

She removes her thin pink jacket with an awkward jerky motion—taking it off like she doesn't quite remember how it is attached to her. When she pulls it over her head, there is a ripping sound as the collar tears. She does not carefully fold the coat or hang it up like she has so many other times. She just drops it onto the dirty sidewalk in a crumpled pool of fabric.

Her hands awkwardly claw at her large beaded necklace. The fingers that had perfected shaping waffle cones in a single twist are now clumsy, almost arthritic, but have lost none of their strength. The necklace snaps, sending a cascade of beads chittering down the street behind her. She grabs the neck of the blouse that she purchased with her mother's leftover Kohl's cash and tears it wide open, exposing her bright green padded bra.

Her left leg starts a shuttering spasm and she almost

loses her balance, but her right foot lands back on the sidewalk and she continues forward. The tattered remnants of her blouse hit the ground. She now is walking through downtown Detroit in only her bra and a black pencil skirt.

Shirley has a much more attractive body than what most people would imagine the owner of an ice cream shop would possess. She isn't a roly-poly grandmother with a quick smile and soft middle. Her retro style actually hides a flat stomach, toned arms and moderately sized, but firm and shapely breasts. A passerby who prefers the company of women would probably enjoy this bizarre striptease in the middle of downtown Detroit, at least until he or she saw Shirley's eyes.

She rips open the three snaps at the front of her skirt, revealing the top of her underwear as the fabric begins to slip off her hips. Her panties are more practical than her outward style, simple blue cotton. Her skirt falls below her knees and she steps out of it leaving her other shoe in the crumbled heap of cloth. In the span of three minutes, Shirley has laid a trail of retro but stylish breadcrumbs leading back to the water fountain.

Her head abruptly snaps to the right as if she were an extra in Michael Jackson's 'Thriller' video. She probably pulled every muscle in her neck and shoulders but she takes no notice. She reaches down, hooks her fingers into the elastic band on her underwear and tears it off, exposing herself to anyone in eyesight.

Her bra is the last thing to hit the street, leaving her

breasts fully open to the warm breeze. If Shirley were still present in her body she might have thought that this is probably the first time her chest has been exposed to the outdoors since she was a toddler.

What used to be Shirley, the owner and sole employee of Scoops, who hoped someday to be known as 'The Ice Cream Lady,' strides down the street completely naked. The only thing covering her now is her distinctive cat-eye makeup. She walks with a steady gate, not quickly, but purposefully. Her journey is only interrupted by the frequent and seemingly random muscle spasms. In another moment, she arrives at the corner of Adams and Clifford, the southeast corner of a large empty lot in the center of downtown.

She begins a slow journey around the perimeter of the open space.

PART I
THE WATER

CHAPTER 1

"Holy shit!" Sarah's voice echoes through the main library, down a flight of stairs, and floats into the kitchen.

"What is it?" Chris turns off the faucet.

"I just discovered something you're going to like!"

Chris walks up the first few steps so he can see into the library and spots his wife above, leaning against the rounded balcony railing. She's looking down at him trying to hide a sneaky grin. Intrigued, Chris quickens his steps. This type of grin always means she's up to something naughty.

"Is it porn?!" He shouts up.

"No, it's-" She stops and looks down at him incredulously. "Wait. How could you possibly have guessed it was porn?!"

He grins and shrugs. "You had a porny face on."

"You're ridiculous."

23

"You know, kinda guilty, kinda excited. We've been married for thirteen years. I know your porn face."

He enthusiastically jogs up the stairs and into the large room. He hops over their coffee table and dodges a beautiful Steinway grand piano on his way to the ladder. In thirty seconds, and slightly out of breath, he joins Sarah on the balcony that encircles the room.

"Funny, you never move that fast when I ask you to help me with the sanding."

"Blah blah, get with the porn. Where did you find it?"

"Well in order to paint this edge I had to pull the bookshelf back a bit." Sarah has been scraping off the old paint and priming the edges of bookshelves encircling the library's second level. "Check it out!"

Chris kneels down and uses his iPhone to illuminate the space behind the shelf, taking time to write his name in the dust.

"Cool! Must be the first time the bookshelves have been moved since they built the place."

"Definitely. Nothing's been touched for eighty years."

Chris reaches under the shelf and comes back with nothing but cobwebs. "Fascinating, but where is the dirty stuff?"

She laughs and hands him the dusty magazine she had been holding behind her back. The cover features a black and white photo of a nude woman relaxing on a chez lounge. "Here ya go husband. You finally found grandpa's porn stash."

"Pep! Magazine: New Spicy Stories and Art. June

1926. This is so cool. History and boobs."

Sarah laughs. "I thought you'd like that."

"So we bought an abandoned eighty-year-old library and the only book in it was pornography from the roaring twenties?"

"You complaining?"

"Hell no! I think it deserves a prominent placement on our shelves."

She rolls her eyes. "Of course you do."

A year and a half into their renovations, Chris and Sarah are finally ready to start painting and hanging pictures. Sarah has spent the last month starting a mural on the rounded walls above the bookshelves on the second level. She's made it halfway around the ring, replicating the city of Detroit as it looked in its 1920's heyday. She is painting one side of the room to show the skyline at night and plans to have it gradually transition to a daytime view on the far wall.

"Wow, this looks great! I keep thinking I'm going to get used to your talent, but I never do. Now if you'd just charge people more than ten bucks for your paintings, we'd have enough money to buy real furniture for this place."

"IKEA is real furniture."

"This beautiful library is made with marble and antique handmade mahogany bookshelves and we're filling it with furniture we assembled with an Allen wrench."

"It's eclectic?"

"It's poor-clectic."

"Oh yeah? I figured when I married a classical

pianist, he'd make all the money and we'd be whisked all over the world to play concerts in Paris and Rome."

"I played in a concert in Rome!"

"Rome, Italy you goof, not upstate New York."

Chris shrugs and heads back down the ladder to the main floor. On his way, he discreetly wipes a splatter of paint off the railing. Sarah is a brilliant artist, but a complete klutz with her brushes. "You knew I was a blue collar concert pianist when you married me."

"When I married you I thought that was an oxymoron."

"And weren't you surprised that there are as many of us classical musicians struggling in the minor leagues as there are in any other sport?"

"It's not a sport."

"Sure it is. And it doesn't matter that I could hit fifty home runs on fastballs if I never learn to hit the curveball. Until I do I'll never get into the major leagues and I'll forever be taking the bus to the theater in my worn-out tux."

She looks down at him as he sits at the piano and opens the lid. He's joking, but she knows he feels a lot more than he's letting on.

Chris is a professional pianist, but not a particularly successful one. He plays concerts of the great piano pieces, but often with 'b' and 'c' orchestras in medium-sized cities: Rochester, Fort Wayne, Macon, even though the orchestras were sometimes only semi-professional. As a soloist, he was paid just enough to survive, if not overly comfortably. He occasionally resorts to taking jobs playing at churches, parties or even auditions for the professional theater companies in the area.

"You're an amazing pianist. I don't think I've ever heard you play a wrong note."

"Yep. I'm a piano machine. Practically perfect in every way," a tiny bit of bitterness sneaks into his voice, but he masks it by playing 'Jolly Holiday' from Mary Poppins. "But nobody in New York or Chicago wants to hear a soul-less computer make music. So I'm stuck playing in Akron for three hundred bucks and a meal stipend."

"So I should cancel delivery on the Faberge eggs I was going to put on this shelf?" She climbs down the ladder and sits next to him on the piano bench.

Chris laughs. He appreciates her poking him out of his impending self-pity tailspin. "Of course, when I married you, you were a fancy architect making six figures a year, not a struggling artist. If anybody should be complaining about not having a sugar daddy, it's me!"

"Touché!" She smiles and looks down at the strange square of contrasting flooring in the middle of the room. It was where the marble staircase connecting the balcony to the main floor was supposed to have been. Since it was never built, they tried to fill in the empty spot with matching hardwood, but it was still obviously not original. After considering putting a rug over it, they gave up and embraced it as a historical quirk. "Are we ever going to finish this?"

Chris stops playing.

"Finish? This place has been under construction for

almost ninety years and it's never been close to completed. I don't know why we ever thought we could accomplish this."

"Cuz we knew we wouldn't get waylaid by the Great Depression and lose all of our money. Crash away Wall Street! When you don't have any stocks, your life is so much more secure."

"You know, when I said I wanted a fixer-upper this wasn't exactly what I meant."

"You wanted space. You wanted character. You wanted something we could afford. King, embrace your kingdom."

Chris stands up and stomps around the room imperiously. "King? That sounds pretentious. I'd prefer to be a dictator."

"Oh yeah?"

"A benevolent dictator though!"

"You're such an idiot." Sarah laughs, tossing a pencil at him.

Chris jumps away from the attack, and sits back down at the piano. Without glancing at the music, he begins to play a section of Schumann, gliding his fingers up and down the keyboard with impressive dexterity and power for his relatively slight hands.

"On the plus side, the acoustics in here are fantastic." Chris says, repeating a difficult passage as Sarah climbs back up to her painting.

"You know-" Sarah stops, knowing Chris can't hear her.

"What's that?" He stops playing.

"There's plenty more sanding to do up here. I can't

do the next part of the mural until we scrape off all of this lead paint. You could come up and help me."

"I was helping! I thought underscoring would make it seem more dramatic."

Sarah rolls her eyes yet again as Chris climbs the ladder and picks up a Brillo pad.

"Don't eat the paint chips husband."

"You're no fun." He starts to scrape and sand the plaster until it is completely smooth, while Sarah follows behind with a bucket of primer. "You know, this mural is turning into a ton of work. Have you considered a nice off-white?"

Sarah laughs. "I'm considering offing my husband at the moment."

CHAPTER 2

If a Detroit Tigers fan leaving after a game at the shiny new Comerica Park walked down Adams Avenue for two blocks, he or she would find themselves in an enormous vacant lot. It's a strangely empty area in relation to the dense city around it. It looks as if someone came along and deleted almost twenty acres out of the middle of downtown. Stretching five blocks in each direction, all the way to the Fisher Freeway, sits an uneven spiderweb of empty streets breaking up abandoned blocks. There are no buildings, no bus stops or mail boxes, just blank space. Some of the streets are still relatively smooth but some have more potholes than pavement. Several of the blocks still sport the faint outlines of buildings long torn down. Other areas are adorned with faded parking spots drawn on the concrete though few cars would dare park alone in the dusty wasteland. There are no security cameras aimed in this direction. There's nothing to guard.

In a couple of spots, crabgrass stubbornly pokes up through cracks in the asphalt. It looks as if nature is slowly trying to reclaim what humanity lost interest in. Yet, the vast vacant space sits in the shadow of modern skyscrapers, busy streets and the MGM Grand Casino.

The juxtaposition of large modern buildings and strangely deserted swaths of land is not unique to Detroit, but this area is a very pronounced example. In the early twenty-first century, the gleaming visage of the city has become dotted with empty lots like liver spots. There are abandoned buildings, abandoned blocks and even abandoned neighborhoods, as if the city is being eaten alive by a cancer metastasizing into almost all areas of the once-healthy landscape.

Many proud citizens of Detroit work feverishly to keep the city alive, but it's too late to reclaim much of its past glory. Hope comes from much smaller successes: a flourishing coffee shop, a craft bicycle store, or even a streetlight being repaired.

More than twenty-five percent of the population left Detroit altogether in the span of four years starting in 2009. The people who remain are the strongest—those willing and able to fight in and for their city, and the weakest—those who were not physically or economically capable of escaping.

**

Kevin usually liked Fridays. He had gym class for

final period so his weekend started early. This week they were doing floor hockey, which was his favorite sport. But that morning his enthusiasm was dampened by a math test. He hated math. Something about long division just made his mind turn to jelly. *Why would I ever need to do that without a calculator? I mean, maybe in the olden days before literally everybody had a calculator on their phone, people needed this? But today, it's a colossal waste of time.*

He couldn't concentrate in math anyway. This was the class he sat behind Karen Tyson. *That* Karen Tyson. The one that single-handedly reshaped his biggest hopes and dreams from football cards and Spider-man comic books to... the *great and powerful bra strap*. The magical bra strap was connected to the even-more-magical bra itself. And the bra touched something so powerful, he could barely even process the thought; Karen Tyson's boobs. He'd never seen her boobs, but the bra strap, like a shining beacon of wondrous light, proved that they were there. *How in God's name could you even pretend to concentrate on long division when Karen Tyson's bra strap was right there in front of you?* He could almost reach out and touch it if he wasn't afraid his heart would literally explode if he did.

And now, he had a test. *Shit*.

The anxiety that Kevin felt before and during the test was only mildly relieved when it was finished. He knew he'd been completely lost on the second half and wasn't really sure if he'd gotten anything right on the first half. As he walked to the gymnasium, Kevin tried to push math out of his mind, not wanting his nervousness about a stupid test to bleed into his enjoyment of floor hockey.

Within ten minutes of running around pushing a plastic puck across the floor of the gym, he was reminded of what was truly important: scoring a goal and impressing Karen Tyson. Not that he thought it would make a difference, not really. Karen Tyson was so far above him in the social food chain, she was completely unreachable. But on some level, her being so far out of reach made his desire feel safer because Kevin had no idea what he would do if he ever caught her attention. So, he focused on scoring a goal and the beautiful fantasy of her being so swept up in his floor hockey prowess that she would hold his hand on the bus home.

He did score a goal. In fact he scored two. But alas, Karen Tyson was not as dazzled by his hockey skills as he had hoped. By the time he got out of the locker room, Karen Tyson was already on the bus and sitting with her impenetrable and terrifying gaggle of friends. Kevin sat down in the third row and pretended not to care.

A moment before bus twenty-eight pulled away from school, Kevin was hit with a shot of blazing panic when he remembered that he had left his earth science book in his locker. *Shit! Do I need it? Oh man, there's a quiz on chapter seven on Monday. But I'll miss the bus!* He stared at the green vinyl seat ahead of him for a moment, thinking. *It's OK, I can just walk home. As long as I get there before Mom does, she'll never know.*

Kevin dashed off the bus and went back into the school heading towards his locker. Even fifteen minutes after the final bell, the hallways were almost empty. It made him wary. Kevin thought the school always felt a little different after the end of the day. In some ways, being in the hall after final period was nicer because he didn't have a class he had to go to, but it also filled him with anxiety. Without all of the structure of the class schedule and without the constant supervision of all the teachers, the empty school felt wrong in some way, unpredictable.

That year his old family dog Maggie had begun to grow cataracts. He loved her with the sureness of a child. No matter what he used to do to the black and white collie when he was an enthusiastic toddler— pulling her ears or poking her eyes—she was always patient and gentle as if she knew the young human didn't know any better. She was a truly kind and affectionate animal. The family loved and trusted her completely, but when she became elderly and went blind and increasingly deaf, things changed. She couldn't see or hear people coming and was frequently startled. Then, one day Kevin reached under the dining room table to pet her, like he had done a thousand times before, and Maggie made a horrible yelp of fear and viciously bit his hand. It wasn't a warning bite, she held on to his hand for several seconds. It felt like an eternity before she let go and her teeth drew blood in several places. Kevin had been shocked. Maggie, the most loving and fundamentally good creature he knew, had become aggressive. She had always been safe and then instantly she was dangerous. The betrayal stung worse than the bite. Of course she hadn't meant to hurt him, she had just been scared. But Kevin would never pet her again without being nervous. Intentionally or not, trust had been broken.

Empty hallways reminded him of Maggie.

This is what the Wild West must have felt like, he thought. *It's like I'm walking down one of the dusty streets in Deadwood.* In this hall, there were no rules, no laws, other than what you could get away with. If he ran into some eighth graders, there would not be any adults who would come to his rescue.

He'd been caught before by Morgan Carver in a situation just like this. One day after school, after most of the teachers had gone home or retreated back to their classrooms to put together tomorrow's lesson plan or grade tests, Morgan and his two zit-pocked buddies pushed him up against a row of lockers. He was completely pinned and had to watch while Morgan went through his backpack.

"Make a noise and I'll punch you in the nuts faggot."

Kevin hadn't made a noise. Not when they smashed his left-over peanut butter and jelly sandwich into his history book. Not when they stole his iPhone. Not when they tossed his notebook onto the top of the lockers where he couldn't reach it. He remembered Morgan's foul breath more than anything else. It was a sour mixture of grape bubble gum and Marlboro cigarettes. Kevin knew his only defense was to try to remain passive and let them do what they wanted.

There were no teachers in ear-shot and he couldn't possibly fight all three of them. He just willed himself not to cry. It didn't work. He helplessly stood there, eyes brimming with tears, desperately trying not to blink. He knew that if he did, he would send his tears cascading down onto his t-shirt, or worse, onto the arms of the assholes pinning him to the locker. He had no choice but to wait for them to get bored of tormenting him. They all knew that he wouldn't tell anybody about what they did. Sure, they might get in trouble, but then he would be even more of a target. They'd find a way to make him regret ratting them out.

So, on that fateful Friday, when Kevin returned to the scene of the crime to retrieve his earth science book, he definitely looked both ways before he raced to his locker.

To his great relief, the hallway was empty and he appeared to be alone this time. But he wasn't going to hang around too long to test the theory. Kevin tossed his book into his already insanely heavy book bag and scurried through the halls and out the front door.

The school had cleared out fast and most of the buses had already left. He could see the beginnings of soccer practice on the field behind the school. With nothing better to do, he sat on the bleachers and watched for a while. He liked walking home. His mother didn't get back from work until about 6:30, so he had almost three hours all to himself. It felt very free, very *adult*.

Of course he knew his mom didn't like him being outside alone, but Kevin figured what she didn't know wouldn't hurt her. *Come on Mom! I'm in sixth grade now. I can take care of myself! Well, unless I get cornered by assholes like Morgan...*

He sat watching soccer practice for an hour or so, doodling in his notebook and playing paper football on the splintery wooden bleachers. When boredom crept in, he figured he'd take a walk. He didn't have a plan. Sometimes he just liked walking. It gave him time to think about important topics like Grand Theft Auto 5 and Karen Tyson's bra strap.

He meandered down Brush Street for a while. This area used to be a neighborhood, but now, once you got past Erskine, it was mostly empty blocks of grass. Most of the houses had been abandoned or burned in the 1967 riots and were torn down years ago, but every once in a while he'd come across one lonely house that survived the blight. It was flat and quiet and—most importantly—if you kept walking down Brush across the freeway, you got to Ford Field.

Ah! That's where I should go! Ford Field. Home of the Detroit Freaking Lions!

He'd only been to three Lions' games, but they were his favorite thing in the world. Each of the games had been Christmas presents from his stepfather. He wasn't so fond of Ted, but it was totally worth it to watch Matthew Stafford throwing touchdowns to Megatron in person. What he loved most was the noise. When Detroit scored it was exhilarating. Hearing seventy thousand people all shouting in unison created something that went beyond sound. It made his chest vibrate. It was *so* exciting.

Kevin liked to walk by the stadium. It was enormous, a vast grand building of brick, steel and glass. He could almost feel the *importance* of what happened here crackling in the air. It was hallowed ground.

As he walked down Brush Street with the stadium looming in front of the billowing fast-moving clouds, he tried to visualize every single touchdown that Megatron, or Calvin Johnson to the boring people who didn't follow the Lions, caught last year.

He had just traversed the overpass over the Fisher freeway when he caught a glimpse of something impossible.

Was that a naked person!?!

Kevin wasn't sure, but he'd seen a flash of what looked to be *skin*. Whoever was wearing it had just ducked behind the parking garage at the corner of Brush and East Montcalm. He—or hopefully *she*—was now out of sight. Kevin's mind raced in a hormone-fueled frenzy.

I think that was a naked person. A naked woman! Maybe it's some sort of protest? Like about not wearing fur or something? Holy shit! Could this possibly be the day? The day I see my first live boob?

He unconsciously quickened his steps, trying to appear casual, but definitely trying to catch up to... *could it be*? He girded himself for disappointment. He'd been fooled before by tan clothing and other annoying tricks of the adolescent mind but when he rounded the corner onto East Montcalm, his heart almost exploded.

That is, without a doubt, a naked woman!! Like, full-on naked. I can see her butt! Oh thank you Jesus for this bounty—or booty!—that you have given me!

Kevin looked around to see if anybody else was in the area. He prayed that some adult wouldn't walk by and stop him from seeing this wondrous thing. He sheepishly continued to walk down the street, trying to catch up and—*oh my God*—see the front of her. He worked hard to appear to be casually taking a stroll and paying no attention to the naked woman in front of him. Kevin surveyed every part of her body that he could see and tried to take mental pictures he could revisit later.

She was probably in her late twenties. She wasn't fat, but she wasn't terribly thin. A survival job behind a desk as a group-sales ticket broker for the Detroit Tigers had softened and rounded her curves just a touch since college, but she was still in good shape. She had short dirty-blonde hair that looked like she had tried to get an aggressive pixie cut about a month ago, regretted it, and was in the process of growing it back out. To Kevin, she was the most beautiful creature that ever existed. Karen Tyson's bra strap be damned.

Her arm twitched out from her side and almost simultaneously, her left foot kicked backwards. She stumbled for a second, and then regained her slow, steady stride west.

Is she dancing? Kevin thought. *Oooooh, that's what it is. She's some sort of weird dancer!*

Ted used to call them Hippie Protest Dance Morons. He said they were all lesbos and tree huggers.

Kevin wasn't entirely sure what all of that meant, but he certainly was a fan of Hippie Protest Dance Morons today.

He had worked his way closer, now only about twenty feet behind her. For a second, his joy and excitement stuttered when he saw her step on a jagged piece of glass from a broken bottle of Bud Lite. Kevin winced and instinctively reached towards her, expecting her to cry out and possibly fall to the pavement. Much to his surprise, she did not. She apparently hadn't even noticed stepping on the broken glass and she kept walking down the road. Her shoulder jumped up for a second then returned. She must have been continuing her choreography, but now she was leaving a bloody footprint every time her left foot hit the ground.

After the brief moment of being fazed by the grossness, Kevin remembered what was important. *What am I doing? I need to get around to the front! There's no way this is going to last long. She's going to see me and put clothes on, or some adult is going to tell me to leave. If I don't see her boobs, I'm going to throw myself onto the freeway and die!*

So Kevin half-walked half-ran ahead, trying to come up with an innocent excuse for stopping and looking at her. Deciding that he was definitely going to have to double-check that his shoelaces were tied once he got a half a block ahead, he passed the Fox Theater and looked down Park Avenue. He stopped walking mid-step. From his spot, he could see into the empty lot. There, marching in a huge circle were several more naked people.

Holy shit! What's happening? Six, seven... ten people?! It totally is some sort of protest! Oh man, I'm going to see so many boobs!

Dropping any pretense, he turned and looked back at the woman he had been following. And there they were: the first real, in-person boobs of his life. They were just the most amazing things he'd ever seen. The excitement he felt staring at her chest was so intense it felt like he was staring directly at the sun. After gawking at her breasts for a time that felt like an eternity and a split second at the same time, he worked his way down her body and saw her... *bits.* Although to his surprise he couldn't really see them, they were tucked behind a small patch of hair. He looked up and down her body over and over trying to memorize the image. He stood in a stupor for a while before he realized that he had been holding his breath for over a minute and sucked in oxygen greedily to keep from passing out.

After regaining his senses, Kevin was startled by the fact that the lady was now very close to him. She must have been ignoring him because there was no way she couldn't see him as she walked almost directly into him. The naked woman was now close enough that if he had the courage, he could have reached out and touched her. Kevin felt compelled to say something, but he had absolutely no idea what people say in this situation.

"Um. Hello. Uh... it's a beautiful nice day huh?"

He turned beet-red from embarrassment, but she

continued to ignore him. *Thank God.* But when he looked to her face for the first time, he took a startled step backwards.

Jesus. What's wrong with her eyes?! They're all white like Maggie's were. Or like some horror movie. That's so gross. Maybe she's wearing special effects contacts? Weird! He stopped his train of thought. *No! What am I doing? Who gives a shit about her eyes?! Look at her boobs!*

Kevin followed her into the empty lot and saw that there weren't ten more 'protesters', but twenty or thirty. And more of them seemed to be coming from everywhere. He watched as a beautiful woman with flaming red hair walked by, followed shortly by an older black gentleman, both just as naked as the first lady.

He stood there for a moment gaping before—with yet another jolt of terror—he realized he was not the only clothed person watching the event. Dotted around the lot were confused residents of Detroit staring at the naked people. To his right stood a young mechanic in greasy overalls and a middle-aged businessman in an expensive suit. Kevin made sheepish eye contact with the mechanic.

"Uh... I was walking to... uh. I'm not-"

The mechanic grinned at him. "You're here to look at the naked chicks. Go ahead kid, I ain't your dad."

*

An hour later, the circle of naked bodies has grown

exponentially. It seems to Kevin that there must be thousands of them now. His twelve-year-old brain is in overdrive. Sure, he has spent plenty of time looking at naked people on the internet late at night. To a sixth-grader who knows anything at all, the Cyber-Sitter software that his mother had installed on his laptop was laughably easy to get around. But this is so different. In the last hour and a half, Kevin has learned the lesson that all boys who like girls learn at some point: seeing a boob on the internet and seeing one in real life is a *completely different thing*. And here they are. Hundreds of them! They are big, small, young, old, fake, real, saggy and just plain weird. He invents the word 'boobucopia' and giggles to himself. Sure, there is lots of stuff he isn't interested in seeing, an old man's droopy scrotum flopping back and forth (*gross*), a woman who kinda looks like his mom (*grosser*), sooooo many penises (*ick*). But all in all, if he has to see some gross stuff to see boobs, it is a deal he would take every time.

Kevin's excitement doesn't wear off quickly, he doesn't think he'll ever get tired of watching this, but he eventually starts to feel a nagging sense that there is something creepy happening. Under all of the titillation there is an unsettling *wrongness* about this whole situation.

The group is also growing exponentially fast. Ten people became a hundred in a matter of minutes. Twenty minutes after that, there are over a thousand naked people walking in the circle. And now it seems to be doubling every few minutes.

The 'dance' hasn't stopped. In fact, the sheer mass of people seems to have intensified the strange spasmodic motions. Arms and legs twitch and flail in random directions. Within an hour, the cluster of bodies which began with a single woman has now grown to include more than five thousand people.

Each of them walks around and around the lot in a huge counter-clockwise circle. They don't fall into step with each other, but they all move at the same consistent and deliberate pace. The order is only interrupted by the randomly snapping muscle spasms that violently contort their bodies.

Step... step... step...SNAP... stepSNAP ...step...step...

As more and more 'dancers' join the horde, they fill in to form a complete circle. They create an enormous revolving wheel of writhing flesh.

Several hundred onlookers have joined Kevin and his new mechanic friend. On their faces shine the whole range of human emotions—excitement, glee, terror, revulsion, despair. Each witness is having their own experience of the event. Some are shouting into their phones or talking rapidly to each other. Others focus on taking pictures. A large number of them just stand in sober silence. As the minutes pass, more people start to crowd around the edges. Many theories on what is happening are posited, but there seems to be no definitive answer. *Is it some sort of a protest? An illness? Mass hysteria?*

A small group of people kneel in a circle holding hands and rocking back and forth. A woman in a corduroy dress leads a prayer. Tears streak down her face as she speaks in a half-murmur, half-moan.

"Lord may you grant us the strength and wisdom to understand what we are witnessing. Give us the grace to comprehend this dark event, this horrible display of wickedness. Jesus, what are you trying to tell us? If this be the end of days, let us be worthy and may you take us to sweet heaven and away from this fetid mortal coil."

The police arrived twenty minutes after Shirley began her walk. They unsuccessfully tried to talk to the naked 'dancers,' eventually trying to arrest one of them for public indecency. They were forced to tackle and handcuff the naked man, but they could not get him to talk. The baffled cops could not get him to do anything except wordlessly strain against them, trying to get back into the circle. Eventually, there were too many naked people to contain. The authorities settled on cordoning off the area with police barriers and just watching. Within an hour, their sawhorses had been overrun by thousands more naked bodies. They had no choice but to keep falling back and bewilderedly ask for instructions over the radio.

The media gets there shortly after the police. Knowing they will get incredible images, they immediately take out their cameras and take gigabytes of photos and videos. Several scuffles break out as photographers jockey for the perfect position. They each dream of taking the one iconic photo they hope to sell to Time magazine for more money than they make in a year. When not trying to interview the nude people, reporters phone their political contacts to try and find out who organized the event. Few of them think to talk to their science editors. The television correspondents call for satellite trucks so they can set up live shots.

Kevin, who remained standing at the outskirts of the circle as it formed, has forgotten all about the fact that he should have been home by now. He should have already received annoyed, then frantic, messages from his mother or Ted asking where he was. But his phone remains silent.

Without really being aware of it, Kevin has fallen into a state of dulled shock. Lulled by the overwhelming strangeness, by the hypnotic circular motion of the bodies, he stands frozen for almost twenty minutes. He remains in his trance-like state until it is brutally punctured by the image of a large tattooed man punching his arm out and slamming an old woman on the side of her face. The force of the impact is shocking. Her head violently snaps to the right. Her grey hair flings across her forehead as if she is at a heavy metal concert. Even in the chaos of bodies, Kevin hears a loud crack on impact. He thinks she must be nearly eighty—small, wrinkled and frail. Her skin sags on her frame like she is melting. Kevin has never seen an old person naked before and he is surprised by what happens to a body, and boobs, when time and gravity do their work. The pit of his stomach drops out like it did when his real father once took him to Six Flags and they rode his first 'adult' roller coaster. He expects her to crumple to the ground, thinking there's no way she would be able to withstand the impact. But neither the tattooed man nor the old woman react to the violence, despite the fact that the woman is now bleeding profusely from her eye and the man's wrist is hanging limply at an impossible angle.

Kevin is stunned. Much like sex, violence in reality is completely different from violence in the movies. His older brother Derek had shown him 'House of 1000 Corpses' one night when their Mom and Ted were away. It was super gross and secretly gave him horrible nightmares, but seeing this casual act of brutality and *injury* in real life is so different. It shocks him to his core. He hears a buzzing in his ears and his vision starts to get darker. With the world starting to swim in front of his eyes, he drops to his knees and leans forward trying to get the blood to go back into his head. He will come to regret this decision.

Trying to clear his mind of the image, he forces himself to read every word on a littered candy wrapper. He takes a few deep breaths. The banality of the unpronounceable ingredients helps calm his mind and after a long moment, the buzzing in his ears slowly starts to fade. His hearing slowly returns to normal and everything seems loud all of a sudden. Still on his hands and knees, Kevin looks back up and realizes that from the ground, he can see a different perspective of the circle. He takes in wave after wave of bare feet, now almost black from walking in the grime and... *could that be blood?* The endless motion is dizzying. He feels a tingling sensation as if all the legs blurring together were bristles on a toothbrush rubbing across the back of his neck.

Through the chaos of the feet, Kevin's attention is called to something different, smaller. Something that used to be a toddler. It is fighting to stay upright in the mass of motion. Kevin gasps. Like the rest of the horde, the child's eyes are white and expressionless, but are no less the eyes of a child who is loved and cared for by somebody.

It's a wonder that the small chubby legs have been able to stay upright as long as they have, though it does not stay up much longer. Kevin watches as a spasming foot kicks out and trips the child. The small body stumbles and falls face-down onto the dirty pavement. No one stops to assist. Nobody avoids stepping on it. Nobody even seems to notice. The thousands of feet just continue their journeys around and around the circle.

Kevin covers his face with his hands and puts his forehead directly onto the dirty concrete causing the wrapper to stick to his sweaty forehead. He almost looks like he is praying. And in a way, he is. He's praying that he will not envision what is happening deep in that circle. He's desperately trying not to picture that child being ground into the pavement. But of course that is impossible.

Perhaps it is a mercy for Kevin when it starts to rain.

*

When the rain begins, the last sliver of sun has dropped below the skyline and darkness has fallen over the city. Dozens of police and TV news lights surrounding the perimeter now illuminate the circle. The powerful lights throw large shadows of the 'dance' up onto the office buildings surrounding the lot. The shadows change fluidly like animation. Sometimes they display abstract shapes created by clumps of torsos and limbs and sometimes they isolate the silhouette of a single body. Projected two stories high, the images swirl with a primitive motion like a post-modern cave painting come to life. Like blood spatter on a wall, it is accidental art created by horror.

Local TV reporters have set up live shots for the evening news, but still fail to make sense of what is happening. In each news van, segment producers are desperately trying to figure out how much to show on television. The nudity is part of the story, but they don't want to spend the next six months being yelled at or fined by the FCC.

"Fuck! What the hell am I supposed to do here?" one producer shouts at an equally baffled reporter.

"Isn't there some sort of policy? Or guidelines?"

The producer rolls his eyes. "Oh sure, just let me check the mass naked hysteria chapter in my editorial handbook!"

Over their heads, the NBC 4 helicopter hovers five hundred feet above, broadcasting the bizarre footage. Crazy Kenny is getting an earful from the station producer who is shouting into his headset.

"Don't zoom in! Pull back asshole. We're live! If I see one more set of dick and balls or big floppy tits on my monitor, we'll all get our asses fired!"

Crazy Kenny in The Chopper, whose regular beat is reporting the Traffic on The Tens, is struggling mightily. This is not his night. He's a one-man operation. He flies the helicopter, he does the reporting, and he runs the high-definition video camera mounted to the bottom of the cockpit. He is perfectly capable of doing each job by itself, but even after three years, he has never gotten comfortable doing all of them at once.

Now, Kenny is failing to describe what he is seeing. And his failure is being broadcast live on TV. He has a vocabulary for traffic: 'It's jammed up like my Aunt Rose after Thanksgiving dinner!', 'It's as clear as my dating calendar!', 'It's a parking lot out there Jim, if I was you, I'd just stay home and watch NBC 4!' He has a vocabulary for the various problems that might occur on the roads of Detroit: accidents, weather, construction, a police chase. But he has no vocabulary for what he is seeing tonight.

What the hell do I call them? Protesters? Crazy people? Freaking zombies? In one ear of his headset, frustrated anchors back at NBC are talking to him live on the air. In his other ear, his producer is screaming instructions that only he can hear. The cacophony makes it impossible for him to concentrate. And to make things worse, it is beginning to rain.

Kenny hates bad weather. The jerk-offs at NBC kept refusing to pay to repair the weather stripping on the helicopter, so every time it rained, he would get cold and wet. Not enough water gets through to damage any of the equipment—because they care about the equipment—but it is always enough to be insanely annoying and give him a perpetual cold.

"Yeah, once again Doug, I can't tell you what the purpose of this... event... is. If it's a protest of some sort, they're being pretty vague about what they're trying to say." Kenny shouts into his head-set. Collin, the pompous head anchor, is continuing to ask him the same questions over and over despite the fact that he doesn't have any answers. Kenny can tell he is making him look like an asshole on purpose.

"I can tell you that they don't seem to be bothered by the-"

A drop of rain hits the bridge of Kenny's nose. There is a cartoonish look of surprise on his face before his expression goes completely blank. He takes his hands off the controls and the self-leveler kicks in. Kenny removes his headset, dropping it to his side with a clang. Voices in both ears of the headset simultaneously ask him why he stopped talking, but Crazy Kenny in The Chopper is no longer listening. He doesn't complete his report or even finish his sentence.

Instead, he begins to take off his shirt.

The rain starts to fall onto the crowd below. The first precipitation comes down in a few random drops, plopping down every few feet. But quickly, the drops build to a pounding, driving rain that crashes over the people below in thick sheets. Within five minutes, the horde is joined by the onlookers, cops, reporters and what remains of a boy who loved floor hockey.

Nobody looks up at the helicopter to see the cockpit

door open and a slightly pudgy balding man calmly roll out and begin to plummet to the ground. None of the people notice that even during his rapid descent, he continues to remove his pants. He gets one foot out before he hits the pavement below and promptly explodes from the impact.

CHAPTER 3

A unique set of circumstances has to take place for a library to be abandoned before construction is even completed and even more unlikely occurrences have to be set in motion for it to remain untouched for more than eighty years. Chris and Sarah jokingly decided that it was fate that led to their ownership of the little library that never was.

Ten years into the twentieth century, Henry Ford debuted his assembly line and started selling Model Ts as fast as he could build them. The automobile industry exploded and Detroit was soon flush with cash and expanding as fast as it could build itself. The industrious city constructed the Michigan Central Station in 1914, a majestic public library in 1921, and the city's first skyscraper, the Penobscot, in 1928, rapidly turning Detroit into one of the largest and most prosperous cities in the world.

The year after the Penobscot tower was completed the city began building a downtown branch of the Detroit Public Library system. It wasn't going to rival the size and scale of the main location on Woodward Ave, in fact it wasn't going to be much larger than a small church, but it was going to be beautiful. European marble and South American Mahogany would create elegant paneling and shelves. The main feature was to be a large open room, two stories tall, with bookshelves covering the walls of two separate levels: the main floor and an oval-shaped balcony. A marble staircase was to have connected the two floors with the card catalogue and librarian desk in the center of the lower level. The library was to have been reached from a marble staircase leading up from the street in a miniature nod to the New York Public Library steps in Manhattan.

On the upper level, there were going to be reading chairs and desks against the railing, allowing patrons to look down on the library floor as they read. There was also a small room off the second level that was to hold the head librarian's office and a special collection of antique books donated specially for this branch from a European estate.

Beneath the Library proper—on the ground floor—was supposed be a level of administrative offices and restrooms. An unfinished basement below would house a large boiler and maintenance equipment.

Construction was nearly completed, save both marble staircases and some of the plumbing, when the stock market crash of 1929 caused the city to postpone, then eventually cancel, any further construction. The library sat ignored and unfinished for more than thirty years of bureaucratic purgatory while the city waited for the economy to improve.

After World War II, the automobile industry had a second boom that lasted for almost twenty years. But in the 1960's, the cancer of economic and racial inequality that lived under the metallic sheen of the cars rolling off the assembly lines finally bubbled to the surface. It eventually exploded in the infamous 1967 riots that burned large tracts of the city to the ground. It didn't create as much as expose the broken industrial economy and Detroit plunged into recession and debt. The city has yet to recover.

In 1969, an opportunistic real estate investment firm bought the unfinished library at a government auction for pennies on the dollar. The company's plan was to wait for the downtown neighborhood, which now housed as many empty buildings as occupied ones, to improve enough to convert the library into condos. Unfortunately, the rest of the company's investments were just as unwise and it went belly-up in 1987.

When there were no takers on the property at its second bankruptcy auction, the city once again took possession of the library and promptly forgot about it. Over the years, new buildings grew up around it. To the west sits a twelve-story office building that has yet to be fully occupied. A beautiful union hall used to sit to the east, but it was torn down in 1993 and replaced with a small parking garage. The four-story garage which stands shoulder to shoulder with the library looks a bit like a concrete fortress. Because the garage mainly serves commuters and closes at night, chain-link fences cover any opening on the first two floors. Many people on that street remark about the slightly sad juxtaposition of the beautiful—if unfinished—façade of the library sitting between the cold 1960's architecture of the office building and the imposing bunker-like inner-city parking garage.

In 2012, with Detroit trying to avoid the bankruptcy that it eventually filed for the following year, the library was auctioned off a third time, for less than the cost of a double-wide mobile home.

Chris and Sarah had no idea what they were getting into when the purchased the library. Sarah had been an architect, so she understood the structural issues in great detail, but she had spent her years designing new buildings for an enormous firm, where a team of lawyers took care of any city regulations and zoning problems. She had never repurposed an incomplete and abandoned building and was not prepared for the great deal of regulatory confusion. They had no idea that in order to live there, they would need to petition the city to re-zone the land for residential use. Because they bought the building at auction, they weren't able to inspect it before they closed the sale, so they weren't aware that the building had never been connected to the Detroit water grid. They didn't know that it would be cheaper to install their own self-contained plumbing than retrofit and connect the pipes to the city pipes. They were unaware that the byzantine building codes would, for reasons beyond their understanding, force them to install a commercial-grade modern fire alarm and sprinkler system despite the fact that the building was now zoned as residential. And they were shocked to discover that the basement had never fully been weather-proofed and flooded every time it rained. Nonetheless, for the adventurous couple looking for a challenge in their second decade of marriage, the library was a dream come true.

The main entrance—the marble staircase that was to have led up from the street—was never built, so the back staircase was the only access point to the grand room. The little flight of wooden stairs was only intended to connect to the administrative offices and bathrooms. They seem small and insubstantial in comparison to the beautiful space they lead up to, but they were just fine for Chris and Sarah. They converted the offices into a makeshift apartment with a kitchen, bathroom and two bedrooms.

Eventually Chris and Sarah embraced all of the unique quirks of their new home and were excited to begin the conversion. But without the money to pay contractors do to the renovations, they knew they would likely spend the next ten years doing most of the work themselves. And they couldn't have been happier.

***

"Why is there never any food in the house?" Chris paws through the kitchen cabinet in search of a bag of chips he was sure he had hidden well enough that Sarah wouldn't have found.

"There's plenty of food!" She replies, looking up from her Kindle.

"Boring food."

Yawning, Sarah tucks her bare feet back under the blanket her grandmother knitted for her when she was a baby. Their couch is cozy and she was lulled by the sound of the rain and her book so she hadn't noticed the room getting dark as the sun had gone down.

When they purchased the building, one of the many things they didn't anticipate was the problem of having *too much* space. Even with a grand piano, the main floor of the library was a large empty expanse. Ignoring Chris' suggestion that they get a pool table, Sarah set up a make-shift living room under the huge windows that looked down over the street. After laying down a thick round rug, she put in a couch, a loveseat, and an easy-chair to surround their TV. The furniture is nice, but not expensive. After winning an argument with Chris, who didn't understand why they would ever want to block the beautiful two-story windows, she installed large curtains that hung down all the way from the balcony to the floor. They weren't cheap. It was hard to find curtains that drop almost fifteen feet. But the room is as cozy as it can be for such an enormous space.

Chris clomps up the stairs from the kitchen below. "We should order food."

"No we shouldn't. You just want to." Sarah smiles without looking up.

"Fair enough." Chris grins, knowing that she has

already given in. "What do you want? I'll pull up Seamless on my phone."

"Whatever you want, surprise me."

Chris sits down and works his phone while Sarah reaches for the TV remote.

"What do you want to watch? Biggest Loser is on tonight."

"Sure, sounds great," Chris doesn't care. His mind is on acquiring calories, not watching people burn them.

"Huh? That's weird."

"Wha?" Chris does not look up from his phone.

"Look."

Chris looks up at the TV. Confused, he turns back to his phone to check what time it is. It's almost eight thirty, but the local news is still being broadcast.

"That's weird. Why is the news still on?"

"I'm not sure it is. Look more carefully."

On the screen is the ABC 7 anchor desk behind a large graphic saying "DOWNTOWN CONFUSION." Sitting on one side of the desk is a watch, a tie and a spray bottle presumably used to wet down that last perfect piece of anchor-hair. Behind the desk sits two chairs. On one chair sits a woman's button-down blouse and a bra. The expensive articles of clothing have been haphazardly tossed on the arm. There's no sound in the studio, but from the slight hiss in the background, they can tell the microphones are still on.

"Uh... what the hell?" Chris says, finally putting his phone down.

"They should have been off the air for two hours. Have they just been showing that the whole time?

Maybe they forgot to switch back to the network? Or they're having technical difficulties?"

"I guess so. But why are their clothes on the chair?"

"Maybe Steve and Sheena's sexual tension got the best of them and they're doing it under the desk?"

Chris laughs. "It's about time. Though I somehow doubt they'd want to broadcast that to all of Detroit. Change the channel, maybe one of the other networks will have something."

Sarah flips through the channels. The national networks—ESPN, HBO, HGTV, all appear normal. But the local networks are either off the air or showing something similar to ABC 7's empty studio.

"Uh... what the hell? Did the TV stations go bankrupt too?" Chris says half-kidding, half-concerned.

"Some sort of natural disaster?"

"In Detroit? How would you notice?"

"Don't be an asshole. All this stuff is digital, maybe a transformer blew or something? Or a crashed computer? Maybe that could cut off all the local feeds."

"I guess it's possible? You know computer stuff better than I do." Chris looks down at his phone. "Speaking of feeds, where is my confirmation from Seamless? Everyone at the Indian place asleep too?"

"The whole city could be having communication problems. Maybe a rat ate through Detroit's single line of internet cable."

Chris laughs. "God knows, the wire is probably strung out of a window all the way from Chicago."

"I thought we were just stealing their Wi-Fi. They'll figure it out eventually. In the meantime, let's just watch an episode of Property Brothers. The DVR still works. I have work to do anyway. This candy isn't going to crush itself."

They settle into a media-addled stupor, staring at multiple screens at once, but not really paying much attention to either. The TV drones on about home renovation while they separately stare at their phones playing the same game.

"That's a nice looking house, but why would they shit it up by having so many cats?"

"Oh, come on husband. Cats are nice! We should get one."

"Are you kidding? All they do is laze about stealing food and knocking things over."

"How is that different from you?"

"I don't shit in a box and ask you to scoop it out."

It's dully pleasant, killing time staring at LCD pixels. It's an easy way to fill their minds with soothing white noise without really admitting that's what they are doing.

***

Shopping can be tedious, especially for a six-year-old in the JCPenney menswear section. Why is Daddy looking at so many pairs of blue jeans? They're sooooo boring. *Chris did not understand what the difference was between one pair of pants and another. He just knew that his dad seemed to have looked through every single pair of jeans ever made. He really did his best to stay patient and sit still. He had promised to stay on the bench and not move. Or else. But the bench was hard and when five minutes stretched into twenty it seemed like an eternity to his child's mind.*

From his height, all he could see was rack after rack of boring clothes. To Chris the round displays of reasonably priced tops seemed as big as houses. In fact they reminded him of the willow trees at his grandmother's house. He daydreamed that he was in a soft and colorful forest. He barely even noticed that he had left the bench when he started dodging in and out of them searching for treasure. He ran past a rack of collared shirts and discovered that it was the secret hideout of Cobra Commander! He was Storm Shadow on a secret ninja mission to track down bad guys. Giggling, he ran down the aisle and ducked into a rack of bulky red sweaters and hid on the floor beneath the Mediums. This would be his home base. He peeked out from between sweaters and secretly spied on a couple of shoppers who were obviously secret Cobra operatives.

But what is that? Is that a toy store? *From his fort, he was able to see through the glass doors of JC Poopy Boring Store and spotted a bright glowing castle overflowing with awesome toys! He had found his treasure!*

Chris frowned. He knew he couldn't go to the toy store because his father would be angry. Mad Daddy was no fun. In fact Chris knew he should go back to the bench before his father gets back from the dressing room. He felt a jolt of anxiety. What if Daddy finds out that I left the bench? *He stood up and looked down the aisle in the direction he had come.* Or was that where I came from? *All of a sudden, none of it looked familiar.* Oh poop.

"Hey there Buckaroo."

Chris heard a man's voice from behind him and turned around to face a pair of khaki pants. He looked up at a large man who was wearing thick-rimmed glasses and a blue polo shirt. He sported a mustache and a thin black comb-over. From his vantage point, Chris could see an old stain on his shirt that had been slightly distended by the gut protruding over his belt. The man looked enormous, like a giant.

"Cat got your tongue?" He grinned down at Chris.

Chris ran through his mental Rolodex. Do I know him? I'm not supposed to talk to strangers, but sometimes I forget people, like Mommy's brothers and sisters. *He looked at the man again. He was smiling, but not really smiling. It was a strange sensation. Chris could feel fear starting to trickle down the back of his neck like cold water.*

"Not supposed to talk to strangers eh?"

Chris shook his head and started to frantically look for his father.

"It's OK Chief. I'm Frank. I work here. See the blue shirt?"

Chris reluctantly nodded. He saw that the man's shirt was blue, but he wasn't sure what that meant.

"Say, what are you doing in the boring old department store anyway? You know there's a toy store right over there."

Chris didn't say anything. He was unsure what he was supposed to do. Frank smiled down at him and kept talking.

"*You know what? If you'd like, we could walk over there and see about getting you a toy? What's your favorite? He-Man? Transformers? I've got all of them you know. Even Optimus Prime. With the trailer that opens up into a secret action base. Would you like to see them?*"

Chris shook his head again. Frank knelt down and leaned in to him. He was so much bigger than the six-year-old boy. Frank's size felt overwhelming, impossibly powerful. He smelled like onions and sweat. Chris tried to place the odor. It wasn't the type of sweat smell he would get from running around the playground, it was the type of sweat he got when he was really afraid.

His mind raced. Why would the man be scared? He was an adult. Adults never get scared. Besides, he was smiling. Who smiles when they're scared? *Chris just felt more confused.*

"*I'm... I'm... just looking for Daddy.*"

Frank put his hand on his shoulder. It felt heavy and strong. It felt hard somehow, like he was almost flexing it. Chris was now truly frightened. He couldn't even put his finger on what was scaring him so much, but something deep and instinctual told him to be very wary of this man. It was a feeling he had never felt before.

"*Well of course you are. Your daddy told me he was going to load up the car and he wants me to take you out to the parking lot to meet him.*"

Chris did not know what to do. He was supposed to do what adults said, but he really didn't want to go outside with Frank. But maybe Daddy *is* out there and will be mad at me for not doing what the adult said? *He was completely lost. He felt tears coming.*

The hand on his shoulder tightened and he felt himself being pushed towards the door. He wanted to scream, but his father had told him 'under NO circumstances do you shout and make a scene in a public place.'

He was being pushed hard now. They were moving towards the exit at a fast walk. Fast for an adult, it was almost running to a child. Chris was trying to keep up, but his feet felt clumsy. He was so confused. He was sweating. He felt a warm wetness starting in his pants. 'Oh no! Not that! I'm a big boy now I don't-'

"Chris! There you are! Damn it! What did I tell you?"

The sound of his father's voice, even as angry as it was, filled Chris with an overwhelming sense of relief. The hand on his shoulder disappeared immediately.

Chris saw his father walking briskly down the aisle towards him. He looked back for Frank, but somehow he was already three aisles away. Just a blue and tan blur. Gone.

"I told you to stay on the bench! What were you thinking?!"

The tears poured out of him. Chris could barely get words out between sobs. "I...I'm... sorry... Daddy. I got... lost... I didn't mean to."

"Who was that guy with you?"

"I... I.. don't know." *Chris wiped the snot dripping out of his nose with the back of his sleeve.* "He... he said he worked here."

His father's face twitched. Was that fear that Chris

saw? Was Daddy...scared too?

"The hell he does." His voice seemed ice-cold. Chris didn't think he'd ever seen him this angry. "That guy doesn't work here."

Chris was now sobbing loudly. He'd lost all sense of self-consciousness. A few other customers milled around looking very interested in the discount blazers next to where Chris and his father stood. They flipped aimlessly through the jackets and pretended not to listen.

"What you did was incredibly stupid. You could have been killed. Or worse."

Chris didn't really know what that meant, but it was scary. But it wasn't as scary as the fear in his father's voice. Not knowing what else to say, Chris just nodded and choked out "I...I'm sorry."

His father seemed to soften just a bit. He knelt down to the boy and gave him a long hug. Chris felt his sobs start to slow down and he felt the terror draining out.

After a bit his father released him and put his hands on his shoulders. They were face to face. His eyes were misty, like he might have cried a bit too.

"You wet yourself."

"I'm... I'm sorry Daddy."

The embarrassment of hearing it out loud is too much for Chris to even process, especially in front of all of these people. He knew his pants were wet. His socks were wet too. He was too upset to feel the shame, but the shame and embarrassment would come soon enough.

"What have I told you about keeping control Chris?"

"I was so... so... scared. I didn't know what to do."

He shook his head for a moment as if he considered

yelling some more, but thought better. Somewhere in his father was a shred of compassion.

"No, it's OK. We'll get you some fresh clothes. It's alright."

Chris took a deep breath. It's almost over. It must be. *He wanted more than anything just to go home and never come back to JCPenney ever in his life.*

"Listen, Chris. Do you know whose fault this was?"

Chris didn't know what to say. Was this a trick question?

"It was your *fault.*"

Chris swallowed but didn't say anything.

"There are all sorts of dangers all around us. People, things, behaviors. They can all hurt you. Kill you even." *He paused for a second to let it sink in.* "You have to be smart. *What happened today was that you did something stupid. I told you to stay on the bench and you left. Whatever happens after that is your fault.*"

Chris felt the tears coming again. He started to feel increasingly guilty for what he did. Anger started to percolate. Anger at himself.

"Do you understand me? This is very important."

"Yes Daddy."

Chris did not understand at all, at least not yet. But, not knowing what else to do, he nodded and wiped his nose with his sleeve again.

"OK. Let's go home."

***

"Chris."

"Chris!"

"Huh?" Chris wakes up next to Sarah on the couch. He'd fallen asleep with his head in her lap. "How long have I been out?"

"About an hour. I think we need to give up on having food delivered. I'll make some sandwiches."

"Do you need help?"

"I just need you to get off my leg before it falls off."

Chris gets up. "You could have moved me."

"You're adorable when you sleep. Like a puppy. At least until you ripped one that made my face melt."

"Lies!"

Sarah gets up and goes downstairs. Chris picks up the remote and switches back to live TV. There's nothing on. Even the national stations are just showing a black screen. No static, no test signal, just blackness.

"Fuck Time Warner." Chris grumbles to himself. "TV's out." He shouts downstairs to Sarah.

"What?"

"TV's out."

"What? I can't hear you."

Chris gives up and checks the news on his phone. According to the CNN homepage, there's nothing much interesting happening. No mention of Detroit at all.

"What were you saying?"

Sarah climbs up the stairs from the kitchen holding a plate with two peanut butter and jelly sandwiches and some sliced cucumbers.

"Cucumbers? What about chips?"

"You have to eat actual food every once in a while husband. No matter how much you want to keep pretending that you're fifteen, you're on the wrong side of forty now."

Chris shrugs. "Look at this. The TV is out. All of the stations, not just the locals. I guess Time Warner is shitting the bed tonight."

Sarah frowns, disconcerted. "What if it's something more serious than that? Terrorism or something?"

"I checked CNN online and there's nothing at all about Detroit. I figure they'd mention something like terrorists. Besides, look out the window, its dead quiet out there. Unless you count the rain."

*

Six hours later, Chris is woken by a noise. Or rather, the absence of noise. Downtown Detroit is usually relatively deserted at 3:00 in the morning. Unless someone is a prostitute, drug dealer or someone in need of their services, there is not much reason to be out. But anyone who lives in an urban environment knows that within a city limit, there is a perpetual drone of noise. It's not always loud, but an ambient level of sound is inevitable and endless. Chris and Sarah have grown used to the hum of traffic, the wail of sirens, the screeching hydraulics of a garbage truck, the clanging of a maintenance crew working on some pipe below the street or just the distant rumble of the elevated train. No matter the hour, complete silence, like complete darkness, is unachievable.

Chris, who had initially struggled to sleep in the city after growing up in rural northern Michigan, has now adapted to the noise and finds it strangely comforting while he sleeps. As if the real world keeps a foot in the door, reminding him that it exists, making his nightmares seem less real.

It was the impossible quiet that woke him up. He had been dreaming of trying to climb down an uneven ladder in pitch black silence. He couldn't see or hear anything, but he knew he was in danger. Deprived of his senses, he felt powerless to protect himself. He put his foot down expecting to find a step that hadn't been there and he started to slip. He flailed out wildly trying to grab hold of something to stop his fall, but his arms were heavy and dull. He could not seem to get them to move fast enough to catch the ladder and he continued to plummet.

When he wakes up, the blankets are completely twisted around him.

Chris hates the sensation of not knowing exactly where he is and what is happening. He finds disorientation embarrassing as if the loss of awareness, however fleeting, not only unnerves but actually emasculates him. Attempting to regain his bearings, he reaches out for Sarah who sleeps to his left. She's not there. This is not unusual. Sarah suffers from occasional insomnia, and Chris is no longer that startled by her not being there. But tonight he is especially disquieted, by the quiet itself.

Throwing on a t-shirt, Chris exits the bedroom and heads up the stairs into the library. No lights are on, but a streetlight's glow through the window creates a soft outline of Sarah.

"Why don't you turn a light on? You look like a Bond villain plotting to laser the White House from space." Chris walks toward her, trying his best to remember where the coffee table is and not stub his toe for the third time this month.

Sarah ignores his joke. "Something is wrong." She doesn't turn to greet him. She remains still, staring out the window.

"What do you mean?"

"Listen." Her voice carries more than a hint of anxiety.

"I don't hear anything."

"Exactly. Where is the street noise? The cabs, the drunks, the sirens. The city is completely silent."

"Yeah. That's what woke me up I think."

"I haven't seen a single car go by. Or anybody."

Chris puzzles for a second. "Well, it is the middle of the night. Anything on the news? TV?"

"The cable's still out."

Chris grabs a blanket from the couch and sits down on the window-seat with Sarah. The large upholstered alcoves are one of his favorite features of the library. He imagines they were originally designed for kids to sit on while they read story books.

"Weird. What about online? I only checked CNN.com, maybe the local news sites will have something."

"I checked the Detroit Times, but there's nothing there."

Chris picks up Sarah's phone and clicks on the Detroit Times website.

"What do you mean? Did it crash? It looks fine to me."

"Look more carefully. It hasn't been updated since 5:00 yesterday afternoon. It's the same with all the local news sites."

"Still nothing on the national news? You check the New York Times?"

"They all look normal. But, there's no mention of what's happening here whatsoever."

Chris stares out the window for a moment. His troubled feeling starts to intensify. He feels that strange pull in the pit of his stomach that he remembers from the time he spent in New York City in the aftermath of 9/11. He hadn't been there on the infamous day—he arrived almost a year later, and there were no bombs going off or terrorists running around—but he remembers the city having that intangible feeling that something was *off*. He could feel an ominous cloud, an ethereal something, created by the shared background anxiety of millions of rattled but resolute New Yorkers as they stubbornly went about their day despite the fearful cacophony of politicians, media and out-of-town relatives.

"Maybe we should go look around? See if we can find somebody who knows what's going on?"

Sarah stares at her husband as if he had sprouted a second head. She was already worried, but now Chris is really scaring her. Her fear bubbles over into anger.

"Is there something about having a penis that makes men idiots? We don't know what's going on out there. Something is terribly wrong. And you want to just walk out into it!?"

"What are you talking about? Do you see any explosions? Did I miss Godzilla walking by? There's no reason to believe there's any danger. Think logically. You're overreacting."

Chris immediately regrets saying that. He knows he's stepped in dangerous territory. Sarah does not like to be told she's overreacting.

"And you're acting like the guy who ends up being chum in the horror movie!"

"I'm sorry I said you were overreacting. I know you just want us to be safe. I want that too."

Sarah catches herself and softens. It's time to prioritize. Their safety is more important to her than scoring a point in an old fight. "Chris, listen. I love you very much and I want you to do something for me: take this seriously. Humor me. If it turns out to be nothing, I'll owe you one. I'll make it up to you."

Her tone gets his attention. He can tell she is genuinely terrified. Sarah, while not immune to a bout of anxiety or two, is rarely scared.

"OK. I'm with you. What do you want to do?"

"Do you still have your hockey stick?"

"Sure. I think it's in the hall closet."

"Get it. We need to make sure all the doors and windows are locked."

Chris looks back at her with a quizzical expression.

"Do. It."

He does. The doors were already locked of course, but Chris locks all of the windows. At Sarah's insistence, though it makes little sense to Chris, he even locks the windows on the second floor. While he goes up and down the stairs, still holding his hockey stick, Sarah works feverishly on her laptop searching for more information. None of the local news sites have been updated since sometime early yesterday evening. There are a couple of reports of some sort of nude protest taking place downtown, but the stories seem vague and half-written. The national sites are filled with the latest political nonsense and a story about Putin's latest shirtless photos, but there are no stories about Detroit.

"There's nothing about it anywhere. It doesn't make any sense. The only thing that's weird is that some of the locals have stories about some sort of nude protest."

Chris pokes his head over the balcony railing. "Nude? Awesome! Let's see the pictures!"

"Easy cowboy. There aren't any. It just says stay tuned for more info, but they never followed up."

Disappointed, Chris continues to check the window locks. "Maybe somebody posted something on Facebook?"

***

Through the night, the circle of exposed bodies has grown immensely. Ten thousand became a hundred thousand, expanding every minute as more and more of the population of Detroit is exposed, transformed, and called by some primitive instinct to join the horde.

The crowd is so large and dense that it's hard to

distinguish individual people. The lot has taken on the appearance of an enormous flesh-colored storm system rotating like a hurricane. And like a hurricane, there is an eye in the center where the ground is still exposed, creating a single perfectly round spot of untouched earth. In this circle of patchy grass and pavement, a single red sneaker sits undisturbed and ignored.

There is a strange order to the human storm. The circle rotates at an almost mathematically consistent pace around a single axis. Its sheer size creates a hypnotic, dizzying motion, as if the entire city was on a turn-table. It looks like the people of Detroit have created a second small planet slowly revolving in opposition to the earth.

The sense of symmetry created by the steady rotation of the perfect circle is shattered by the chaos of the individuals within. Each naked figure's intermittently spasming limbs constantly hit, shove or trip one another. It looks like a riot, teeming with angry elbows, fists and feet. Yet the fighting is slow-motion and the individuals are not responding to each other. One person hitting another does not cause a retaliation, or a reaction of any kind.

There is no cause and effect—the people are merely taking random actions. Chris would say they look like video game characters controlled by someone who was just mashing random buttons—like a mom trying to play Mortal Combat.

All the unclothed people might appear sexy from afar—so much naked flesh—it's an unbridled bacchanalia of skin. There are no rules, just a massive collection of people devoid of modesty, boundaries or inhibitions on a scale unrivaled by even the greatest of Roman orgies. But the titillation breaks down on closer inspection. There is no passion or enjoyment on their faces. Just blank, lifeless expressions and empty white eyes. They are merely bodies in motion, moving flesh. It is not sex, it is horror.

And the bodies are already beginning to break down. People, who had been mostly sedentary for their human lives, begin to show their fragility. Feet unaccustomed to walking over anything other than grass or carpeting are being damaged by the unforgiving pavement. Without the protection of shoes, they are becoming raw and beginning to blister. Corns wear down to soft skin and the soft skin bruises and cracks. Then they start to bleed.

Shirley's body has been walking barefoot for nine hours. The soles of her feet are cut in multiple places and are being slowly eroded by the asphalt, glass, dirt and trash. The toenail of her left big toe was torn back when she stepped on the edge of a curb. Her pinkie toe shattered when it was stomped on by another nameless foot. No longer able to hold its shape, it flops lazily like a deflated balloon every time she takes a step. Shirley would be in excruciating agony if she still felt pain. She should be hobbled and exhausted. But she is still upright.

Many in the horde have not been as lucky. Hundreds of the weaker bodies—the elderly, the children—lost their footing and have been trampled. Endless rows of feet mash the fallen into pieces. The pieces mix with dirt and debris to form slippery patches of a horrible paste.

***

Chris finishes his sweep of the building and pours himself a glass of water from the kitchen sink. Taking the stairs back into the library, he discovers Sarah staring dumbfounded at her computer. All the lights are now on. When she looks up and sees Chris holding the water, her eyes widen and her hands unconsciously grip the side of the table. She speaks slowly and clearly, almost in a monotone.

"Chris. Put down the water."

"Huh?"

"The glass of water. Put it down and step away from it."

"What are you talking about? It's just water."

"Chris! Fucking listen to me! Put down the goddamned water!" She's shouting, finally having lost her cool.

Chris slowly and carefully puts down the glass, giving Sarah the 'you're losing your mind, but I'm going to calmly and nicely take care of you until you take your meds' face.

"OK. Water is down. What's going on?"

"Did you drink any of it?"

"No?"

"Did you touch the water at any point?"

"I don't think so? Why?"

"Thank God. It might just be a hoax and I'm

overreacting. I hope that's what it is, but I think there's some sort of contagion in the water. I think that's what's going on."

"What kind of contagion?"

"I don't know but they say it's apparently super dangerous."

"Who's *they*?"

"People on Facebook."

Chris releases a relieved breath. "Oh. The great titans of medicine and journalism on Facebook. Well why didn't you say so?"

Exasperated, but unwilling to be pulled into an argument, Sarah plops her husband down in front of her computer. He reads her Facebook feed:

> *Doug Cartman: What happened to the TV? Do the stars really dance if I can't see them?*
> *Becky Dawson: Lions are totally going to win. Tom Brady is so overrated.*
> *Paige Brewer: DON'T TOUCH THE WATER IN DETROIT! Tom's National Guard unit just got activated. They told him the water is contaminated! We're being quarantined! Not a joke.*
>> *Adam Smith: For real? Are you kidding?*
>> *David Spacey: Hoax.*
> *Becky Ulmer: Has anybody been able to reach anybody in the city. Carl's phone just rings and rings. Does anybody know if there's an outage or something?*

Alan Carrol: I hear there are naked people downtown! Why wasn't I invited to the party?

> *Patty Granger: Leave it to you to be the first to know...*

> *Arlene Carrol: I'm pretty sure he has a Google alert for #nude.*

Nina Venet: Just heard a rumor that we should avoid the water. #Detroitwaterconaminated #sowhatelseisnew

Ken Wojciechowski: Uh... a tank just rolled down my street. WTF?!

Ken has posted a picture of a large green tank rumbling through a neighborhood. The juxtaposition of the huge piece of military hardware on a quiet suburban street—the sheer size of the tank in relation to the Prius parked in the driveway—reminds Chris of old news footage he'd seen from the riots. He frowns and keeps reading. Under the picture:

> *Sarah Smith, Linnet Frankel, Bob Wojciechowski and 4 other like this.*

>> *Michael Lee: Really? No joke?*

>> *Ken Wojciechowski: Yeah, they're on megaphones saying not to leave our house or use the water. They say it's dangerous.*

>> *Tom Helmut: Probably trying to cover-up the poison they're putting into the sky with con-trails. #repealobamacare*

> *Michael M. Bulston: My Wicked tour heads to Dallas this week. Gonna get me some BBQ! I think I'm on for Boq for the Wednesday*

*matinee. #stagedoorismyfrontdoor #tourlife
#workingactor #grateful #productioncontract*
*Derek Freeman: I think I just heard gunshots.
So much for the suburbs being safer.*
*Christine Winter: Why the f*ck won't they let
me on the highway? Ugh...*
*Scott Wolvington: My puppy just pooped on
the couch. #adorable*
*Trig Roland: Look at my hamburger! It is
magnificent! Look at it!*

Chris looks up from the laptop. "Sarah, it's just internet rumors. Sure the picture of the tank is weird, but you know how easy it is to Photoshop something like that."

"Maybe, but this is what I wanted to show you."

Kelly, Sarah's old college roommate, has posted a link. The headline reads 'HUNDREDS OF THOUSANDS MISSING IN DETROIT. GOVERNMENT COVERS UP MYSTERIOUS OUTBREAK.'

Sarah clinks on the link. A blog appears showing a series of photographs of military hardware blocking highways and bridges into Detroit.

"What is this? Some sort of conspiracy blog?" Chris says with more skeptical bravado than he feels. "More con-trail nonsense?"

"I don't think so. These pictures don't look fake. Read."

GOVWATCH readers, we are picking up

numerous reports of an unprecedented outbreak and government cover-up in Detroit, Michigan. GOVWATCH has been flooded with pictures and videos of a huge military crackdown surrounding and apparently quarantining the largest city in Michigan.

According to both eyewitness accounts and our own transcripts of police and military-band radio, we are dealing with a virus or parasite causing bizarre effects on people who come in contact with water, either rain or city water. Reports started to taper off significantly after rain started falling over much of Northern Michigan.

If you examine the photos of the military blockades of the bridges and highways around the city, you'll note one interesting thing. There are plenty of people backed up attempting to get into the city, but only small pockets of citizens are attempting to exit the city. What happened to everybody in Detroit? Where are they?

And lastly, why haven't you seen this on CNN, Fox News...or any mass media outlet??? Why are all of the Detroit metropolitan TV stations off the air? Why isn't this outbreak the biggest news story since 9/11? It's obvious that the government has decided to keep this from its citizens. Why? To avoid panic? To prevent concerned citizens from trying to get into the city and those within the city from breaking quarantine? To *protect financial interests in the domestic and international stock markets? Only time will tell...*

(UPDATE: 8:43 PM) As of this evening we have had two reports that the quarantine is being enforced by any means necessary, up to and including the use of lethal force. In case anybody is confused, that means the United States Government is threatening to kill its own citizens. What is going on? GOVWATCH has been attempting to get answers from the 'authorities' but we have been ignored.

Rest assured fellow patriots, they will not be able to keep this under wraps for too long. When a city disappears, people tend to notice. Keep refreshing for more updates.

Sarah hits refresh on the computer. The browser spins for a second and the page is replaced with an error message:

Error. The server at http://www.govwatch.org can't be found, because the DNS lookup failed

Sarah hits refresh again, and gets the same result.

"Maybe it crashed from too much traffic?" she says while clicking back to Facebook.

"Wait a minute. What the hell? Scroll back up."

They stare at Sarah's Facebook feed. It now reads:

Becky Dawson: Lions are totally going to win.

Tom Brady is so overrated.
Michael M. Bulston: My Wicked tour heads
to Dallas this week. Gonna get me some BBQ!
I think I'm on for Boq for the Wednesday
matinee. #stagedoorismyfrontdoor #tourlife
#workingactor #grateful #productioncontract
Scott Wolvington: My puppy just pooped on
the couch. #adorable
Trig Roland: Look at my hamburger! It is
magnificent! Look at it!

"They deleted all the posts about the... whatever this is! How is that possible?"

"Even if it's possible, there's no way that it's legal."

For the first time, Chris finds himself truly frightened as well. "Assuming this is true, the depth and scope of this cover-up is staggering. I mean, its audacity is ridiculous. Because no matter what the government tries, whichever shady agency it may be, a problem of this magnitude could not possibly stay a secret for more than a few hours, days at the most."

"What do you think it means?"

"I have no idea. Water-borne virus? Shady cover-up? It's all a little X-Files, don't you think?" He pauses to think for a moment. "But if there really is a quarantine, it seems like an act of desperation. What could possibly merit all of this?"

Sarah shakes her head. "Maybe it's all just some big hoax. I mean, do you really buy that the government would—or could—cover this up? What would be the point?"

"I don't know. The money thing seemed most plausible I guess."

"What do you mean?"

"If there is some sort of disaster, it could crash the international stock markets. Remember what happened after 9/11? People lost a shit-ton of money."

"Sure, but if this is really happening, they can't hide it forever."

"Of course, but maybe they don't have to. They just have to delay the news from getting out until they can freeze their assets internationally and shut down the exchanges domestically or whatever. Right now, I don't think anybody knows what's actually going on, and nothing crashes markets like uncertainty."

Sarah gives him a skeptical look. "You're a finance expert now?"

"Remember when we lost the remote? The TV was stuck on CNBC for two hours. I'm pretty sure I have a good understanding of international trade markets now."

She is too frightened to give his joke more than a nod and a smile that comes out as more of a grimace. "It doesn't make any sense."

"What of this does make sense to you?"

"None of it. But we should behave as if it's real. I'd rather be a red-faced dupe than... an infected or whatever."

"Yeah."

"So, what do we do?" Sarah knows this is the obvious if somewhat unanswerable question, but somebody has to ask it. "Call 911? Or 311?"

"I think they shut down 311 last year when they ran out of money. Besides, nobody in any official capacity is going to give us information. They've stopped the media, legit and otherwise, from reporting it. They've somehow been able to remove information from Facebook, they're definitely not going to answer questions."

Sarah nods. It doesn't seem possible, but based on what they've seen, he's right.

"What about calling your folks? They're on the other side of the country. Their TV probably works. Maybe they know something we don't?"

"Yeah, that's a good idea."

Chris picks up his cell phone and attempts to call her parents in Wyoming.

"Not going through. I can't get a signal."

Sarah checks her phone too. The same.

"Did they shut down the cell networks?"

"I guess they'd have to." Chris thinks for a second. "Oh, let's try the hard line."

Like the fire alarm and sprinkler system, the strange building codes created by the conversion from a public to a private building forced them to install a traditional telephone line despite it seeming unnecessary. They never even bothered to install an actual phone, but in the back of a closet, Chris finds a cheap plastic telephone they bought at a dollar store to test the line. He plugs it into the jack.

"Shit. No dial tone. Try e-mailing them. They won't get it until the morning, but at least it's something."

"They won't get it at all," Sarah says with a mixture of frustration and anxiety.

"Why not?"

"The internet is down now too."

"All of it?"

"Yep, the modem's not getting anything from the cable line. I already rebooted. I think this means we're officially cut off."

Frustrated, Chris sits down on the arm of their couch. Something in his 'man brain' is struggling with the growing sense of danger and his being completely at a loss for what to do about it. His father always told him even in danger, or perhaps especially in danger, a man is supposed to be able to reason out the situation logically. You're supposed to be able to figure out a plan that guarantees the safety of yourself and your loved ones. But tonight he can't think of anything to do. The situation is so bizarre he doesn't have enough reference points to put together a plan of action. It temporarily short-circuits his ability to act.

"I need a drink." Chris says finally.

"You need to help me find our flashlights and any candles we can find." Sarah's brain has no such male limitations. She doesn't need all of the data, she's working more on instinct than logic.

"Why? What do we need those for?"

All of the lights abruptly shut off. Power to the city of Detroit has been severed and they are swallowed up by darkness.

"That's why. If they're truly trying to stop all traffic and communication out of the city, they've got to shut off the electricity too." Lighting her way by her iPhone, Sarah walks down the stairs into the kitchen, where they keep the flashlights.

Chris heads to the linen closet where he remembers they stashed some candles last Christmas. They continue their discussion, now shouting between rooms.

"Even if they think they're protecting people outside of the city, what about the people *in* the city? They can't just abandon us. Where's the CDC?"

"No fucking clue." Sarah shines her flashlight on Chris and hands him another one. "Let's find those candles. We should save the batteries. We don't know how long the power is going to be out."

"It's almost dawn. We'll have light in a couple of hours."

"What makes you think the power will be up before it gets dark again?

CHAPTER 4

"**O**W! OW! OW!" *Mikey was shrieking.*
Sarah's heart started pounding in her chest.
Mikey had only been out of her sight for thirty seconds,
a minute tops. FUCK. Scrambling up the embankment
while pulling her pants up, she slipped and almost face-
planted into the steep wet carpet of rocks and leaves.
With a flash of dexterity she didn't have time to
appreciate, she managed to grab on to an exposed root to
keep her balance. Adrenaline coursed through her
teenage body as she desperately tried to get to the top.

They were on a brother-sister camping trip. That's
all that Mikey wanted for his ninth birthday. Not some
wimpy day hike like on a school field trip, but a full
week in a national park where he would get to camp in
a tent and cook marshmallows by the fire. Most
importantly, it had to be with his kickass older sister
Sarah. The only girl he knew that wasn't gross or

worse... girly.

Not a lot of nine-year-old boys want to go camping with their sisters and even fewer seventeen-year-old girls would, secretly, be just as excited. But Sarah was thrilled. She enjoyed being outdoors, but even more — she loved her little brother. Being eight years apart in age helped them avoid most of the typical sibling rivalries and petty arguments about toys or chores. He was a bright and enthusiastic kid. Something about his child-like optimism and love of life helped ground her when she stepped into the bleak world of teenage angst and perpetual misery.

Mikey looked up to Sarah because she seemed so adult. She drove a car, she had a job, she had money so she could buy all the candy she wanted. She seemed to be so mature, but she was still cool. Most adults seemed to talk at him not to him. They always treated him like he was either much younger or much older than he was. They looked at the top of his head or at their own feet, as if looking him in the eye would be weird or dangerous. To Mikey, it felt like adults didn't remember what being nine felt like. Sarah was different. She made eye contact with him. She talked to him like he was her equal but in a way that made it clear that she understood, and more importantly, was interested in the intricacies of his nine-year-old boy's thoughts.

They had long discussions about the various bugs and worms he discovered on their father's farm. He was obsessed with insects, the weirder the better. He spent hours reading books well above his grade level to learn as much as he could about the insect world. Sarah often helped him navigate the bigger scientific words. She would pronounce the words for him, and then he would explain what they meant to her, because often he had already heard them on a Discovery Chanel or PBS program. He had posters of spiders, beetles and dragonflies tacked over every surface of his bedroom. Finding his enthusiasm irresistible, Sarah had cemented her status as the coolest sister ever when she presented him with a live ant colony on his eighth birthday.

"Ooooooooooowwww!"

Sarah could hear fear in Mikey's voice. She tried to run faster up the steep wooded slope and tripped on a stick, banging her shin on a rock. Seventeen was an awkward age for Sarah. She had one foot in adulthood, but another still firmly planted in childhood. Her favorite doll still sat on the same desk as her college applications. Hanging out with Mikey usually made her feel very grown up, in control—powerful even. But in that instant: alone in the woods and responsible for keeping her brother safe, about to face some sort of injury she wasn't qualified to treat—she felt very much a child. She was not ready for this. She had just stepped behind a tree to pee and now Mikey, the child she was supposed to keep safe, was wailing in pain.

Sarah finally reached the top of the ridge and looked down to see Mikey sitting on the ground holding onto his leg. Blood was streaming down his calf and was starting to saturate the top of his sock.

"Oh my God! What happened?" She knelt down next to him looking for the source of the blood. How deep is the cut? Did he break his leg!?

Mikey's words came out in broken little spurts between sobs. "I...I...I climbed... that rock...and...and...slipped." A new gale of sobs began. He seemed so young to her. He really was small for his age.

Sarah cursed herself for not bringing first aid supplies. As an adult she would always wonder why her parents didn't insist that they bring them. Perhaps they didn't care about first aid due to some 'farm-tough' vanity. 'We're tough country folk. Just rub some mud in it' or some bullshit.

She tore off a piece of her t-shirt and started to wipe the blood off his shin to get a look at the wound. She winced when he whimpered from the pain, but knew she had to see what they were dealing with. When she did, Sarah almost laughed with relief. He was cut for sure, but it wasn't that deep. There was a gash about four inches long, but it was shallow and already starting to clot. There was a startling amount of blood, but it was just that: startling.

"Shh... shh... it's OK Mikey. You're going to be fine. It's just a cut."

Mikey looked up at her. The sobs started to thin out. He was more frightened than in pain and when she said it wasn't that bad, he trusted her.

"OK. Let me just wrap this. It will stop bleeding soon." She tied the piece of fabric tightly around the gash. "See, now, you look badass!"

The swear word broke through Mikey's sniffles. He almost started to grin.

"I'm... a... badass." He tried out the swearword and waited to be admonished. When he wasn't, the grin spread. "Bad... ASS!"

"Alright, alright. Let's not take that term home to Mom. But we should start heading back."

Mikey's face fell. "What? No! We just got here. I don't wanna go home. You promised! A whole week!"

"Mikey you got injured. We don't even have any Band-Aids."

"No! I'm fine! See, I'm not crying. It's OK. Pleeeeaasssse can we stay?"

It was just a cut. He had indeed stopped crying and was walking around in circles, as if to prove he was alright. Sarah could never seem to say 'no' to Mikey, even when she knew better. Why not stay? The weather was great. They were having fun.

***

Chris has fallen asleep on the couch again. He snores lightly, leaning up against Sarah's leg. She's still awake, deep in thought, but her mind is confused and chaotic. She tries to wrap her head around what is happening to them, tries to make plans, but her thoughts are too filled with jumbled questions without answers, conflicting emotions and upsetting memories. She looks at her phone. It's still at least an hour before dawn.

She carefully gets up and sits down on the window seat to stare out into the blackness. Not only is the street unnaturally quiet, it is now completely pitch black. All of the lights in the city have gone out. Streets that haven't been truly dark since the invention of streetlights have been erased into inky blackness. All the porch lights, the headlights of cars, the neon ATM sign in the deli window, the dingy billboards lit from below... all those millions of light sources she no longer even noticed are gone.

The only sound is the persistent rain pounding the pavement.

Sarah has an intense sense of claustrophobia. Even in the large room, even in a vast and seemingly empty city, the silent darkness surrounds and envelops her. A single candle burning at her side is the only thing that prevents the oppressive void from swallowing her whole. She hears a rapid tapping below her and nervously looks around for the source of the noise until she realizes that it is her own foot nervously knocking the wooden trim.

Knowing it is a waste of batteries but not being able to stop herself, she turns on the large flashlight beside her. The light now seems incredibly bright. Sarah has never been afraid of the dark but she is immensely grateful for the beam of illumination she holds in her hand.

She thinks of Luke Skywalker's lightsaber, not just light, but a powerful weapon against evil. She remembers the real belief she had as a child that light could protect her from all evil. The monster under the bed, the ghosts in the closet and even the *nothingness* from her favorite movie 'The NeverEnding Story' could all be held at bay with the single flick of a switch. The pink flashlight she kept under her pillow had magical powers. She wasn't afraid of the dark—even as a little girl, she was too rational for that. But she was afraid of the unknown, the danger she couldn't see, the doom that crept in shadows. The dark couldn't hurt her, but ignorance could. She no longer believes that her flashlight is magical of course, but nothing in the known world could pry it from her hands this evening.

She pulls the curtain back and shines the flashlight onto the street one story below. The light catches the rain illuminating each droplet for a fraction of a second as it plummets to the ground. Sarah spotlights a crosswalk sign, a parked Hyundai Elantra, a blue mailbox that she had forgotten was there. Then, directly below the window, a face.

"Shit!" Sarah shouts much louder than she means to. She scrambles back from the glass. The flashlight drops to her side.

"Wha? What's going on?" Chris snaps awake at the sound of her cry. He immediately grabs his hockey stick and stands up, banging his shin on the coffee table again. With panic coursing through his body, he doesn't feel the pain, but somewhere in his subconscious he knows he'll have a pretty impressive bruise tomorrow.

"There's someone out there!" Sarah shines the flashlight back out the window, but the face is gone. She arcs the beam down the street to her left, nothing. Then she turns it to the right and spotlights the somewhat flabby naked body of a middle-aged woman walking down the street towards midtown.

Chris scrambles to her side straining to see. "What the hell is she doing?"

"I have no idea! Jesus, why is she walking in the middle of the street completely naked? In the rain!"

Chris shouts towards the woman through the glass. "Hey! Lady! Are you OK?"

The woman does not respond. But as she continues walking down the street, her arm snaps out to the right. A few steps later her shoulder twitches.

"This is so freaking weird. What is she doing? Is she having convulsions? Dancing? Maybe she couldn't hear me?" He starts to open the window.

"Are you crazy?!" Sarah pushes him back forcefully. "It's raining! You were just going to stick your head out there? Jesus Christ! You've got to be smarter than that!"

"Fuck. Yes, you're right. I'm sorry." He puts his hand on her shoulder. "Look. I know this is weird. I know you're scared-"

"Hell yeah I'm scared! I'm scared about whatever the fuck is happening, but I'm even more scared that you're not scared enough!"

"Sarah, I know things are confusing, but we're safe. We're here in our living room. I don't see anything trying to attack us. There's no gun to our heads."

"The water."

"What?"

"The *water* is the gun to our heads. If there's some sort of virus or contaminate in the water that is so dangerous the US Government would abandon an entire city..."

Sarah trails off not knowing exactly how to formulate the thought, not knowing what the true implications may or may not be.

"Maybe, but that lady was in the water and she seemed OK." Chris looks out the window trying to see the woman again, but she's long gone.

"OK!? Walking completely naked down the street in the pouring rain, twitching like Urkel being hit with a taser?! Does that seem 'OK' to you?"

"Well, no. Obviously not. But, I mean... I don't know."

"Exactly. We don't know. We have to be smart. We agreed on this. Dangerous until proven safe. You got it?"

"Fine. I got it."

They stand silently looking at each other for a moment before Sarah goes back to the window and shines the light out into the street again.

"Look! Someone else is out there!"

What used to be a teenage boy walks down the center of the street. Naked, blank-faced, he slowly works his way down the road. His right elbow jerks out then falls back to his side.

"Hey! Hey you!" Sarah calls at the boy through the window.

He does not respond. Sarah shines the light in his face, trying to get his attention. No response.

Chris leans toward the glass. "Shit. Look at his eyes! They're all white. What the fuck happened to his eyes?!"

They watch in silence as the boy walks down the street and out of sight.

Chris shines his own flashlight out the window. He

can feel a part of him still trying to avoid the gravity of the situation. A part of him doesn't want to look like an idiot when this all turns out to be nothing, so he wisecracks.

"So this is what happens when you get exposed to the water? You take off all of your clothes and boogie down Broadway?"

Despite herself, Sarah grins. "It's more like zombie krump don't you think?" She thinks maybe he's right to try and diffuse the tension a bit. It's too easy to be paralyzed by fear. She's embarrassed by being so scared. She's annoyed with herself for shouting at Chris. There is another beat of silence. "I'm sorry I snapped at you."

"I get it. I was being stupid. We're going to have to be a lot smarter to..."

"Survive." Sarah says flatly.

"Fuck, that's bleak." Chris shakes his head and lets out a sigh. "But yeah I guess so." He sits back down on the couch and turns off his flashlight.

Sarah takes one last look out the window and chokes back a horrified sob. "Oh no!"

"What is it?"

"It's a kid. A toddler."

Chris gets back up and joins Sarah. Together they watch the solitary child unsteadily totter through the rain.

"We have to do something!" Sarah says. A tear of desperation begins to form in her eye. She already knows what Chris will say. And he will be right.

"You know there's nothing we can do. You said it yourself. We have to be smart. Whatever is happening to these people, we can't help them. Not while it's raining. And probably not even after it stops. We don't know shit about viruses or whatever this is. We also don't know what *they're* going to do. They could be dangerous."

Sarah does not reply. Her lack of action is her response. Chris takes her by the shoulder and sits her down on the couch, then slowly closes the curtains. They sit together in silence. Dawn is right around the corner.

CHAPTER 5

T*his can't be happening. I am not a monster. I will not do this.*

When Lawrence Thomas joined the National Guard out of high school in 1990, he envisioned directing traffic during a power outage or stacking sandbags during a hurricane. 'A couple of weekends a year,' they said, 'It will help you pay for college'. And it did. He spent three years serving in the guard before attending Michigan State. It wasn't too bad. Basic training was hard, but after spending most of his two years of service working in the kitchens, his obligation was only a couple of weekends here and there. He was technically in the Individual Ready Reserve for five more years, but after he was officially discharged in 1999, he was free and clear. Not a bad deal, he thought. He graduated college with a degree in English and history and taught sophomore English at a public high school just outside of Detroit. When the wars in Iraq and Afghanistan started, he was pretty nervous that he might be re-called, but by then he was already thirty and was teaching full-time so he was low on the list for deployment. By 2015, Lawrence hadn't thought about his National Guard duty in years. He was forty-three and pudgy. Curly grey hair had sprouted out of his temples and he had settled in nicely to his suburban life with his wife and seventeen-year-old son. It occasionally made him shake his head with wonder that his son was now only a year younger than he was when he joined the Guard.

The night the water turned, Lawrence was headed home after moderating a student debate competition at the school. It was already eight o'clock and he was tired and hungry so he was trying to decide how he could convince his wife Dianne to let them order a pizza when the call came. She would tell him that he shouldn't be eating pizza at his weight and blood pressure, but if he were able to craft the right charm offensive, he might be able to pull it off. He had decided on singing "let's get a pizza" to the tune of Marvin Gaye's 'Let's Get It On' when his cell phone rang. He looked down at the caller ID and it was a restricted number. *Damn, did I forget to pay Comcast?*

"Hello?"

"PFC Lawrence Jones?"

"Uh, yeah. Who is this?"

"You are hereby recalled and ordered to report to Selfridge Air National Guard Base."

"Huh? Sir, I was discharged sixteen years ago. I'm

retired."

"This is an emergency recall. Report to Selfridge."

"When?"

"Immediately. This is a top secret mission. If you have any communication about this engagement with a civilian you will be subject to a court martial."

"Uh... What's going on?"

"Code Orange."

"What? Is this a joke?"

Lawrence did not get a response. The line was dead.

*

"Private! You will fire your weapon or you will be shot yourself!"

Ten hours later, Lawrence found himself in full combat gear holding an M15 assault rifle. His flak jacket was too tight—maybe he had gained more weight than he thought. He felt dazed by the flurry of activity that greeted him when he got to the base. He was barely out of his car when people started throwing equipment at him and shouting orders. Somebody roughly pressed a rifle into his hands and ordered him to get on a bus.

Most of the men he rode with were just as confused as he was. Charles, who sat next to him in the third row, was sixty-eight years old and hadn't even thought about the guard since he was discharged in 1975 after Vietnam. They were all trying to ask question of their C.O.—who looked to them like he had just started shaving—but he refused to answer. They were told to 'sit down and shut the fuck up' until they reached their posts.

Their post turned out to be the northbound lane of Route 5. It was still dark. Dawn was coming soon, but they were lit from behind by huge arc-sodium flood lights. Lawrence was pressed up against an improvised road-block that consisted of an armored personnel carrier and a Dodge minivan. The National Guard had blocked Route 5 fifteen miles outside of Detroit and was on orders to prevent anyone from leaving the city by any means necessary. He stood there for five straight hours while he listened to his superiors argue with each other. They were getting more and more disturbing orders over the radio and he could tell they were frightened.

Lawrence stood there until his legs felt like jelly. He was shouted down every time he tried to ask what was happening, why he was there, and why his orders were getting more and more drastic. He knew the situation was barbaric, but eventually the fear hidden behind the eyes of his commanders made him keep his mouth shut. He had no choice but to remain silently standing there becoming more and more confused and more and more afraid.

Now he was being forced to kill or be killed.

This can't be happening. I am not a monster. I will not do this.

"Private! Do I sound like I'm fucking joking!?"

Lawrence hadn't really believed that there even was such a thing as a 'Code Orange'. It had been whispered about when he was enlisted, but it seemed like one of those rumors that got started to scare rookies. Code

Orange was a complete, permanent quarantine to be maintained with lethal force. They were abandoning anything and everything within the hot zone. And tonight, the hot zone was the entire city of Detroit.

He heard a click behind his ear. It was the unmistakable sound of a pistol being cocked. He felt the cold barrel on the back of his neck. In front of him, a small crowd had gathered on the road. About twenty-five men, women and children stood looking back at him demanding to be let through. Some of them shouted curses at the soldiers, while a couple of others had tearfully fallen to their knees. They were begging to be let out. They were innocent civilians and they were pleading with them... with *him*. Lawrence tried to avoid eye contact with the desperate and—Jesus help me—innocent people on the other side of the line.

"You have until the count of three to open fire or I will fucking grease you and do it myself!"

Lawrence put his finger on the trigger of his rifle and put his sight on the largest, most aggressive-looking man in the crowd. He was wearing a denim jacket and a Detroit Tigers hat. He was shouting at the soldiers behind the barricade, foaming with rage. Spit rained out of his mouth and collected on his scrabbly beard as he demanded to be let through.

"Three!"

The barrel of the pistol felt alive with the promise of pain, like a hornet's tiny feet crawling down his neck. It was a completely unnerving sensation—that it could sting him at any moment. If he tried to swat it away, he would definitely be stung, but there were no guarantees that remaining frozen would keep him safe either. And in this scenario, the sting would be fatal. Reluctantly, Lawrence took a deep breath.

"Two!"

In that instant of indecision, Lawrence thought of his family. *Were they in the quarantine zone?* They were a half hour drive out of the city center, but he didn't know where the military considered 'ground zero' so he couldn't be sure. Either way, he knew he couldn't help them if he was dead.

He took a deep breath. *Jesus forgive me.* The man wearing the jean jacket—the man he was seconds from shooting—hesitated for a second and looked down. There was a little girl pulling on the pocket of his jeans. The man knelt down and hugged her. She was obviously his daughter and he was quietly comforting her. *Lord, I can't do this.*

"One!"

The last thing Lawrence heard was the gunshot that sent a bullet into the back of his spine. He didn't feel pain, just surprise. He only realized that he had fallen to the pavement when he noticed that he was looking straight up at the sky as the first hint of dawn approached. He had never looked directly up as the sun rose or set. He had always just looked at the horizon. This new perspective was beautiful really. On one side of the sky, it was still fully night-time. Clouds were blocking the stars so it was pitch black. On the other side, the hint of light, the hint of color peeked into the periphery of his vision. Between horizons is an expansive slow gradation of dark to light that seemed to be increasing in intensity as if the day were an electric range slowing cycling up. The irony of watching the day powering up as he powered down made him grin for a moment. If he read this in one of his student's creative writing assignments, he would have told him or her that the thought was a little 'on the nose.'

Lawrence listened with dull, fading ears to gales of automatic gunfire as the other Guardsmen opened fire on the crowd. The last thing he thought was '*is it starting to rain?*'

CHAPTER 6

The sun begins to rise over the city as the rain tapers off. It's a Saturday. The warm light fights its way through the clouds to illuminate the quietest rush hour in history. There's still gridlock up and down 94, but it's not moving. Tens of thousands of cars sit abandoned on the highways and streets. A garbage truck rests up against a park bench. It had rolled over the curb after its driver suddenly opened the door and stepped out of the cab. A torn remnant of a filthy green shirt remains on the steering wheel. The engine has been idling all night, its endless low rumble joining hundreds of vehicles that were left running, creating a strange monotone chorus. Their occupants never bothered to turn them off when they abandoned them, intent on getting to the circle. One by one, the engines eventually sputter and die as they finally run out of gas.

The vast network of streets is littered with countless discarded articles of clothing. Shoes of all shapes and sizes dot the pavement. Briefcases, eyeglasses, watches, rings and even a few wigs lie in filthy puddles of rainwater.

The last of the precipitation comes from the tail of a large weather system working its way from the southwest to the northeast, depositing rain as it goes. Water vapor gets sucked up from Lake Michigan and heads high up into the clouds to mix with moisture from all over the Midwest. The trillions of molecules of hydrogen and oxygen eventually become too densely populated and re-combine as water. Soon they plummet down in droplets of rain, falling over a large part of the country. The rainwater runs into puddles, streams, rivers and lakes from which the whole process begins again.

From above, the streets of Detroit appear completely abandoned. There are no lights. No cars, buses or trains are moving. Normally at this hour pedestrians and vehicles would be constantly moving through the grid like blood through arteries. Not today. But the streets are not completely abandoned. Every once in a while, a solitary naked straggler can be seen headed for the center of town. Not everyone got exposed at the same time of course, so the few people who might have had a cold and had gone to bed early, blissfully unaware that the city was falling around them, are exposed by drinking their morning coffee, washing a dish or brushing their teeth. They may have stepped into the rain to retrieve a morning paper that was never even printed. However the story plays out, the last one percent of the once-great city gradually joins the circle.

At 10:07 AM, as the sun burns through the last of the clouds, the tall man Lawrence the National Guardsman died to avoid killing arrives at the horde. He had been able to duck under the bullets, but he could not avoid the rain. The man, now sans his customary Tigers cap—and everything else—merges smoothly with the parade of feet. His daughter would get there twenty minutes later, slowed by her shorter legs. The circle has grown so large that the five empty blocks can barely contain the masses. Some people on the edges of the horde run into the corners of the surrounding buildings causing pileups. The pressure from all of the arms and legs and torsos causes the bodies in front to be mashed into the obstacle and break into pieces.

At the corner of Cass and Columbia, Bookies Bar and Grille sits alone in the desert of pavement. It's so isolated that its owner decided to run a shuttle bus between itself and the sports stadiums and theaters a few empty blocks away. The two-story brick building now finds itself flush with customers in the ever-expanding pathway of the circle. Bodies begin to pile up as they crash into the dingy exterior walls. The facade had been adorned again and again with hand-painted advertisements for Coca-Cola, General Electric or smaller local businesses for nearly a century. Now it is painted with blood. As more and more bodies push against the brick, the force increases and increases until the building itself shudders, raining dust and bits of plaster onto the people below. Eventually, Bookies Bar and Grille gives way, collapses onto itself, and is overrun by the naked 'dancers'. Their feet continue up and over the rubble, eroding the mound of brick until it crumbles into dust. In time, the building will merely be a bump in the pathway of the population of Detroit.

And the circle continues its slow, inexorable rotation.

***

When morning comes to the library, Sarah has returned to her post on the windowsill watching an occasional nude person blankly stumble by. She did not sleep. She wonders when she might ever feel safe enough to sleep again.

Chris arrives from the kitchen and hands her a can of Diet Coke.

"It's not coffee, but it's caffeinated and it's probably not contaminated." He opens a can of his own and sits down at the piano.

"There weren't any cold ones?"

"No power, no fridge. Remember?

"Right. Duh. Thanks."

Chris begins to play a Chopin etude. It's a beautiful and sad piece. His fingers dance up and down the keyboard with uncommon dexterity, but the music sounds flat and dull. Chris stops playing. His heart is not in it.

"So." He puts the cover down over the keys and turns to face Sarah.

"So." She replies.

"I suppose we should figure out what to do. This is what we know: something has contaminated the water. The city water, the rain, pretty much anything wet."

"Well not everything. We drank the soda and we seem to be OK. So, let's say any water that wasn't self-contained when whatever happened... happened."

"Right." Chris pauses for a moment. "So, if we trust that website we assume that when people get exposed to water, they start acting crazy. Take off all of their clothes, go outside and do a, what did you call it? Zombie krump?"

"Don't forget the eyes. Their eyes go white. I guess they roll up?"

"Yeah, and they're non-responsive." Chris sets down his drink. "So is it fatal? Are they going to die?"

"I've never heard of anybody coming back from something like that." She hears the stupidity of what she just said. "I mean, I guess I've never heard of anything like this at all, so how would I know?"

"So if you touch the contaminated water, you turn into a zombie."

Sarah shoots him an eyebrow. "What I said was a joke. We're not in a Romero movie. They're not zombies. They didn't look interested in eating anybody's brains."

"You have a better name for them?"

"I don't know. These are people... I don't want to write them off like that. 'Zombies' sound evil or something."

"'Fred and Gingers' then?" Chris mimes putting on a top hat and dancing with a cane.

"Really?"

"They seem to like to dance?" He plays a little bit of 'Cheek to Cheek' on the piano.

"You're an idiot. But at least it's better than 'zombie'. OK. So do you think they are dangerous?"

"They didn't pay any attention to us last night. But we have no way of knowing how they are going to react to us if we meet face to face. Besides, we don't know if they can spread the disease or whatever. They might be infectious. If we're smart, we assume they're dangerous until proven otherwise. Let's steer clear of them as much as possible."

"Yeah," Sarah sits down at the piano with Chris. "OK, so water is bad, Fred and Gingers are creepy at best, dangerous at worst. What about the police, the government, the CDC? When are they going to rescue the uninfected?"

"You'd think they'd try and get a message to us. Over the emergency broadcast system or something? Even if we are quarantined, they'd want to give us instructions right? But they turned off all communication and power."

"But what about the battery-powered radio? They might broadcast to that."

"Makes sense to me. But then again nothing has made sense in the last twenty-four hours."

"Hold on, let me get it." Sarah climbs the ladder to the balcony and carries down the small radio that she had been listening to when she was painting. When she turns it on, they hear nothing but static.

"Try the other stations." Chris says helpfully.

"You think?" Sarah says with a touch of annoyance. She spins the dial. Nothing. She switches to AM, still nothing.

"Either the radio is broken or nobody is broadcasting."

"It worked yesterday. I don't like this at all. The AM broadcasts pick up stations as far away as Cleveland. You don't think they're affected now too?"

Chris noodles on the piano while he thinks. "We have to assume that, at least for the time being, we're on our own."

"Shit."

"Yeah." He continues pushing the conversation ahead. "So let's take stock of what we have."

"We have some food, not a lot. We should have gone to Costco last weekend after all. More importantly, we don't have a lot of water. Safe water at least. You *had* to talk me out of using bottles."

"It's incredibly wasteful."

"True. And now we have almost nothing to drink."

Chris improvises on the piano for another moment then stops. "We have plenty of water to drink!"

"Huh?"

"We know the city water is compromised. And so is anything that's exposed to the rain."

"Right."

"But we're not hooked up to city water!"

"Our water tank! On the roof! It's weather-proof

right?"

"It should be. We'll have to check it carefully for leaks before we can trust it, but it should be OK!" Chris gets up and starts pacing around the room. He starts laughing at the absurdity of it. Soon Sarah is laughing too.

"So we're saying the Kafka-esque bureaucracy of the Detroit zoning laws that made it impossible for us to hook up our building to city water might have just saved our lives?"

"Looks like it."

"Well fuck. I don't even know how to process-"

A loud rumble rolls through the city. Sarah stops talking.

"Thunder? That's weird. I thought the storm had passed. The sun is out."

Chris listens closely. "Doesn't sound like thunder to me. The pitch is off. "

"Well that's ominous. It doesn't matter right now. We need to go up to the roof and check our water supply."

"OK. But we better be damned careful."

*

Wearing a poncho tied tightly around his face with a pair of eye goggles, Chris slowly pokes his head up through the trapdoor that opens onto the roof. He carefully surveys the roof for any puddles or water droplets that might have been trapped after the rain. Thankfully, the drainage is good and the midafternoon sun has dried the black tar surface. Not that Chris and Sarah are taking any chances.

"We look ridiculous."

"We look like people who want to survive. Of course I'm already sweating my balls off."

They climb out of the trapdoor both wearing ungainly improvised rain gear. They only had one poncho, but they fashioned another one—and improvised wading boots—with heavy-duty trash bags and duct tape.

They do a survey of the skyline looking for clouds that might have accompanied the thunder. The clouds they discover are black and billowing up from several spots on the ground.

"Look, smoke." Sarah points to the north. "Looks like it's coming from the highway. Accident?"

"Over there too. Must be a pretty big fire. That's a lot of smoke. At least it's a ways away. Let's keep moving."

Looking carefully before taking each step, they work their way to two large water tanks. One of them is the type of classic round wooden water tower that can be seen dotting the rooftops of many buildings in cities across the country. It's roughly the size of a mini-van and looks like an overgrown wine barrel turned up on its end. Chris always liked the old wooden towers because when he was a kid, he was obsessed with GI Joe comic books and his favorite character Storm Shadow—a badass ninja—kept a secret lair in a fake water tower on top of a skyscraper in Manhattan.

Alas, there was no Ninja in this water tower. In fact,

upon closer inspection, it's clear that it contains nothing but probable death. Its old wooden top has corroded with time and the dark murky water inside is exposed to the rain. The water is not only useless, but dangerous.

This does not surprise or concern them. This tower is only hooked up to the unnecessary and expensive sprinkler system that was mandated by the Detroit building codes. They fought the zoning board hard on this one because it cost them almost thirty thousand dollars in extra expenses to have it installed and it broke their hearts to cut holes in all of the original molding to run the pipes. The only good news was that they were able to re-use the original water tower to supply it even if it was too old and leaky to be safe to use as their drinking supply.

They were also forced to install a high-tech fire alarm system with emergency strobe lights (in case of a power outage or deafness), and a computerized fire box that automatically called the fire department if smoke was detected. Chris and Sarah joked that at least they had the most fire-proof house in all of Detroit. It was small solace for the unanticipated loan they had to take out, but they eventually accepted that it was all part of wanting to live someplace unique.

What they are actually here to check is the large hard-plastic water tank that sits beside its older wooden counterpart. This tank is also round, but it is made of thick black polyethylene standing almost six feet high. It is designed to hold 2500 gallons of clean water to use for cooking, cleaning and showering. Each month or so

Chris slipped the parking garage attendant next door twenty bucks to connect a hose to the garage's water supply and fill up the tank. It took about four hours to fill, but it was a lot cheaper than retrofitting the plumbing to commercial code and connecting it to the city water directly.

"Looks like it's about three quarters full. Should last us for a while if we're careful," Chris says, tapping the side of the plastic tank.

"Not until we check every inch of it for cracks or leaks. If any rain got in last night..."

"Right." Chris slowly works his way around the exterior of the tank. "Hopefully we'll find a way to get out of the city long before we use this up."

"I'm not sure how. We don't have a car and I don't think Megabus is running today." Sarah carefully checks the connections on the pipe that runs from the tank into the building.

"Look out there. There are thousands of abandoned cars. We can take one of those."

"Duh. Of course. I keep forgetting to re-adjust my Western ethics for the apocalypse. But let's not forget the possibility that we'll run into the military trying to keep quarantine."

"We're obviously not infected, they can't turn us away."

"I'm not so sure about that."

From a distance, they hear a whooshing rumble. The sound reminds them again of how unnaturally quiet the rest of the city is as they both look up to find the source of the noise. In the horizon they see a dot.

It's a plane. They rush to the edge of the roof which gives them a pretty good view all the way to the river.

"A rescue plane? Looking for survivors?" Sarah says hopefully while shielding her eyes from the glare of the sun.

"I doubt it. It's too small, too fast." He squints. "Oh shit. It's a fighter jet. F18 I think."

"How do you just know that? You play piano. You don't know anything about planes."

"Comes with the penis. All men think fighter jets are awesome." Sarah rolls her eyes as he continues. "But it does beg the question, what do they need a jet for?"

The question is answered when one side of the Ambassador Bridge explodes in a huge ball of flames. The four-lane suspension bridge—built in 1929 connecting Detroit to Windsor, Canada—shudders and begins to collapse into the river. Another missile streaks across the sky and slams into the Canadian side. The second explosion lights the sky and an entire mile of bridge falls into the water. It disappears into a cloud of fire and dust never to reappear. Chris and Sarah see the explosions before they hear the noise a split second later. It is terrifyingly loud.

"Fuck." Chris says quietly.

"What the hell!?" Sarah says a lot less quietly.

"So that's what we were hearing before. It wasn't thunder. They're blocking off all access to the city."

"They can't just- Why would they do that? That's crazy!" Sarah is shouting without realizing it.

"Yeah. They're scared shitless."

Sarah has a sickening sensation in the pit of her

stomach, feeling a sense of permanence for the first time. "Do you know what this means?"

"They've finally found a way to stop Obamacare?"

"It means they're serious about stopping infected people from escaping. Dead serious."

Chris nods. "If we want to get out of the city, we should do it now before they find a way to cut off everything."

"I don't think that's a good idea. We can't go up against the freaking military."

Chris looks at Sarah incredulously. "What do you mean 'go up against'? Look, they might want to check us out or do a screening, but they're not going to stop perfectly healthy citizens from leaving. They're there to keep us safe. They're going to help us. They'll listen to reason."

"Reason?! They just blew up the bridge with a fucking missile! That website said they were killing innocent people!"

"Come on, that was one random conspiracy blog. Look, whatever they're doing, it will make sense once we understand. It has to. It will be OK."

They are silent for a moment. Chris looks at his feet. Sarah stares in the direction of the smoke rising from the bridge, but she's not actually seeing anything. She's deep in thought.

Finally, Sarah breaks the silence. "We are at the mercy of everything. The military, the water, the... whatever the hell happened to the people. I think you vastly overestimate the amount of control we have right now."

CHAPTER 7

"OK. Look this over and see if I'm missing anything," Sarah passes the 'shopping' list to Chris.

TARPS
RAIN GEAR
WEATHER STRIPPING/SILICONE
DUCT TAPE
NON-PERISHABLE FOOD
BOTTLED WATER
FLASHLIGHTS/LANTERNS
BATTERIES
DEODORANT
CONDOMS

Chris looks the list over. "Condoms?"

"Well, I don't think they're going to mail me my next batch of birth control pills. You think me getting preggo is going to help things?"

"Oh, duh." He stops and looks Sarah in the eye. "So we have a deal right? Before we go after supplies, we see if we can get out of the city."

"Yes, and when we can't get through, we find a store, get provisions and get our ass back to where it is safe."

"They're going to let us out. Have a little faith in my shining oratory."

"We do this carefully or not at all. Do you understand?"

"Yeah, of course. We'll be very careful, I promise. We will be safe."

Sarah frowns, but eventually nods. They don't have a lot of options. "We should get some sort of weapons."

"Weapons? What for?"

"For whatever. I don't see a lot of police around. There must be other people who haven't been infected and they might not be as interested in law and order and rational oratory as you are. I'm not sure calling 911 would do us much good."

"Did it ever? I bet the police response time is about the same now as it was last week."

"True enough. We're better off safe than sorry. You understand me husband?"

Chris nods then looks out the window, staring at the sky for a while.

"I wish we had a better sense of the weather. There

aren't any clouds, but if a storm comes through, we're dead."

"I think we're probably not going to hear a weather report for a while. We're going to have to do it the old fashioned way."

"How's that?"

"Just what you're doing. Meteorology by eyeball."

*

Looking like they're dressed for a hurricane, Chris and Sarah emerge from the library. They've lived on this street for the last year and half, but today it looks and feels completely unfamiliar. Without people walking by, without cars fighting through traffic, without stoplights and meter readers and all those things that used to fade into the background of city life, the street might as well be the moon. It's motionless, unexplored, unfamiliar territory.

In Sarah's mind, it feels like a corpse. She finds herself thinking of her favorite uncle who died when she was eight. She loved him dearly but at the end of his slow death from cancer, her parents had stopped allowing her to visit him in the hospital. They thought she would be frightened and confused by the beeping monitors, tubes and wires poking out of him, the IVs slowly pumping several different colors of fluid into his brittle body and the machine breathing for him. She didn't understand why they were keeping her from Uncle Tim. It was confusing and seemed mean, like she was being punished for something and she didn't know what she had done wrong. When he eventually died, despite her sadness, she was excited to see him at the funeral. She looked forward to seeing her friend again even though she understood it would be for the last time.

When she got to the viewing, she knew that he would be dead and she was only going to see his body. She knew he wouldn't be able to talk to her or tell her stories like he always did. But she was horrified to discover that the person she used to know, the person who had thoughts and feelings and hopes and dreams, who always kept candy in his right pocket for his favorite niece, was truly gone. Without the blood being pumped through his arteries, without the thousands of neurons firing imperceptibly fast, without... life, his body didn't resemble the person she knew at all. It was just a mound of room temperature flesh. It *looked* like him, but it was not him. It was a perversion. It was disturbing. It hurt her feelings. She wasn't able to figure out who she was hurt by... her parents? God? Nature? But she felt like his body continuing to exist without *him* was wrong. It was a violation of life.

Now, her neighborhood felt like another cadaver. It looked like their street, but it definitely didn't *feel* like their street.

"Sarah! Puddle!" Chris shouts.

"Shit!" Sarah narrowly avoids stepping in a pool of water that had filled one of Detroit's labyrinth of potholes. She stops for a second to allow her heart to stop racing. "God, we need to be so careful."

Moving more slowly than before, they continue

down the block looking for a suitable car. They eventually come across a pickup truck that had run into a newspaper stand after being abandoned while still in gear.

"That would help us if we have to go off-road," Chris says.

"And carry a lot of supplies."

"Right. Let's check it out."

After walking around to the driver's side, they discover that since the truck had idled all night, it had run out of gas.

"Shit. Not a lot of pickups in the city."

"Hold on," Chris looks in the bed of the truck and finds an emergency gas can. "Not a lot here, but certainly enough to get us there and back. See if you can pop the gas cap for me."

She finds the lever next to the driver's seat. There is a click as the door opens. Just as Chris starts to reach for the gas cap, something also clicks in Sarah's mind.

"Wait! Stop!"

"Huh? Why?"

"Look and make sure there isn't any moisture trapped in there before you touch it! Without much ventilation, it's going to dry slower than anything else."

Chris, who hadn't even been looking, pulls his hand back as if it was on fire. "Holy crap. You're right. We need to slow down and think through everything before we do it."

There are indeed still a few drops of water clinging to the lip of the door. Sarah hands Chris a pair of thick rubber gloves she usually used when cleaning the stove.

Chris puts them on, carefully twists open the cap, and begins fueling the truck.

After emptying the can, he throws his hockey stick in the back of the truck and joins Sarah in the cab. She is in the process of getting rid of a torn pair of tighty-whiteys that she found at her feet. Grimacing, she wishes she had another set of rubber gloves. *Ugh.* She reminds herself to pick up Purell at their first stop and starts the engine.

The radio had been left on when its previous owner bailed, and they nearly jump out of their skin when loud static starts. Her heart racing, Sarah mashes the power button more forcefully than necessary.

"We should check and see if it picks up anything." Chris turns the radio back on and spins the dial back and forth but he gets nothing but monotone static. There aren't even little spikes of static that come from picking up radio signals from too great a distance to be coherent. There seem to be no signals whatsoever.

"Wait a minute." Sarah starts to fiddle with a small electronic box on the dashboard. "This truck has satellite radio! They'll still be broadcasting."

Chris switches inputs on the radio to the satellite receiver. The white noise is replaced by silence. Chris flips through a few stations and is greeted by Bruce Springsteen belting out 'Jungleland,' then a section of Yo-Yo Ma playing the 'Bach Cello Suites'.

"Oh man, that's a relief," Sarah says, putting the truck in gear and navigating around a taxi cab that had run into a planter in the median.

"Let's check one of the news stations," Chris uses

the touch-screen to flip out of the music channels into the news and talk stations. They find nothing but silence. "That's weird. Why are the talk stations down, but the music stations running? The Feds again?"

Sarah scrunches her forehead. "Wait. Try the BBC news service, there's no way the feds could shut down the news stations in Europe."

Chris finds the station and it too is silent.

"Well that's unsettling." Sarah mumbles.

"It doesn't necessarily mean that they're not broadcasting, it could be that the government just blocked access."

"Maybe. Or it could mean that the virus or whatever is global."

Sarah keeps creeping them down the street. It's a difficult task to drive in Detroit on a regular day, but Sarah has to avoid hundreds of abandoned vehicles scattered over the roads like leaves. She winds her way down alleys, over medians, on the sidewalks and down the wrong sides of streets.

"Never thought I'd be off-roading in midtown." she says with a grin. "Reminds me of when I was a kid on the farm."

"Don't remind me. I can't believe you survived driving that four-wheeler like a maniac." Chris never understood Sarah's parent's willingness to let her drive tractors, ATVs and snowmobiles all over their property when she was as young as nine. He grew up in a suburb so the idea of letting your child tool around on vehicles designed for adults seemed crazy. Even now the idea still made him a bit nervous. So cautious in every other way, Sarah had developed a sense of invincibility behind the wheel that just doesn't seem safe to him.

"Man I wish our phones had signal. I don't know how we ever navigated without GPS."

Chris attempts to make himself useful by searching through the truck. It's filled with duplicate copies of work orders and crumpled fast-food wrappers, but Chris eventually finds an old dusty map in the glove compartment.

"Ah ha! No GPS, no problem. We can pretend it's the 90's."

"Lucky us."

"The 90's were awesome. So, since we know they've bombed the highways, let's take route 5 and see if we can get out of the quarantine on a side road."

"OK. There's a Costco in Livonia. We can go there after we hit the roadblocks."

"Proverbial or literal?"

"I guess we'll find out."

*

Forty minutes into a trip that should have taken twenty, even with traffic, they notice the first signs of trouble. They had weaved for miles through the strange landscape of abandoned cars, clothing, purses, backpacks and other possessions. It looked like God had pressed pause on the world and deleted all of the humans. Chris made a joke about the Rapture that Sarah didn't think was that funny. But, just before they got to Farmington, things changed.

In front of them, the cars have clumped and created a huge traffic jam. Both directions of the highway are filled bumper to bumper with cars that had been attempting to drive northwest, out of the city.

"Well that's different. These people seem to have been trying to leave."

With the road now fully blocked, Sarah stops the truck. They have to continue on foot. Turning off the ignition, Sarah glances nervously at the sky. Chris, having already checked for clouds, nods grimly and steps out onto the road.

"Looks like we're near the perimeter."

"There's nobody here. Maybe they got through?" Chris says hopefully.

"There was nobody anywhere else either."

They walk slowly between rows of cars trying to see down the road, hoping to spot what kind of barrier prevented the cars from leaving.

Sarah grabs his arm and stops him. "Uh, Chris. Is that a bullet hole?"

There is a large round hole in the windshield of a Subaru Outback parked to her right. The glass had splintered out from a three inch impact near the rear-view mirror.

"I don't know? Maybe? Let's keep moving."

"I don't like the looks of this one bit."

Reluctantly, Sarah continues walking between the rows of cars. After another fifty feet, she can almost see what might be an improvised barrier a half mile or so up the road. She stops and reaches into her bag for binoculars.

"Fuck. Sarah get down!" Chris abruptly grabs her by the shoulders and pulls her to the ground.

"What is it?!"

Slumped between an old black Saturn and a green Kia SUV is the body of a young woman. Her head seems to have exploded. Blood and brain matter are sprayed up the windshield of the Kia. It had obviously rained and the water had washed the detritus down the glass, thinning the blood until it covered the entire hood and much of the ground below with a sticky reddish-brown residue. The windshield wipers had trapped several bright white chips of skull and some spongy grey bits of brain matter.

"Oh Jesus." Sarah fights hard against her sudden urge to throw up. "What happened to her? Her head looks like it fucking blew up."

"She's not alone."

Chris can see at least four other bodies draped over cars or lying on the ground between them and the barricades.

"This is a massacre. All these people! What happened?"

She sees a hand limply sticking out of a window and a set of feet poking out from under a pickup truck in a pool of drying blood. She turns around searching for something to look at that isn't a picture of horror.

"They shot them. Probably with rifles. High caliber sniper rifles maybe."

"Again, you're apparently a military expert? How do you fucking know that?!"

"Xbox. Call of Duty."

"You know that from a fucking game? Jesus. That's sick!"

"Maybe, but it's no less true. We have to get out of here. You were right. There's no way we're getting out of the city."

Sarah, still a little light-headed, starts to head back in the direction from which they came. Taking dazed, shuffling steps, she walks back towards their truck.

"Sarah! Keep your head down!"

She crouches below the tops of the cars and keeps moving. She does not say anything. Chris follows behind her for a moment. After two minutes of silence, he somewhat meekly speaks.

"Jesus, Sarah. I'm sorry. You were right. I never should have brought us here. I'm sorry you saw that. Fuck, I'm sorry *I* saw that."

"Do you think it's like this everywhere?" She speaks in a flat monotone, as if she can't think logically and process her emotions at the same time.

"I don't know. I mean, they blew the bridges, they blocked the highways. We're already on a side road."

"Maybe we could sneak through the woods somewhere?"

"I thought you didn't want to leave at all?"

Sarah shakes her head. "I didn't. But whatever's inside the city has scared the shit out of the freaking military. Enough to commit murder. Guns or outbreak. Pick your poison."

"What do you think we should do?"

"Well, we walk a hundred yards in that direction

and we get shot. Back in the city, who knows? I'll guess I'll take possible death over certain death."

Chris thinks for a moment and can't find a flaw in her logic.

"Works for me. Let's get the fuck out of here."

*

Twenty minutes later and five miles away from the perimeter, Sarah pulls the truck to the side of the road and silently starts to cry. Chris tries to think of a way to comfort her, but after a minute, starts to cry himself. After quietly holding each other for a time, Sarah looks up with dry eyes and puts the truck back into gear. It's time to keep moving.

*

When they arrive at the parking lot of the Livonia Costco, Chris hops out of the truck and flashes Sarah a brave smile he only half means.

"Ah Costco, where would we be without you? Did you remember our membership card honey?"

"This isn't funny." Sarah says morosely.

"Oh come on. Haven't you always dreamed of doing an 80's movie shopping montage? Running through a store taking whatever you wanted?" Chris grabs a shopping cart, starts to run and rides it off of the curb like a kid.

"You're an idiot, husband."

"That's why you love me!"

Sarah knows he's faking his good cheer, but she appreciates it anyway. After a few minutes she does feel better, OK at least. Though she knows she's going to have to re-calibrate her concept of 'OK'.

When they get to the entrance of the store, they realize that while the front door is unlocked and welcoming—because there was nobody to lock up the night before—it's gloomy and dark inside. The wall of sarcastically large flat-screen TVs that normally light up the front entrance like Times Square are all dark. No power. Luckily for Chris and Sarah, the warehouse is at least partially illuminated by a bank of battery-powered emergency lights. It makes it possible for them to move around but the normally cheery, if somewhat chaotic atmosphere of Costco is now a bit creepy.

They each grab a cart and begin working their way through the aisles together. Chris plops three enormous bags of rice into his cart with a clang.

"So I don't understand why we didn't see anybody on the drive. I mean there have to be other survivors like us. There's no way everybody got exposed."

Sarah thinks for a second. "I think more people were infected than you're thinking. It was pouring last night. When was the last time you didn't get at least a drop of rain on you when it was coming down like that?

"Sure, but a lot of people wouldn't go outside."

"You're right. I'm sure plenty of people didn't leave their house, but how many of them didn't take a shower, water the plants, or brush their teeth?

"Or have a cup of coffee or wash their hands after

taking a leak. Yeah, I see where you're going."

"I mean, making contact with water is hard to avoid even if you're trying not to. And the government shut down communication so I doubt many people got the warning we did."

Chris mulls it over in his head remembering something his middle school biology teacher said once.

"We humans, despite all of our advances in technology and food science, are still remarkably dependent on clean water. I know most of you only survive on Mountain Dew, but would you believe even that great elixir is still mostly water? And we are too. You and I are 60% water. That's right. Water. Not bones or muscle, or fat and certainly not brains. Yes, I'm taking to you Mr. Wells. So what does this mean? It means that water is the most important factor in our survival. Humans can survive indefinitely without power, shelter and companionship... even MTV. Without food we can survive for weeks, if not months. But without safe water, we're dead in a matter of days. Think about that next time you pee in the pool."

"OK. I'll accept that a high percentage of people would get exposed. But here's the other thing that's really eating at me: where are all the infected? I mean there are almost seven hundred thousand people in this city. If they all went crazy and started their own zombie rave, where are they? It's such a huge amount of people. We haven't seen a single person since last night."

"I don't know. The population of Detroit has been dropping like crazy anyway. Maybe white-flight went post-racial."

"Sarah, this is serious."

"I know. These are important questions, but we have no way of answering them right now. Let's focus on the task at hand: Gatorade. Come on, if you ignore the fact that the world is ending, apocalyptic freedom can be fun!"

After loading the first two loads of supplies into the back of the pickup, they start to relax a bit. They race carts down the aisles, lob stuffed animals at each other like grenades and laugh hysterically when Sarah climbs on top of a palette of canned corn and drops an enormous bag of flour onto the cement floor causing an explosion of white powder that ends up making her look like she'd just been pushed into a snow bank.

"Why did you do that?" Chris chokes out between gusts of laughter.

"I've wanted to do that since I was a little kid! Of course now I'm a vandal." Her smile fades a bit. "Crap, now I feel bad. It's going to be a pain in the ass to clean up."

Chris slowly stops laughing. "Nobody is going to clean it up. I don't think there is anybody left to care."

Sarah stops too. The mood has been shattered. "Maybe not for a while, but eventually people will return."

"I dunno. I've been thinking about the satellite radio stations. They're not all run out of Detroit, they're run from all over the country. All over the world. The freaking BBC. They stayed on the air all through World War II. Nobody's home."

"But what about the music stations. Somebody's still running those! Only DJs survive?"

"There aren't many DJs anymore. Most of the music stations are all run by computers. They'll just keep playing an algorithm of songs until their power gets shut off."

"Do you know that or are you just talking out of your ass?" Sarah says grumpily.

"A little bit of both I think." Chris says honestly.

Thump.

"Quiet!" Sarah sets down the huge jug of olive oil she had picked up.

"What? Why?"

Thump.

"Shut up! Listen!"

Thump.

Chris and Sarah instinctively duck down and hold their breaths. A loud noise is coming from the back of the store, but it's too dark to see what is making it.

"What do we do?" Chris whispers to Sarah.

"Well first off we can give up on the pretense that whoever it is doesn't know we're here." Sarah says in a normal voice. "We've been cackling like hyenas for an hour."

"Right. OK." Chris stands up and calls out "Hello?"

Thump.

"Is anybody there?"

Sarah grabs Chris' hand and they duck back down. Sweat has somehow magically appeared on her brow. It drips onto the cement floor, leaving a trail behind her.

Keeping her eyes peeled for movement, she motions for Chris to pick up his hockey stick and circle around the back of the store while she circles around the front.

She whispers in his ear. "You be quiet and try to get behind it. I'll be loud and try to keep its attention."

Chris nods and takes off behind the shelves. Sarah stands up and walks directly towards the noise.

"Hello? I don't want to hurt you. My name is Sarah."

Thump.

As she gets closer, she can tell that the sound is coming from the offices in the back of the store. The offices are behind a solitary red door set in a two-story white wall. A dry erase board on the wall lists the store's checkout scanning leaders. Odell M is in the lead averaging 29 items per minute. Sarah thinks that Odell might be holding that record for a long time.

"We're just here to pick up some food. There's plenty for everyone. There's nothing to be afraid of." Sarah is a good liar. To everyone but herself that is. She is definitely afraid.

Thump.

Only thirty feet from the door to the employees' area, Sarah notices a large panel of one-way glass that she figures the security guard must sit behind watching for shoplifters. *Are Coscto security guards armed?*

When she reaches the door, she puts her back up to the wall next to it like she sees cops do in movies. She spots Chris coming down the aisle to her right.

THUMP.

The sound of something hitting the door just inches

from her face causes her to make a small involuntary squeak. Chris reaches the other side of the door and holds his stick at shoulder-height ready to swing.

"We don't want to hurt you. We're going to open the door OK?" Sarah is starting to sound almost as scared as she is. Leaning against the wall gives her a chance to look at the hinges directly next to her ear. The door opens out towards her. It doesn't appear to have a lock. *Why doesn't whoever is behind the door just turn the handle?*

THUMP.

For a moment, she wonders why they didn't just run away. There was no reason to investigate the sound. No reason to put themselves at risk. Except they have more supplies to get. Or maybe this might be a survivor who can help them, someone who knows what's going on.

She knows their options are fairly limited now. So, using hand signals to warn Chris, she silently counts down from five and pulls the door open, tucking behind it as a shield.

Out stumbles the completely naked form of Tom Middleton, Assistant Manager. He's forty-five, overweight and balding. Two dark stripes of curly hair crawl up his large pimply back like a vine and blend into the back of his comb-over. His hands and forehead have been cut, presumably the source of the messy spatters of blood smeared all over the inside of the door. He had obviously been running into the door over and over for hours.

'Tom, Assistant Manager', completely ignores them

and starts walking towards the exit of the store. Without thinking, Sarah steps out from behind the door and stands next to Chris. They look to each other as if the other one should have a plan for this. Neither of them do.

'Tom' gets a few steps away from the office and his leg abruptly kicks out, hitting a display of coffee. The enormous cans are sent clanging everywhere. There is a distinct cracking noise as one of 'Tom's' toes snaps from the impact. One of the containers rolls across the cement floor and stops at Sarah's feet. The former Assistant Manager who had eyes on becoming the Manager Manager makes no sign that he is in pain or that he is even aware that he has injured himself as he heads for the exit. He continues to completely ignore Chris and Sarah.

"Wait! Hey... uh... Sir?" Sarah doesn't know what to do. She doesn't have a lot of context for naked men dancing through Costco. But something in the back of her head makes her feel like she should do *something*. "Hey wait! Stop!"

Chris, not entirely sure what to do either, jogs ahead and tries to catch up with him.

"Chris, be careful! Don't touch him! He could be infectious!"

He looks back at his wife and gives her a 'what am I supposed to do here?' look. He steps in front of 'Tom' and tries to slow him down.

"Hey buddy. Where you going? Are you OK?"

'Tom' advances closer to Chris who keeps backing up, trying to keep some distance between them. Chris raises his hockey stick and attempts to stop his momentum with the blade. 'Tom' walks right into it and keeps pushing. Chris has to plant his feet and lean into the stick to stop him. The man ceases, but he keeps dumbly trying to push his way to the door.

Chris becomes increasingly conscious of the man's nakedness, the hair nestled on the shelf created by the protrusion of his gut. His uncircumcised penis dangles ever so slightly to the left. Chris feels a sensation he could only describe as 'icked out.' His arms flail wildly and Chris is almost grazed by a bloody hand. He grimaces but is able to keep the stick on the man's chest, preventing him from getting closer.

"No offense buddy, I don't want to hurt you, but I don't want a hug. At least until you put some pants on."

Sarah catches up and stands next to Chris. She stares into the naked man's eyes. His pupils are missing, his eyes are just blank white orbs streaked with red veins.

"I think his eyes rolled up! That's why they're all white."

Despite her fear, she finds herself musing that perhaps the most 'human' part of a body is the eyes. Eyes convey so much thought and emotion. They tell truths that can't be as easily faked as words or even actions. Sarah remembers the line in 'Jaws' about sharks having 'dead eyes, doll's eyes.' She knows that somehow it is possible to discern consciousness, intelligence, mood, even good or malicious intent purely by looking into a creature's pupils. When something dies, that intangible light is extinguished.

It's both indescribable and unmistakable. Without pupils, the incredible conduit of information is completely cut off. Looking into the whiteness where 'Tom's' eyes should be sends a chill down her spine. There's just nothing.

"Are you in there man?" Chris grunts, struggling to keep him back with the stick.

"He's not. Let him go."

"But he might just be sick. I don't think he's trying to hurt us. What if we-"

"Let's just let him go. We can't help him."

"How do you know that? We're not doctors. Maybe he can be cured?"

"I just know OK? I can feel it. Maybe a doctor could help, but what could *we* do? Let him go."

Chris steps back and to the side, lowering his stick. 'Tom' continues his journey through the door and out into the parking lot. He's headed off in the direction of the circle and in a moment he is gone.

She nods to him as if to say 'thank you for listening to me and not doing anything stupid.' Chris lowers his hockey stick.

"Nice guy. Quiet. Touch of the zombie."

Sarah can't contain a grim giggle. "Let's hurry up and get the fuck out of here."

"Agreed. Let's get this stuff onto the truck. I didn't find much for weapons. Is there a gun section here?"

Sarah laughs. "In Costco? You think they sell twelve-packs of handguns? If you want an arsenal, you need to go to Walmart."

***

"My leg hurts."

Mikey sat by the fire precariously balancing a marshmallow on a stick. Sarah was amazed that this meal hadn't fallen into the fire yet, like his last two, but Mikey refused to accept her help. He was going to cook his own dessert.

"Should we go home tomorrow and get you some Tylenol?"

"No, no. It's OK. It just hurts."

"Tomorrow morning, when there is more light, you have to let me take off the bandage and look at it."

"But it stings!"

"I know. But you have to. I check it tomorrow or we go home. Understood?"

"Fine."

Five nights in the woods with Mikey had been almost as much fun for Sarah as it had been for him. They hiked for miles then followed a stream down to a pond and attempted to fish. They were woefully unsuccessful, but Mikey was undeterred. He did catch a huge bullfrog and paraded it around like he was holding the Stanley Cup. When he returned it to the pond, Mikey marked the spot where it had ducked under some mud and decomposing leaves with a pile of rocks. He wanted to remember where he was so they could visit the frog next time they went camping.

Mikey and Sarah had long chats about life. He was remarkably astute and intuitive for his young age. She assumed he would never understand some of the things she told him about her life, but she found him surprisingly easy to open up to. She told him about the pressure she felt to get into college and told him about her teenage boy troubles—at least the parts that were PG-13—and to her surprise he understood more than she expected him to. He listened to her dilemmas and didn't try to solve them, he just nodded and empathized. He had a natural wisdom and she realized that Mikey had at least a toe in adulthood too. Sarah was proud of him and thought he was going to grow up to be a great guy someday. They sat in front of the fire for a while in silence. Each deep in their own thoughts, but both enjoying the experience immensely.

Sarah found herself refreshed by being out in the wilderness. After thinking about it for a while, she thought that she wasn't so much 'outside' as she was inside the woods, inside nature. Perhaps nature is the real environment and that all of the buildings that people created were really the 'outside.' *Then after contemplating this for a while, she laughed out loud. She sounded like a stoner but she was only high on fresh air and burnt marshmallows.*

It wasn't until the next morning that the trip turned sour. Mikey didn't seem quite himself when he woke up. When he helped her pack up their little tent, he seemed groggy and distant.

"Are you OK? You seem a little off this morning?"

"Huh? Oh, yeah I feel kinda spinny."

"Really? Come here."

Sarah put her hand on his forehead. He was burning up. She was surprised how obvious and unnervingly hot a real fever is. She remembered checking herself for a fever plenty of times trying to convince her mother she was too sick to go to school but it never felt like this. This felt serious. She winced and her stomach involuntarily clenched.

Sarah sat him down and removed the make-shift bandage from his leg. What she saw made her light-headed. It looked raw and hot. Pus oozed from the gash which was obviously infected. All of the happy ideas Sarah had been thinking about that morning disappeared in a puff of smoke. Her ideas about spending more time in nature, her nagging fear that Tommy was ignoring her in English class and her despair about her fucking history paper that was due next week all dropped away and were replaced with a singular purpose.

"OK. We're going home."

She expected him to protest, to remind her that they weren't supposed to go home until tomorrow, but he just nodded. That scared her more than the infection itself.

They had five miles of trail to walk before they could get back to her car.

***

Chris and Sarah load the truck with as many supplies as it can hold. They got everything on their 'shopping list' and added any fresh food that hadn't gone bad. They found some bread, cake, fruits and vegetables that looked like they hadn't spoiled yet. They knew that in a matter of days, anything that wasn't pre-packaged would be very difficult to come by. They might not have access to fresh produce, dairy and meat for a long time. Even in the era of bioengineered, packaged and preserved everything, without freezers and refrigerators, their food options were going to be very limited, especially in a city. They were facing a world without cheese, without real cream in their coffee, without fresh vegetables, without hamburgers. Chris spent a moment staring sadly at the huge refrigerated cases filled with steaks that had already started to rot.

With all of their supplies tied down, they wind their way back through the streets of Detroit.

"So, you know how we've been talking about this in terms of survivors and... I dunno, *not* survivors?"

Chris nods. "I don't like the term, but I don't know what else to call them. I mean the infected obviously aren't dead."

"Well that's the thing. I think they are."

"They can't be. At least not yet. We just passed our friend from Costco marching down the street. It might be fatal eventually, but you're not dead if you're walking around. Not really."

Sarah pauses for a second, trying to form her thought. "When I saw his eyes, I knew he was dead. I could just feel it."

Chris starts to say something but Sarah cuts him off.

"OK, I know that's not scientific. So let's look at it that way. I mean, he felt no pain, he had no response stimulus. No sense of self-preservation. I didn't see any kind of real consciousness there."

"That doesn't mean he's dead."

"Maybe, maybe not, but I don't think he's human anymore. My gut says he's moving, but he's not alive."

"So you're actually talking literal zombie. Come on Sarah. That's ridiculous. There's no such thing."

"Well yes and no. There obviously aren't zombies in the 'Day of the Dead' sense, but I just remembered something that Mikey told me once."

"Mikey?" Chris gives Sarah a look. She almost never talked about him and he had learned early in their relationship not to bring him up.

"Yeah. When he was little, he was obsessed with bugs and insects."

"I remember you told me. The grosser the better."

"He once cornered me for almost an hour and described in great gory detail about some types of parasites that can infect insects and literally turn them into zombie kinda things. They can control their behavior and even make them move after they're dead. It was the dancing that made me remember. The spasms. Mikey said the insects did that after they got infected. They'd spin in circles endlessly or just twitch over and over. Like something was pulling random levers in their brains."

"That's nuts."

"Yeah, it happens to bees and ants I think. Maybe roaches. I don't really remember much except for the story Mikey told me about this parasitic fungus that takes over carpenter ants. It infects the poor bastards and uses chemicals to literally control their minds. It forces an ant to act all crazy, leaving its colony and using its pincers to grab onto the underside of a leaf and just hang there forever. Once it dies, the fungus spreads all over the ant's body and starts shooting spores out to infect the other ants."

"That's fucking creepy."

"Yeah, that's why a little boy would be so excited about it. Point is, whether it's larvae or a fungus or whatever, there is such a thing as a parasite that causes behavior like this."

"But insects. Not people, not even animals."

"Yeah. I don't know. I'm just saying that if there was some sort of new parasite in the water... a parasite that infects humans?"

"So do they die? Do the parasites kill the insects?"

"I think so. There's no cure as far as I remember."

"What you remember from the musings of an eight-year-old hopped up on candy canes."

Sarah puts her hands up as if to say 'this is what I got, take it or leave it.'

Now back downtown, Sarah turns a corner off Elizabeth St. and on to Grand River Avenue. She abruptly slams on the brakes.

Neither one of them is able to say anything because they have no words for what they see.

Passing before their eyes is a wall of flesh. Only ten feet in front of them, an endless moving mass of naked bodies marches past, teeming with motion. There is a staggering number of bodies, a tangle of torsos and limbs. The wall spans the width of the entire street, like an incredibly dense protest march. Chris and Sarah can't see how large the group is because they can't see a beginning or an end, just countless forms passing in front of them.

"Back up." Chris says quietly.

"What?"

"Back. Up."

The truck idles right on the perimeter of the lot, but the circle is continually changing size as the people start to clump, then disperse. It looks like a great flesh-colored organism, an enormous round creature, expanding and contracting as if it were breathing. It seems to take a deep breath and begins to swell, sending a large wave of former humanity spinning toward them.

Sarah sees the tide starting to grow, threatening to envelop them. She feels the sinking feeling of inevitability. It reminds her of being caught in an undertow—knowing she's about to be sucked under, but being powerless to do anything about it. She knows she needs to move but she is paralyzed. She's not thinking clearly.

"Fuck. Look out!" Sarah starts to lay on the horn. It's loud, but none of the horde seems to pay any attention.

"Stop! You'll draw more!"

"More!? How could there possibly be more?!"

"Reverse! Back up! Back up!!" Chris is now shouting. Sarah stares dully at her hands and feet, not remembering how they are supposed to work together.

They are enveloped by the bodies. Arms, legs, torsos and faces start to pound the truck. There's no intent behind the impacts, merely that the truck is an obstacle in their journey around and around. Inside the truck, the hits are teeth-chatteringly loud. The bodies start to climb over the truck. The pounding horde is so dense that it's instantly dark in the cab. Sarah is frozen in a scream while Chris tries to put the truck in reverse from the passenger side.

A crack appears on the windshield. The weight of the circle is becoming too much for the glass.

"Sarah!!"

She is finally spurred to action when an elbow hits the driver's side window and it explodes inward, showering them both in shattered glass. Still screaming, but having regained motor control, she slams the truck into reverse and starts backwards.

The tires spin and the engine roars. The truck starts to move in a jerky motion as if they were going over huge potholes.

"Oh God. We're running them over!"

"Fuck it! Keep going!!"

The truck eventually catches traction and peels back away from the crowd. The spot where they just were—and the people they ran over—are immediately enveloped by the circle. As if they had never been there at all.

Sarah keeps driving backward as fast as the truck can go, bouncing up onto a curb and running into a mailbox, showering them with letters and magazines that will never be delivered.

"Stop! Stop!" Chris tries to grab the wheel. "They're not following. Stop."

The truck comes to rest about fifty yards from the

circle. They sit in silence for a minute watching the nude people march by. It almost looks like a demented parade.

"Are you OK? Are you injured?" Chris asks.

"I'm fine. You?"

"I'm alright."

They both take a deep breath and wait for their hearts to slow down. Or at least slow enough to feel like they're making individual beats instead of a frantic blur of pumping blood.

"I guess we found the Fred and Gingers."

Chris is relieved to hear his wife's voice sounding almost normal. He's never heard her really scream before. An actual scream doesn't sound like it does in the movies. A real scream is a terrifyingly alien sound. It doesn't sound human at all. Her scream tapped directly into some sort of instinctual panic that couldn't be replicated by anything other than a loved one in true danger. It shook him to hear that sound come out of her.

"Well I've seen enough to know that we are fucked."

Sarah looks at him. Her eyes are wide. She looks like a child.

"Is this the end of the world?"

Chris considers the question. He's heard the phrase 'it's not the end of the world' more times than he can count, and it's never really been up for discussion. He always said 'Of course it's not the end of the world.' But today, he is forced to really think about it. He knows he is not qualified to answer it, and that it was probably rhetorical anyway, but he knows he has to say something. And as he says it, he knows it's the truth.

"Not for us. Not today. Let's get out of here. Let's go home."

PART II
THE LIBRARY

CHAPTER 8

June 25, 1967

Things had gotten completely out of hand. This was not a demonstration. This was not a protest. This was not a disturbance or even a riot. Sammy found himself in the middle of outright warfare.

When the shooting started, Sammy dove to the ground and tried to get under a 1964 AMC Rambler. Its windows had already been smashed out but he hoped the large engine block would provide some coverage from either the sniper's bullets coming from behind him or the National Guard firing back towards him. Sammy could hear bullets whizzing over his head like a flock of angry hummingbirds. He closed his eyes and tried to pray, but the only thing he could think about was the fact that he was hiding under a car assembled in Wisconsin and Canada. His father, who had spent most of his life working on the Ford assembly line, would have been pissed. He knew it was a silly, if not insane, thing to have needling his consciousness when he was just a stray bullet from death, but he could not rid himself of the thought: *What was a Rambler doing here in Detroit? What am I doing here?*

When he left his home an hour before, it had been against the tearful protests of his mother.

"No, Sammy, no! It's too dangerous. Half of the city is on fire! The police are beating people. You can't go! Please!"

"Mom. I have to. David is out there. He's going to do something stupid. He's going to get himself arrested... or killed. I have to find him."

"You're only sixteen. You're just a child. It's not safe! If your father were here-"

"He's not. So I have to be the man of the house. David's out there all alone. I'm not going to let him die out there. I'm sorry Mom. I love you, but I have to try."

As he listened to the echoes of the screen door slamming and his mother's muffled sobs, he scanned the horizon. It wasn't hard to figure out where the action was. Countless sirens pierced the air. He could smell the smoke and see the orange light glowing in the sky coming from the fires that were tearing through the streets and neighborhoods. Fear gnawed at him, but his fear for his little brother outweighed his fear for himself.

David had already been an angry kid when their father was killed while trying to stop a robbery at their corner deli. It took the police four hours to respond to the shooting. David sat there with his father's body, watching as a pool of blood slowly spread over the dirty linoleum in the snack aisle. He held his father's hand as it grew cold knowing that nobody cared that he had died. In fact, officially, nobody even knew they existed. Like many of their friends, they had been left off of the 1960 census entirely. David was tired of the racial epithets. He was tired of being harassed by the police. He looked down the road at his future and saw no opportunities, only poverty and racism.

Over the years David had hardened. His outrage turned icy, cold and unpredictable. Even though Sammy was the older brother, he was a bit frightened of him. His younger brother was so smart, truly gifted with intelligence and wisdom beyond his years. In a fair world he would have had unlimited potential— far beyond his own, Sammy thought. But after their father died, David stopped going to school. To Sammy it seemed like he had given up on the idea of his own future. David would not participate in a game he knew was rigged. It broke Sammy's heart.

He begged David not to go out into the streets that night, but it was impossible to stop him.

"David! You can't go out there!"

"Why not!?"

"They're destroying our neighborhood!"

"We got to make then listen! They don't give a shit about us. We're people, not rats!"

"But-"

"We gotta fight man! How long do they expect us to live in this segregated shithole? Terrible schools, no jobs... police beat us for no reason and nobody gives a fuck!"

"I know. But there's a better way..."

"How? By shuffling along with a big smile, playing their little game? They don't want nothing to change. It's the same racist shit it's always been."

"David, you're right. Of course you're right, but-"

"Don't you ever want it to get better? You want to be an old man someday and look back to see that nothing's different but the code words? They're not going to give us anything. If we want to be free, we got to take it by force."

Before Sammy could say another word, David was out the door and gone.

Wishing he had come up with something better to say to David, Sammy worked his way down 12th Street in a haze. It was no longer a street, it was a battlefield. The previous night's rioting had left most of the stores completely looted and destroyed. Several of them had been hit with Molotov Cocktails and burned to the ground. Twenty-four hours later, the rubble still smoldered because nobody had bothered to put out the flames. So much of Detroit was on fire that it had run out of firefighters. *Besides, this is a black neighborhood and the fire department has priorities,* Sammy thought bitterly.

He walked over broken glass, rubble and burning trash. Most of the surviving buildings had been boarded up with spray painted signs that read 'black owned' or just 'black.' Sometimes the signs prevented the arson and looting. Sometimes the rioters didn't notice, or care.

As Sammy walked south, he caught up with the rioters. The firebombing seemed to have picked up where it left off the night before; growing, metastasizing, consuming blocks like a cancer made of flame. That night, the warfare had continued to spread south in three different paths that formed a triangular wedge of inferno and destruction that pointed straight at Downtown Detroit like a burning arrow.

Within minutes, he was swept up by the angry mob. Hundreds of men and women advanced down the street screaming and throwing rocks and bricks at the police who had set up barriers further down the road. Fighting his way through the crowd, Sammy scanned their faces. He saw sweat, blood, dirt, fear, sadness and rage. He saw the fury and desperation that he had seen simmering just behind the eyes of his friends and neighbors for years finally escaping.

He did not find what he was looking for. He didn't see David anywhere. But it was so dark, so loud, and so confusing he may have walked right past David without noticing. Sammy couldn't be sure he wasn't in the mob. He had to keep searching.

On the next block, Sammy looked to his right down the cross-street and saw an image that he thought only existed in the news reels from Vietnam that he saw in school. The street was engulfed in flames—an entire neighborhood of neat brick homes was burning to the ground. Gouts of untamed orange and yellow fire belched fifty feet into the sky. The heat was oppressive even a hundred feet away.

Where are the fire trucks? Isn't anybody going to try and save them? These are people's homes!

Almost as if to answer his question, someone pushing through the mob knocked into his elbow. Stunned, Sammy gaped at him. The skinny man wearing a sweaty yellow bandana was struggling to carry at least a dozen mismatched rifles.

Sammy backed away quickly. *What is going on?! What the fuck is going on!? This can't be happening.* He backed into an alley and started to run. He wanted to circle around to get ahead of the rioters, to a place where there was still law and order. He honestly wasn't sure if the police would be a friend or an enemy, but he knew he didn't want to be in that mob.

He ran down a deserted alley for three blocks and re-emerged further down 12th Street. He assumed that he would now be behind the police lines, but instead found himself smack dab in the middle of no-man's land between the police and the advancing rioters. He stood there frozen, staring at the huge pack of white-helmeted cops. Sometime during the day they had been joined by a squad of National Guardsmen called in by Governor Romney. They were standing on the bed of a large green military truck. Mounted on its back was an enormous and fierce-looking machine gun. When the flickering glow from the fires in front of them lit the men's faces, Sammy saw the mirror image of what he had seen in the mob. Sweat, fear and hate.

To Sammy, it seemed that hundreds of years of history and context had been dissolved by violence. In that moment the righteousness claimed by both sides seemed irrelevant. Perhaps all of that would matter again in the morning, but all Sammy cared about was survival.

"Hands up nigger! Make a twitch and you die! You hear me?! We're not fucking around!"

It took Sammy a moment to realize it was he who was being shouted at through a bullhorn. He raised his hands high above his head and froze.

That was when the shooting began.

He watched as a bullet shot from behind him tore a hole through the shoulder of a very surprised-looking cop. The injured man abruptly sat down on the pavement in a way that would be comical were it not for the blood.

Sammy dove under the AMC Rambler as the National Guard's machine gun started roaring in response, sending a hail of bullets at the top of a building to his left. Tracers lit up the sky and pieces of brick and plaster rained down from the façade. More rocks and bullets flew over his head in the opposite direction from the rioters. Sammy had been completely forgotten when the fighting began.

Knowing he had to get out of there, Sammy crawled on his hands and knees out from under the car and ran back down the side street as if his life depended on it. In fact, it did. He ran not really knowing where he was headed. He just had to be away from the sirens, the fire, and the gunshots. He eventually stumbled onto

Grand River Avenue as it crossed diagonally over Trumball. He wanted to go home, but was too frightened to head back north, so he followed Grand River Avenue all the way down to where it ended in midtown.

As he slowed to a jog and then a walk, police, firemen and National Guard troops were mobilizing and heading north and east. Moving in the opposite direction were scores of wounded people, scrambling to get away from the violence. Hundreds of people, mostly black, were being loaded onto stretchers with gunshot wounds and broken bones. Most were dazed and bleeding. Some had obviously been beaten and many others seemed to be suffering from burns or smoke inhalation. While he was watching, he saw at least five stretchers go by covered with white sheets. The fabric covered the faces of the dead, but it didn't prevent their blood from seeping through the cloth, creating slowly expanding bright red splotches. The blood seeping into the fabric made the red color seem unnaturally bright and cartoonish. It reminded Sammy of a clown's face paint.

Thousands of people, almost entirely black, had been arrested and were roughly being handcuffed or chained together, loaded onto buses or just being locked down and ignored. He could hear a woman wailing with grief. Nobody seemed to be listening as she screamed over and over that her baby had been gunned down in her own bedroom by police haphazardly shooting into a neighborhood. He watched a car fight its way through the crowd driven by a middle-aged white woman in horn-rimmed glasses who was holding a pistol in the same hand with which she held the steering wheel.

He kept searching for David, but he knew his chances of finding him in this chaos were slim. He felt the fear, the horror and the sadness, but his feelings seemed to be growing duller. He couldn't tell if it was because of the smoke, or from his own clouded mind, but Sammy gradually began to see the world through a thick haze. Eventually the persistent sounds of sirens, gunfire and screaming seemed to blend into the environment so much that he didn't even notice them anymore. Nobody paid any attention to the dazed teenage boy as he continued walking slowly down the street.

Is that a-? Sammy had never seen a tank in real life before. Of course he'd seen them in movies or on his neighbor's old black and white TV, but seeing one in real life was an altogether different experience. And this one was not rumbling up the street in a Fourth of July parade. In that context, he would have been impressed, even excited by its size and obvious power. That night, he wasn't impressed; he was intimidated by the huge green monstrosity charging into his neighborhood. The barrel of its cannon loomed over Grand River Avenue looking aggressive, malicious. The tank didn't seem to care what side it was on, it didn't care who was right or wrong or justified or monstrous. It wasn't there for ceremony. It was there to destroy, to maim, and to kill.

Sammy had always loved playing with his brother's

toy M26 Pershing tank, running it over the living room carpet killing Nazis who camped out in a secret base on the couch cushions. He always fought his imaginary wars in Asia or Russia or the moon or some other far-off place. He never imagined the war taking place in America, and certainly not on the streets of Detroit. He was getting a little old for playing with toys, but even if he wasn't, he knew his days of playing war were over. He stared at the tank as it disappeared down the street and without much thought, continued walking south.

After crossing the Fisher Freeway, the street came to an end in a huge empty lot. Even in all of the chaos, he was startled by the huge black space in the heart of downtown. *Why is there nothing here?* He stopped walking and turned around to look back uptown. What he saw took his breath away. Coming from three different points in the horizon were advancing walls of flame and destruction. The city glowed with firelight and mountainous thick clouds of smoke choked the skyline and blocked out the stars. He had the sickening sensation that each of the rivers of destruction were headed in his direction, as if they were moving towards this very spot. As if this very stretch of abandoned pavement had some sort of magnetic pull that drew devastation and ruin to itself.

He sat down on the dirty sidewalk and put his head in his hands. There in his home of Detroit, there in that spot, society had broken down. *Is this the end of the world?*

***

The next morning Chris plays the piano with a furious intensity, practicing the difficult passages over and over, refining his fingering, and slowly working up to tempo. The music is the one thing that still seems normal to him—the only thing that still seems sane. He rehearses like his life depends on it, perhaps because it's the only thing his life *doesn't* depend on at the moment. But of course, he is practicing for a concert that will never take place.

Sarah sits at a table on the other end of the library. It took years for her to get used to listening to him play—to be able to do anything other than watch his fingers and marvel at the sounds he was able to make with such ease. It was one of the things that drew her to him when they first met.

***

The year after getting her master's degree, Sarah was a young intern at a prestigious architectural design firm. The job was hard to get—there were almost three hundred applicants for the single unpaid position—but Sarah was an overachiever. It was obvious to her interviewers that she was brilliant and dedicated. Unlike many of the other applicants she was also charming and sociable. It was clear she could collaborate with her co-workers and that was an advantage in a field filled with talented people who did not play well with others. But what really intrigued them was that beneath the friendly smile and quirky-smart sense of humor was a drive unmatched by the other twenty-four-year-olds vying for the job. By the time the firm's Christmas party rolled around she had already established a reputation as a rising star. There were half-awed, half-annoyed whispers that she would be offered a job when her internship ended.

Despite her obvious talent, she never balked at menial tasks like sorting mail or answering phones. She never complained about staying late or working through the weekend. She looked as if she needed to be in motion 24/7. When she was tasked with arranging the Christmas party, she threw herself at it with this same zeal. She even went as far as to call the University of Michigan School of Music to hire a pianist to play the cocktail party.

Chris arrived at the event feeling completely out of place. The building was opulent and the people at the party were wearing suits and cocktail dresses that looked like they cost more than his rent. He was just a gawky kid in a wrinkled tuxedo. Despite feeling like a rat who had sneaked into the kitchen, he was more than happy to get paid three hundred dollars to play a couple of Christmas carols for drunken executives. Chris wasn't the first recommendation when Sarah called the piano department, his professor had recommended a classmate who was a more gifted pianist. But when she turned it down, Chris got the call. He didn't mind, he knew that this would probably be the case for most of his career. He'd take the jobs that the stars didn't want.

Playing a cocktail party was not a glamorous gig.

Nobody at the firm paid much attention to the pianist, but Chris was used to being ignored. Corporate partygoers tended to focus on the cocktails and cock tales. They mostly talked about who was sleeping with whom and whose wife was the wiser. But, there was one person at the party who was paying attention. Sarah was enraptured. While she listened and watched, the rest of the party seemed to fade into the background. All she could hear was his music. All she could see was that man. He was still practically a boy, still sporting a touch of teenage acne and wearing glasses five years out of style. There was a mustard stain on the collar of his tuxedo that looked as if it had been there for a while, but Chris made that piano purr. The poor baby grand spent most of its days sitting in the lobby as a decoration, ignored and un-tuned. But with his hands on the keys, it sung like it was meant to when it rolled out of the Steinway manufacturing plant in Astoria, New York.

Sarah worked up her courage and brought him a drink.

"Hi there. You're really terrific. I brought you some eggnog. Is that OK?"

Chris smiled, not missing a beat of 'Have Yourself a Merry Little Christmas' while he talked. "Of course. Thank you. I didn't know anybody was actually listening."

"I am. I'm Sarah."

She offered her hand to shake, but then realized how silly that was because his hands were occupied. She blushed and rolled her eyes at herself. Chris grinned and reached his right hand out for the shake while somehow covering all of the notes with his left hand.

"Chris."

He spent the rest of the evening dazzling her by working little musical commentaries into his Christmas carols. When the douchey guy from accounting, still sporting his high school class ring, made a drunken pass at her, Chris worked Springsteen's 'Glory Days' into the harmonies of 'Silent Night'. The chorus of 'Ding Dong the Witch is Dead' found its way into a verse of 'Jingle Bells' when Sarah's canker sore of a boss spilled a martini down the front of her ostentatiously expensive dress.

Sarah laughed and laughed at her co-workers who were oblivious to Chris' musical subversion. They were puzzled by her mirth. Sarah had been charming and warm as a co-worker—she was the type of person who smiled easily, but she almost never really laughed. She giggled frequently, but it was never really because she was actually amused. It was for their benefit—to smooth out a bad joke or to ease the tension in the room. She was very much attuned to the emotional needs of others, but didn't seem to have any herself.

But that night she wasn't laughing for them or for Chris, she was laughing from a part of herself so deeply buried that she hadn't really remembered it was there. Chris didn't think his game was actually that funny, but he was delighted to bring such obvious joy to the beautiful woman who had sat down on the piano bench with him. He was very conscious of the feeling of her leg against his and even more conscious that the hem of her skirt seemed to creep its way up her thigh just a bit more every time she laughed. He couldn't make jokes fast enough.

Sarah had been a very serious person in the years after what happened to Mikey. She had turned from a decent, but not perfect, student into an obsessive overachiever overnight. When she got to college, she held a perfect 4.0 with many notations for extra credit projects. She joined the debate team, the chess club, the technology committee and was well known for her volunteer work. She rarely slept more than five hours a night, but seemed to be pulling from an endless reserve of energy. Sarah did anything, everything, that could keep her busy.

Very few of her friends noticed the tremendous amount of guilt Sarah carried with her. Had they known, they would have expected her to fall into a pattern of self-destruction, alcohol, drugs, sex or even just isolation. Sarah was the opposite. She was friendly, popular and successful. What could be wrong?

It was Chris who intuited what was happening almost immediately. He had spent most of his time in classical music, a world filled with obsessive over-achievers trying to hide something behind their twelve daily hours of violin practice. Concealing something from themselves or someone else, or both. Sarah had the same feel about her. Or perhaps it was just that he noticed that despite her warm gregarious exterior, she had a strange way of avoiding being looked at. It felt like eye contact made her really uncomfortable. She always cleverly drew his attention away from her face—pointing out a cute dog or a new restaurant—if his gaze became too fixed. He wasn't sure if she even knew that she was doing it, but it became clear to him. Sarah, who appeared to be the 'golden-child,' the rising star of the office, the intern everybody knew would be the boss someday, was really a woman in a great deal of pain.

Sarah cried for almost an hour after the first time they made love. They had waited for almost a month before they took the relationship into the bedroom. She had offered sex to him on their first date in a jarringly matter-of-fact way, but Chris turned her down. He suspected she might have been play-acting what she thought she was supposed to do, and that her true desire didn't seem to be present in the offer.

Instead they dated. Chris took her bowling, to the aquarium, to the ice-skating rink. They did silly, almost child-like activities and spent most of their time roaring with laughter. By now, Chris was not surprised that Sarah hadn't done any of these activities since she actually was a child. The innocent happiness seemed to sneak up on her, but her joy was fresh and genuine.

About a month after they started dating, they walked home in falling snow after an evening at the movies. They had seen Jurassic Park 3 and Sarah had been completely dazzled by the special effects.

"I just don't get it. How did they do that?"

"Where have you been? You realize this is the third Jurassic Park movie right?"

"I haven't seen the first two. I mean, I haven't seen a lot of fantasy movies."

"Because they aren't black and white documentaries in French?"

Sarah punched his arm softly and took his hand.

"Seriously, what's the last movie you saw that had anything magical in it, or you know, anything fun?"

"Well-"

Chris put his hand on her lips. "Wait, let me clarify. What is the last movie you watched for actual fun, not for enlightenment or artistic pretention?

Sarah raises an eyebrow and grins. "Artistic pretention? You realize you're a classical musician right?"

He laughed. "Answer the question woman."

"The NeverEnding Story?"

"That was from like 1984! You haven't seen anything for fun since the Reagan administration?"

"I saw Tom Hanks in 'Philadelphia'?"

Chris stopped walking and looked at her incredulously.

She laughed. "OK fine. Not necessarily fun, but it was popular at least?"

He threw his hands into the air with mock frustration. "Oh I give up."

They walked together quietly holding hands for a while.

"We should... uh... go back to my place."

"You mean...uh."

"Yes. I think we should have sex."

He laughed. "Oh is that all?"

"Sorry, I kinda suck at subtext."

Chris took her other hand and looked at her seriously. He brushed a snowflake off her forehead, while he debated what to say.

"Are you sure?"

This time Sarah looked him in the eyes. He could see tears starting to build, but she squeezed his hand.

"I'm completely terrified. But yes. I want this. Do

you?"

Chris smiled at her. "Absolutely. Sarah I love you."

A tear escaped out of the corner of her eye. "I love you too Chris."

The sex was beautiful. It was slow and passionate, but also slightly silly. They giggled like teenagers and they connected physically and emotionally like adults. It was sexy and it was light. The passion was unmistakable to both of them. When they finished, holding each other in the darkness, Sarah's tears started in earnest.

Chris didn't know then, though he suspected, that despite the fact that she was twenty-four years old, that it had been her first time. She didn't cry because she was sad, or because she had been saving herself—she hadn't been. She cried because she had, almost accidentally, allowed herself to be happy. She allowed herself to be in the moment... even if it was just for that moment. She allowed herself to forget.

She knew she was going to marry him that night. Somehow he understood what she was going through. He was able to soothe her enough to slow down. To stop running, even for the briefest of moments. The sensation was completely overwhelming. She hadn't told him much about her past, and she wouldn't for another six months, but he had already been able to diagnose her type of self-destruction as 'self-distraction'. Perhaps this had been obvious to some people who came across Sarah at college, grad school and her internship. Perhaps she was the last person to know what she was doing to herself, but Chris was the first person who cared enough to tell her.

Sarah didn't slow down right away. She finished her

internship and worked her way from Assistant to the Associate Designer to Principal Designer in six years. They thought she was crazy when she quit her six-figure, corner office job to go back to school to learn how to paint. They thought she was having some sort of mental breakdown. Chris, now her husband, knew it was actually the end of her breakdown.

***

Chris stops playing for a moment. "Do you think they're all there in that lot?"

"Who?"

"The people. The Fred and Gingers."

Sarah looks up from the blueprints she's laid out on the floor. "Well, we haven't seen any of them anywhere else. It's been a week since anyone has wandered by. I guess so?"

"It's not like we've left the house in two weeks, since Costco. We wouldn't really know if they'd moved unless they marched down our street."

"Yeah."

"I wish we knew what they wanted. Or why they gathered in the first place. It doesn't make any sense. What would be the purpose of gathering the entire population of a city in some abandoned lot?"

"What makes you think there's a purpose?

"I don't know. Why would everyone go to the same place? How would they all know where to go? It's like magic."

"It's not magic. It's not uncommon in nature."

"What are you talking about?

"Monarch butterflies."

"Butterflies? More bug trivia?"

"Well, you know that Monarchs migrate every year right?"

"Sure. They have to go someplace warm. They'd die in the cold." Chris shifts on the piano bench to face her.

"Well they don't just go to the south. They go to a specific forest in a specific town in Mexico. Every single monarch butterfly in North America flies thousands of miles to congregate all together in the exact same spot every year. I think there's another meeting place in California but I don't remember where. The point is they all get together. They congregate. When they do there's so many of them they literally cover every inch of the trees."

"How the hell does a butterfly know where to go? Do they even have brains?"

"Even the scientists aren't entirely sure. But it has something to do with magnetic poles and instinct I think."

"So are you saying that the Fred and Gingers are acting like bugs?"

Sarah sighs. She feels like she knows just enough to be even more confused. "Honestly, I have no idea what I'm saying. It's all speculation anyway."

"We're never really going to know what's going on are we?"

"Probably not."

"I wish we knew *why* this is happening."

"I wish we knew a lot of things."

Chris starts playing again, but softly. "I wish we could communicate with the outside world. So we could tell our folks we're still alive."

"What makes you think they're still alive?" Sarah says grimly.

"Yeah."

With nothing more to say or at least nothing more he wants to say, Chris returns to practicing. Sarah stares at the architectural designs of their library while absent-mindedly chewing on the cap of her pen.

She's identified some important truths about their home. The basement is a lost cause. Because the foundation had never been truly weather-proofed, it is too consistently flooded to risk using, especially now that there was no power to run their sump pump. The roof is in decent shape, but they would need to invest some time in making sure that every crack, seal, hinge or joint is absolutely water tight. They had already put tarps over the entire surface of the roof, but she wanted to go over everything again with silicone.

They had considered sealing all of the windows too, but knew they would need some ventilation. So they ended up sealing most of them, with the exception of the large windows in the library proper because they were under eves. They did go through the trouble of extending the eves with two-by-fours and plywood covered with more tarps. Sarah had plans to design a more permanent solution, but it was good enough for now.

Their water supply would be sufficient for a while

at least. They agreed on a strict rationing system because, while they had plenty to drink between the water tank and the bottled liquids they had acquired, they also needed water to cook, clean, shower and flush the toilet. They agreed on very short showers once a week. They save this soapy water for cleaning clothes and dishes. Their showers' brevity is not difficult to maintain as they have lost access to their water heater which was stored in the basement and not worth risking using. They still use the toilet, but flush as infrequently as possible using the water they had already used for showering and cleaning. It's Spartan, but certainly better than using a bucket.

Trash and recycling is no longer being picked up of course, so whatever they can't re-use they now put in bags and deposit into abandoned cars. They decided against putting it on the street because they hope to eventually have a better solution and don't want it getting exposed to the rain and becoming untouchable. Chris points out that it a good idea not to leave it outdoors and attract rats. If rats survived that is. It ends up not being a major concern because they create a great deal less trash than they used to. There are no more takeout containers or junk mail. There are no more impulse buys or electronics to be thrown out when the latest upgrade comes on the market. Most of what they have to throw out is the packaging their food and drink comes in.

The biggest concern Sarah has is the impending approach of winter. She knows that winter in Detroit means snow, sleet and ice that without plows and salt, and a half million people shoveling their sidewalks, would probably cover every inch of the city until springtime. Rain they can avoid but snow-cover means they will be completely trapped until it melts. She figures that they only have a month, two if they are lucky, to prepare.

Sarah also knows they need a lot more supplies. They lost a good portion of their Costco loot off the truck when they were overwhelmed at the circle. They have to be prepared to be trapped for months and they don't have nearly enough food. They will also need a source of heat. The library's boiler, like its water heater, is in the now-inaccessible basement. There is a fireplace in the main library, but the risks of leaving the flu open to the weather are too great. Besides, they have nothing to burn. So, they are not only going to need a heat source to keep them warm, they are also going to need something to feed it. They need oil, gas or kerosene and they need a lot of it. She has no idea how they are going to find, transport and store thousands of gallons of fuel.

Perhaps the saddest thing that was destroyed on the way back from Costco, was the camping stove they found on Aisle 4. They might have been able to keep using their normal range if the building had been hooked up to the gas lines, but of course it never had been. They didn't think it mattered very much to have an electric stove—at least until the power was permanently cut off—but now they have no way of heating food and water. Chris tried to make coffee one morning over a candle and just ended up singeing himself and his coffee pot and was rewarded with a beverage that was barely lukewarm.

It is inevitable that they are going to have to venture out again soon. But another of Sarah's frequent trips to the window shows yet another cloudy day. The clouds that feel like a permanent fixture in Detroit during the winter seem to be gathering already. They are left with no choice but to sit through another day unable to leave the library because it might rain. Another day trapped.

After a half hour, Chris stops playing. He sits stretching his fingers, staring blankly into the distance. He knows he's only practicing for himself, but decades of discipline make him continue. *Maybe I should start writing music?* He doesn't voice the idea out loud. It's too scary. Calling yourself a 'composer' comes with all sorts of pressure and judgment. But then again, there probably aren't a lot of people out there to judge his writing.

Sarah breaks the silence. "We should have gotten a treadmill or something. I'm going to get so fat."

"I dunno about that. You've never been fat a day in your life. Besides, once we finish off the jerky we're pretty much vegetarians by default."

"Well, the word vegetarian would imply that we were eating vegetables. Right now, we're pretty much carb-itarians."

"You know, if we cleared out all of the furniture, we could set up a great floor-hockey rink!"

"Oh sure, here you grab that end of the piano and I'll get the other one. Should we take it up the ladder?"

Chris grins. "Fair point. Plus it would only be one-on-one. There's only one sport that's really good one-on-one."

Sarah sniffs. "Well, that and tennis."

"Oh right! Let's get a ping pong table! And an air hockey table."

"Great! I'll put them on our list right after food, heat and other things we need to stay alive."

They return to silence for a moment. Sarah stands up and starts to pace around the room aimlessly. There's not much to do other than sit or walk around. "We need to find a way to contact the other survivors in the city."

"What makes you so sure there are any?"

"Oh come on. If we survived, somebody else did. I mean it would be the height of arrogance to think we were the only people in the whole city smart enough to not get exposed."

"I'm sure you're right. But the phones are down, the internet is down, radio is off the air and the power is out. What's left? Smoke signals?"

"Maybe? We could start a fire on the roof?"

"Sarah. That's insane. Plus who would be out looking for smoke? I mean, if someone is smart enough not to be exposed, they're not going to be walking around taking pictures of the skyline, they're going to be hunkered down like we are."

"Yeah."

"I know it sucks, but we have to be patient. There's nothing we can do right now but wait."

***

Nearly a month after it formed, the circle has finally stopped growing. Eventually all of the stragglers who could physically make their way to the lot joined the masses. In fact, the circle is ever so slightly getting smaller. Hundreds, thousands of the exposed have fallen, tripped up by a stray foot or hand or just literally broken down from a month of walking. The older tendons and joints started to wear down first. Each of the fallen were trampled and stomped into the bloody mud beneath them. The bodies are beginning to look less and less like people every day. They are dirty, emaciated and suffering from profound dehydration.

Not all of the infected even made it to the circle. Thousands more remain where they were exposed, trapped like Tom the Assistant Manager, mindlessly unable to escape their houses or cars or fenced areas. Yet, even a month after being exposed, they still try.

A relentless rumbling noise radiates from the lot. It's the sound of a million feet hitting pavement over and over. Each foot hitting the ground by itself is almost silent, but combined with the cacophony of two hundred thousand other footfalls in that exact instant, the sound is audible for almost two blocks. It's not a crisp disciplined marching noise. Instead the steps are random and chaotic, causing the sound to congeal into a low-frequency thunder.

Over the weeks, a new sound joined the footfalls and gradually increased in volume until it was as loud as a rock concert. It rose to such a frantic pitch that long-term exposure would have caused hearing damage. The sound is not coming from anything human, or even ex-human. The decaying flesh at the bottom of the circle has provided a breeding ground for hundreds of millions of flies. Great dense clouds of large black house flies buzz over the heads of the Fred and Gingers. They climb all over the bodies. They walk all over their arms and legs and faces. At times they are so thickly packed in the air that they literally block out the sun, throwing sections of the circle into shadow. The deafening buzzing noise roars on endlessly, raising and lowering in pitch and intensity at random intervals. The flies are not bothered by the end of humanity. They're feeding, breeding and thriving.

***

November first goes by without anybody noticing. Nobody stresses about paying their rent, the Lions are not worried about dropping out of playoff contention... again. The days are growing shorter and the air is growing colder.

Chris and Sarah have still not been able to leave the library. They got close one morning, but in the time it took them to get their weather gear on, clouds rolled over the lake threatening death-bringing precipitation. Sarah wanted to risk it, but Chris talked her out of it. They are growing increasingly frustrated, increasingly nervous and increasingly bored.

"You know what they forget to warn you about in

all of the apocalypse movies? Boredom." Chris deals another hand of blackjack to his wife.

It's late morning. The sun is shining, but a couple of clouds to the northwest keep them trapped indoors. Chris and Sarah sit at a table with a bowl of chips and a bottle of Johnny Walker Blue.

"Boredom? Every time it rains, we're in mortal peril of being Gingerized!" Sarah folds.

"I think I'd be Fredized."

"Indeed. Who says English doesn't have masculine and feminine verbs?"

"Ok, so there's the occasional mortal peril thing, but what about the rest of the time? No TV, no internet. No contact with anybody but each other. And we can't go out because it's too dangerous to leave the library."

Sarah stares sadly at all of the empty bookshelves surrounding them. "And let's face it, we keep calling this a library, but there are barely any books to read."

Chris smiles. "You *had* to get a Kindle."

Sarah doesn't respond. Instead, she bites her lip for a second scrunching up her face.

"You're either deciding something or you've got gas. What gives?"

She laughs. "Well, I was going to save it for your birthday..."

"Save what?"

"I have a surprise for you."

Chris sets down his cards, intrigued. "Really? Awesome! What is it?"

"We would have to go outside for a second." Chris

starts to protest, but she interrupts him before he can speak. "Don't worry, we're not going anywhere far. We're literally just going next door."

Chris thinks for a second, weighing the risk. "I don't know. There are clouds."

"Oh come on! The clouds aren't over us. We're going thirty feet tops. If it will make you feel better, we can put on our weather gear."

Chris hesitates. "Just next door? Nowhere else?" Sarah nods. "OK. Fine. Let's do it."

Ten minutes later, they stand at their front door, staring out the window.

"Looks clear to me. Clouds over there, but they don't look that threatening."

Chris shakes his head. "Boy, if you get us killed for something stupid, I'm going to come back to life just so I can strangle you."

"Come on husband! It's totally awesome. You're going to love it."

"What is it?!"

"I told you it's a surprise! Come on."

Sarah opens the door and they step onto the deserted street. She takes him by the hand and walks him to the entrance of the office building that sits next to the library.

"What are we going to do here? I've been trying to avoid cubicle farms my whole life."

"Trust me. It will be worth it."

They walk through the main entrance and step into the lobby. A large desk dominates the open room that is strewn with random bits of clothing. Most of the clothes look like they were owned by the security guard and the receptionist who normally would be sitting sentry at this hour. Behind the desk, two elevators lead up to the office floors above.

"We're going up to four."

Chris starts walking in the direction of the elevators. Sarah watches him for a second and laughs.

"Where are you going? There's no power dummy."

Chris shakes his head. "Oh right. Of course. Man, you spend years taking stuff for granted. It looks almost normal in here. My subconscious forgot that the world ended. I almost signed in at security."

"The stairs are over here."

"Wait, so you've been here before?"

Sarah ignores him and pulls him into the stairwell. They climb up four flights of stairs and Chris reaches to open the door.

"Hold on. You need to close your eyes."

"What for?"

"It's a surprise. Just do it!"

Chris closes his eyes and she guides him into the large open room. There is a field of almost identical cubicles buttressed by small offices on the east and west sides of the building. There are no lights on, but the cloud-spotted sun shines through the floor-to-ceiling windows and illuminates the room. At this hour it should have been jam-packed with miserable office workers and temps making and receiving phone calls. Today it is silent.

"Keep your eyes closed. Take three more steps forward... Good. Now, listen to me closely and follow my instructions. OK?"

"OK. Tell me what to do."

"Keeping your eyes shut, count to fifty, then open them."

Chris laughs. "This is ridiculous wife. Alright. Fifty...forty-nine..."

When he finishes counting and opens his eyes, Sarah is gone. On the desk in front of him sits a laser-tag gun and a vest with a sensor on it. A note reads: "Put on the sensor. Pick up the gun. You are already being hunted."

Chris cackles with glee as he puts the vest on, grabs the gun and ducks down. He runs down the aisle and dives under a cubicle.

A half hour later, after crashing her way over the top of the Assistant to the Executive VP of Marketing's desk, Sarah shoots Chris for the final point. His vest flashes and makes a sad beeping noise.

Laughing, Chris picks up a foam stress-ball from the debris she knocked off the desk and tosses it at her. "You cheated!"

"You're dead bucko! Dead people can't talk."

"Fine. Fine. You win."

"Well I win the first event."

"First?"

"This is your birthday triathlon! Duh!"

"Wait. When on earth did you set this up?"

Sarah laughs. "I have lots of time while you sleep in until eleven every morning like a teenager."

"I'm a musician! I don't work on a nine to five schedule." He stops. "Wait a minute-"

"Don't worry! I was careful! We should keep moving. We have much more to do!"

Chris kisses her on the mouth. "You are amazing wife. Well, what's up next?"

"Follow me up to the fifth floor!"

They take the stairs up another flight and find another floor filled with more identical rows of cubicles. A series of arrows have been drawn on the carpet with green duct tape that map out a twisting track through the workstations. At their feet there are two children's tricycles.

"Oh, this is awesome. Where did you get these?"

"Never you mind that. Three laps around. Follow the arrows."

They sit down on the tricycles looking somewhat ridiculous. Chris teeters on his seat like a circus bear.

"This isn't fair! I can barely get my knees under the handlebars."

"What's that? Oh, sorry, I can't hear excuses."

Sarah tears off, headed down the carpet leaving Chris laughing and desperately trying to get his bike in motion. He feels a bit like Danny Torrance riding his big wheels through the Overlook Hotel. Feeling the illusion of speed because he is so close to the ground, he takes tight turns down corridors of desks. He almost topples over taking a sharp left turn, but eventually is able to catch up with Sarah. Giggling, she has acquired a ruler and tries to stick it into the spokes of his tricycle. Chris responds by squirting her with a huge bottle of hand cream he swiped from one of the desks.

It was a close race, but Chris manages to squeak out

a victory by knocking a stack of files off a shelf and into Sarah's path.

Out of breath from the pedaling, Sarah throws a couple of folders at him. "You cheated husband!"

"What's that? Oh, sorry, I can't hear excuses!"

Another stack of papers gets tossed at him. He just grins. "So, we're tied. What's the final event?"

"Bowling!"

"Bowling? How do we bowl??"

"Sixth floor. Let's go!"

When they reach the sixth floor, Chris sees that Sarah has set up two bowling lanes in the aisles between the cubicles. At the end of the aisles, in front of the windows, there are two sets of 'pins' made up of glass vases, computer monitors, lamps and other things she knows the little boy in him would love to smash with a bowling ball.

"Oh no way!" Chris says with glee.

"I found the ball in one of the executive offices. It was kind of obvious what we had to do."

"Of course."

"OK. Me first."

Sarah rears back and rolls the ball down the carpet as fast as she can. It doesn't go straight at the 'headpin' that was actually a glass trophy won by the original owner of the ball, but it does crash into an old CRT monitor and a ceramic bowl making a tremendously satisfying shattering noise. Glass flies everywhere and Chris and Sarah cheer.

Picking the ball up and inspecting the wreckage, Chris counts the 'pins.' I'd say you got four, but I'll give you a bonus one for smashing the monitor."

"OK. Five is the number to beat. Let's see what you got hotshot."

They walk down to Chris's lane and he takes aim at a tacky crystal sculpture of a dolphin and a large glass bowl of jelly beans at the head of the pyramid of pins.

"Oh I've got this."

He pulls the ball back and throws it with every ounce of strength he has. The little voice that tells fortyish-year-old men to over-exert themselves to impress women is very a loud one. Two things happen in that moment. One, Chris pulls every muscle in his back. And two, the ball doesn't roll down the carpet, instead it catches on his finger for just long enough to send it flying high into the air, and grazing the dusty ceiling tiles. It drops down with a tremendous bang five feet in front of the pins. Then it bounces over them and slams into the floor-to-ceiling windows. They explode with a thundering crash raining glass down six stories to the street. There is a terrific cracking noise when the ball hits the sidewalk and splits into two spinning pieces.

Chris and Sarah freeze for a second, processing what just happened. Then they burst into hysterical laughter. Tears stream down their faces as Sarah falls to the ground clutching her stomach. Chris tries to reach down to her, but is stopped by the clenching pain in his back. This causes them to laugh even more hysterically. It takes three minutes for them to collect themselves enough to speak again.

"I'm too old to have fun." Chris clutches his back

and tries to stretch.

"You would have done the same thing when you were twenty."

"Of course, but I wouldn't have thrown my back out!"

"Let's get you home and give you some Advil He-Man."

"Yeah." They walk towards the stairwell for a moment. Chris grabs her shoulder and stops her. "Hey. Do you know how amazing it is to be your husband?"

"Almost as amazing as it is to be your wife. Now kiss me for real you doofus."

*

The next day, the boredom returns with the grey and cloudy weather. Chris noodles on the piano while Sarah re-reads a paperback novel she found under the bed.

Chris sighs. "I tell you what I'd give my right arm for: a cold beer and a Redwings game."

"Then we need to get serious about finding a generator."

"How's that going to help me watch the Redwings?"

"For the cold beer dumbass."

Chris sighs. This is a conversation they've been rolling over and over for two weeks.

"We'd have to keep it fueled. Where are we going to get enough gasoline? Plus it's going to be noisy. We don't want to attract the Fred and Gingers."

"The dance party doesn't seem to have much interest in us. Or in anything."

"Look, I know that I didn't take this seriously right away. But you were right the first time. We can't take any unnecessary risks. We've all seen this movie. People make mistakes. People die. We can't take chances."

"The mistake would be not preparing for winter. How do you expect us to stay warm? With a generator we could get electric heaters, refrigeration, lights, power."

Chris pushes his chair back from the table. Annoyed.

"You think I don't know that? Every day, all I think about is how to keep you safe. Fed. Warm. I *know* we need it. But last time we went out, we almost died. I'm not in a hurry to go back out there. You step in a puddle you die. A drop of rain hits you in the head, you die. There's fucking zombies out there! And who knows what else?! I can't keep us safe outside of the library!" Chris' face is red, he's on the verge of tears. He stops to catch his breath.

"Are you finished?"

Chris sits back down and puts his head in his hands.

"First off, you're being sexist. Why is it your job to keep us safe? To keep *me* safe? That's bullshit. We keep each other safe. Our survival depends on both of us, not just you. You're being an idiot."

"Yeah." Chris replies without looking up.

"Secondly, obviously you're right about all of the danger. Do you think that I of all people am not aware of what can go wrong when we venture out?"

Chris swallows. Of course she knows. He feels stupid for not handling the subject with a little more tact. It's been a long time, but some wounds will never truly go away.

Sarah continues. "But there are short term dangers and long term dangers. If we starve to death, or freeze to death, we're still just as dead. We're running out of supplies and we're running out of options. We don't have a safe choice right now. We just have dangerous and more dangerous."

Sarah pauses and waits for Chris to respond. He doesn't. She keeps going.

"We have to move. Soon. Tomorrow. Even if it's cloudy. We're playing Russian Roulette waiting for a bright sunny day when we might not get another one before we're buried in snow. A generator, food, water. Maybe some fresh books. OK?"

Chris mumbles a reply.

"What's that?"

"Well, even if the TV isn't broadcasting anymore, if we have electricity my Xbox will work."

Sarah smiles. "Now you're talking."

CHAPTER 9

The morning the water went bad, Sam Jones—who stopped going by Sammy decades ago—woke up knowing he was going to have a good day. It began much like every other Friday for him, but he knew this one was different. He woke up at 7:45 AM and snuck into the shower as quietly as he could so he wouldn't wake Helen up. After thirty-seven years of marriage, he knew better than to wake her during his morning routine. She worked second shift at the Super Associated grocery store and didn't get home from work until after midnight on weekdays. So they made a deal; he wouldn't wake her up when he left for his job, if she didn't wake him up when she got home from hers. They had been on this routine for almost twenty years and it worked just fine. But Sam knew that this would be the last time he would have to sneak out in the morning.

He put on his Detroit Department of Transportation uniform in their small but cozy living room. He stopped for a second to look in the mirror. There he was, Sam the number 125 bus driver. He'd softened in the middle and his temples had turned grey but he was still just as tall as he had been as a gawky twelve-year-old standing in a crowd of 25,000 people to hear Martin Luther King Jr. speak at Cobo Hall in 1963.

Sam had driven the same route six days a week since 1988. He never made more than thirty-five thousand dollars a year and he never made a speech or changed the world, but he was proud of the career he had chosen. And more importantly, he had earned the respect of the people in his life.

He'd developed long friendships with his regular passengers. He would miss Josh the bike repairman who always wanted to talk about the Pistons but never seemed to get any of their names right, and Mrs. T who would take the bus to the market for a bagel and a paper every single morning. Sam told her one day that she could have her paper and a bagel delivered if she wanted, especially after they had celebrated her eightieth birthday. She scoffed and said that the day she couldn't go out and get her own breakfast was the day she should curl up and die.

He wondered if Josh or Mrs. T would even recognize him out of his uniform. Would they know it was him if he wasn't behind the big wheel? Would he recognize himself? He pushed the thought down. *Retirement starts tomorrow, this is a good thing. This is a happy day.*

There was a card from Helen sitting on the counter next to his lunch bag. He opened it and as soon as he began to read, he was interrupted by a voice coming from behind him.

"You worked hard for forty-two years. I'm proud as hell of my handsome husband. I can't wait to spend the next forty-two with you all to myself. Happy retirement, old man."

Sam turned and, through the film of tears in his eyes, saw Helen standing behind him with a tiny cake in the shape of a bus.

"You realize in forty-two years, I'll be a hundred and six?"

"I'm game if you are. Get out there and drive safe. I'll be here with a bottle of champagne when you get home."

Sam smiled and put on his cap. Feeling a little self-conscious, he surreptitiously picked up a napkin and dabbed his eyes. He started to discard it, but then thought better. He folded the napkin and tucked it into his shirt pocket figuring this probably was not the last time he was going to cry that day.

It wasn't. Josh handed him a bottle of scotch when he got on the bus on Fort Street. Mrs. T brought him a bouquet of flowers that she had picked from her own garden. By five o'clock, his dashboard was covered with gifts from his regular passengers. He subtly used his napkin on at least five occasions to discreetly wipe tears out of his eyes.

At six o'clock, Sam finished the 125 loop for the final

time and pulled the bus over on a side road overlooking the Fisher Freeway. It was time to hand the bus off to Brett, the evening driver. As always, he was sitting on a bench waiting for Sam with his customary mug of coffee. Sam collected as many gifts as he could carry into a plastic bag. He had to leave some flowers, but he figured maybe Brett could take them home to his husband. With one last glace at his old seat, he exited the bus.

"Pretty good haul you got there."

"I had no idea. Wow. People really came out of the woodwork for my last day."

"Congrats my friend." Brett held out his hand and Sam shook it. He was surprised to feel something in Brett's hand.

"What's this?"

Brett had given him what looked like a DDOT GoPass card that passengers swipe to get to the bus. But this one wasn't white, it was silver.

Sam turned it over. "Wait a minute! Is this a free-for-life pass? I didn't even think these were real!"

"They're not... officially. But you should never have to pay for the bus. You've given the city enough. Enjoy your retirement Sammy. You're a free man."

Before Sam could say anything else, Brett hopped onto the bus and drove away. He watched as the green and white 125 bus disappeared down the street for the last time. He remained sitting on the bench for a moment unsure of what to do. He had the rest of his life to spend however he wanted and now he couldn't think of anything to do next. Obviously he was going to go home, Helen was waiting, but he felt like he should do *something* to commemorate the moment. Nothing came to him, so he did what he's done after his shift every day for the last forty-two years; he walked over to the Mobil station across the street, bought his after-shift doughnut and used the restroom.

Because he didn't have any opportunities to take a leak other than his lunch break, he always had to pee after his route. There was a time when he could wait until he got home, but now that he was in his sixties, his bladder didn't hold out like it used to. So every night he used the bathroom at the gas station before hopping on the 160 bus to take him home.

After saying hello to Kendra the attendant like he always did, he grabbed the key and walked behind the building to the dingy unisex bathroom. A single florescent light flickered and buzzed over the toilet and a small rusted sink. A cracked mirror hung over the ancient porcelain basin. The decrepit state of the bathroom never bothered Sam that much. He'd seen worse. He was old enough to have lived through the time when—just a few states to the south—people his color had separate bathrooms that were lucky to have running water. When he finished his business, he washed his hands thoroughly while staring at himself in the mirror.

"What are you gonna do now Sammy old boy? You made all sorts of plans for how you're going to get to retirement, but didn't make any plans for what you're going to do *after* retirement." He grinned at himself and made a grunting noise. "Well, I guess you can sleep in tommorroooouhhhh..."

He never finished his sentence. The air continued out of him like a groaning sigh, but the words were gone. The face looking back at him in the mirror went slack as the expression drained out of his eyes. His mouth went limp leaving his features blank and masklike. His eyeballs started to look up as if he was rolling his eyes, but the pupils did not come back down. They continued to roll up and into his skull until they were turned almost completely backwards. The mirror showed only bright white sclera with red veins running through it. Sam's eyes were just a bright white wall. Empty.

His leg abruptly kicked out and hit the small trashcan below the sink. It made a loud clanging noise as it crashed into the grimy wall. A tile shattered and rained bits of porcelain and plaster onto his shoes. Shoving the door open with his shoulder, he stepped into the light of the sun which had just begun sagging in the sky. His green cap lay abandoned on the edge of the sink. His bag of gifts sat on the ground outside the bathroom door ignored. His arm twitched sideways as he began to walk northeast.

Sam's Detroit Department of Transportation shirt hit the pavement ten yards from the bathroom door. The uniform that Sam had maintained with pride for years now dangled green buttons that had been roughly torn from the fabric. The seam in the shoulder ripped open as Sam violently removed it. His white starched undershirt was next. He always ironed his undershirts even though Helen teased him about it.

This too was torn off and discarded, exposing his large belly. He carried his weight pretty well, but forty years of sitting behind a steering wheel all day had helped him acquire an extra thirty pounds around his midsection. He had been embarrassed by the fact that his stomach protruded over his belt so he always wore a shirt a couple sizes too large to make it look like the shirt was just 'poofing' over his belt and not filled with his love-handles. When he removed his belt, his stomach settled down, causing a small crease between his belly button and his penis.

His pants fell down with a clang. He had always carried a lot of change in his pockets. It was just one of the things that made his day easier because it allowed him to make change for passengers who sometimes came on the bus without their monthly bus passes. It was against policy to make change, but his riders appreciated it.

He stepped one foot out of his pants and left a shoe on the sidewalk. For a while he dragged the pants along the ground streaming coins and keys behind him. Then, he was only wearing his faded white briefs. In a moment, the briefs were torn off too and were left on the ground with the pants and the other shoe. Sam was completely nude—even his watch and wedding ring fell to the ground, discarded. His penis, which was normally tucked neatly into his briefs, swung lazily from side to side as he walked down the sidewalk. His testicles, which dangled lower than they did when he was young, tightened and crept back up in response to the slight chill in the late afternoon breeze. There was a loud honking noise as he stepped off the curb and into traffic.

"Watch where you're going you fucking lunatic!!" a driver in a Mercedes shouted as he swerved to avoid Sam.

The naked man paid no attention to the cars honking at him. He just steadily headed Northeast. As he traveled, there were more confused, frightened or angry shouts from the people driving by or crossing the street to avoid passing him on the sidewalk.

"Jesus man! Put some pants on! That's disgusting."

"Mommy? What is that guy-"

"Look away Kelly! He's just a homeless junkie."

He did not seem to notice the shouting as he made his slow journey through downtown Detroit. He continued to twitch and spasm as he walked, every five or ten seconds flailing an arm or a leg out. It took him fifteen minutes to reach the abandoned lot. When he arrived, on the other side of the open space, Shirley had just started her first lap.

***

High above the silent city, a tiny speck of dust flies through a cloud. It comes in contact with a miniscule amount of water vapor which freezes and crystallizes. The weight of the ice crystal is soon too much to sustain flight and the first snowflake of winter begins its long gradual descent. Flitting and twirling out of the clouds, it looks down on the dark grey skyline of Detroit. The snowflake makes a lazy circle down and down until it is caught in a draft rising up the side of the Marriott building. It picks up speed as it is sucked down and around the tower before being set free to gently float northwest on a breeze off the river. It flies over the immaculately manicured divide of Washington Blvd. and almost lands on the roof of the Leland hotel before a tiny gust of wind pushes it over a pipe and around a chimney. The snowflake flies into the open air and looks down over a sea of twisted, crumbling bodies.

The circle is now nothing but a fetid landscape of horror. Bodies that were once young, virile, and attractive are now gaunt, bruised and bony.

Sammy, or Sam, looks a lot different than he did when he discovered the lot on a horrible night almost fifty years before. In fact, he looks a lot different than he did a month ago when he returned to the lot after being exposed. His features seem to have been sucked into his face. His eyes retreated further into his skull as they dried out. His skin has contracted so much that despite having been relatively heavy-set when he died, the outlines of his bones now visibly protrude through the cracked leathery skin covering his frame. Much like normal cadavers, it appears as if Sam's hair and nails have continued growing, but it is just an illusion. His drying skin had merely shrunk around his follicles exposing more of his curly graying hair.

The snowflake meets its demise when it is stepped on by what now could only loosely be described as a foot. The skin and muscle have worn down and hang in shredded pieces like a sweater that has started to unravel. Protruding bone takes most of the weight, and it too is showing signs of wear. What used to be clean white bone is now scarred and grimy. It is blackened by the unspeakable slurry that coats the ground. Human slurry.

The people are weaker now. Even without pain, fatigue or consciousness, the human body has limits. They have become frail. The former citizens of Detroit are now intensely dehydrated and malnourished. The circle has been revolving for almost two months. They can no longer be considered human. In fact, no reasonable person would even consider them alive. But some new sort of programming, either instinctual or parasitic, has taken over. And now the programming has finally changed.

Sammy is leaving the lot for the final time. His single body, one of over half a million, finishes its rotation past Montcalm Street and instead of continuing over Clifford Street towards Columbia, it starts to travel north. It takes the highway overpass towards nowhere in particular. Towards anything. Towards food.

Within ten minutes, two more head off in random directions. Then ten. Then a hundred. As if some sort of biological alarm clock went off, the circle begins breaking up. The great rotating mass slowly loses its organization and spins out like a hurricane dissipating, sending expanding spiraling waves of Fred and Gingers to flood the city.

They, or whatever is in the driver's seat of their bodies, are hungry. No distinctions are made about the food source. Anything made of flesh will do. Like a giant cloud of locusts, there is only the single desire to consume. The bones of Detroit will be picked clean of every last morsel.

***

That same morning Sarah sits on the floor of the library with the street map they found in the truck and a sharpie. She has circled several options.

"OK, so I know there's a hardware store on Gratiot, but I think we'd be smarter to go to Home Depot."

"So much for supporting local small businesses."

Chris stands over the map feeling slightly useless. He never remembered where anything was. His parents always teased him that he needed road flares to find the bottom of their driveway.

"A big store is going to have more options. I think we should get two generators. So we have a backup."

"Makes sense. Let's suit up."

***

The creature that used to be Milly Smith shuffles her way down Woodward Ave. She had been a thirty-seven-year-old stay-at-home mom. She had given birth to two children in her twenties who were now middle-school-aged and had figured she was off the baby train. That was until a week before her thirty-fifth birthday, when she discovered she was pregnant with twin girls. Surprise. Now instead of Pilates at 1:00 PM and a large glass of pinot noir at 3:00 PM, she was chasing around a pair of toddlers. She wasn't sure if she was more exhausted because she was ten years older than last time she chased a toddler, or because this time everything was in stereo. Tasks like meals, diapers, baths and story time were now either doubly chaotic or had to be performed twice. She soon discovered that she wasn't skipping her large glass of Pinot Noir after all. Hearing her father's voice judging her in the back of her head, she wondered if this made her a bad mother. A recovering alcoholic, he would have given her a long talk about responsibility. He would have droned on about slippery slopes and learning from his mistakes using a thousand words where ten would suffice, but his tendency to pontificate made her wonder how much of it he actually believed. Nonetheless, his voice weighed on her, even from the grave. This usually led to another glass of wine.

Milly was exposed to the parasite when she washed her hands after having her 'mommy tinkle time.' She had dropped the twins into their playpen for their forty-seventh viewing of 'Finding Nemo'. Twenty minutes after washing her hands, she joined the circle. 'Finding Nemo' ended a half hour later. Nobody ever returned to turn off the TV.

Now, the body that Milly Smith used to inhabit is just a horrifying shell. So withered and desiccated, all of her bones look like they are trying to push out of her skin, trying to escape. Her skin has become hard, brittle and somewhat translucent like untanned leather.

Milly has no thought, no self-awareness, but whatever is still commanding her body to keep moving is hungry. Navigating by instinct and smell, she finds herself in front of a dog tied to an old out-of-service parking meter.

Cooper was a six-year-old German Shepherd who lived for the twice-daily walks his owner would take him on. The street seemed like a magical place filled with endless fascinating smells. There were old smells, new smells, layered and complicated smells that seemed to bring the sidewalk alive with a rainbow of odors.

Another dog was here. What is that? A half-eaten candy bar. I want it! A human peed on that bush. I must pee on it myself. Oh boy a squirrel!

Cooper thought nothing of being tied to the parking meter. It was part of the routine. His owner would go in for a cup of coffee and newspaper every afternoon. He didn't notice anything was amiss until he was very hungry and tired of being wet. Cooper did not conceive of time the same way humans do, so he did not know he had been tied to the post for almost nine hours.

Two months later, when Milly discovered the rotting, liquefying corpse of what used to be Cooper, she did what her hunger compelled her to do. She began to eat.

***

Chris and Sarah walk out the front door of the library. Their weather gear has improved. They have thick green raincoats and wide-brimmed hats. Their garbage bags have been replaced with rubber wading boots designed for fly-fishing. The new gear causes them to walk more slowly and is very hot despite the cold weather, but they feel a little less susceptible to death-by-puddle. They have to abandon their pickup truck because of the broken window, but they find a working van two blocks from the library. They hop in and head off in the direction of Home Depot.

"Even if we get the generator, we still need a long-term solution to our fuel problem," Chris says, keeping his eyes peeled for Fred and Gingers. They haven't seen them anywhere but in the circle, but he sure as hell does not want to get caught in the horde again. "Running a generator all winter is going to use up a ton of gas."

"I think we could set up a siphon to get it from all the cars but we'll need some way to store it. I'm sure they'll have some large gas cans at Home Depot."

"Sure, that will work for a while, but it's not going to last very long. Besides we're going to be exposed to the weather every time we need to siphon more gas."

Neither of them have a good solution. They continue in silence as the van crawls through the streets of Detroit.

"Look!" Chris points out his window. "Dogs. A whole pack of them."

"Weird. I guess they weren't affected? Maybe the parasite, or whatever it is, only affects humans."

Chris stares out the window watching the dogs root around in a pile of garbage. He counts six of them made up of several different breeds. A German shepherd, a collie, even a maltipoo. They're dirty and bedraggled, but seem to be surviving. This pack has adapted to a human-less world. He wonders what became of all of the pets who weren't able to adapt or even escape from their homes or cages. He frowns knowing there's nothing to wonder about, they died. *What did these dogs need to do to be the ones who lived? What had they gone through? Were the survivors or the dead the lucky ones?*

Sarah interrupts his thought. "I wonder if they're dangerous."

"Fifi's gone feral? Maybe? ...Probably."

"We should get a cat."

Chris rolls his eyes. "Cats are awful."

***

Fifi hasn't gone feral. At least she hadn't gone feral completely. It hasn't been an easy couple of months for Fifi, who actually went by Elly before the water turned, but at least she wasn't tied to a post to starve to death like poor Cooper. She's hungry, dirty and starting to be cold more and more often, but she still has not given up hope that her owner will come home from work and give her a treat.

When she comes across a human for the first time in two months, she's really pleased. Her tail wags and she goes right up to the man and licks his hand. Perhaps too many generations of breeding for friendliness and adorability has left Fifi with too little survival instinct.

Her last thought is to be confused about why the human just bit her.

***

They left early wanting to make sure they didn't get caught out after dark, so when Chris and Sarah arrive at the Home Depot parking lot, it's only 10:13 AM. Sarah parks and grabs a flashlight out of her backpack.

Chris climbs out and pauses. "You know, even if we can get a generator into the back of the van, we're not going to have room for much else. We need food and water too. We're going to have to make three or four trips at least."

He looks over to discover that a smile has crept onto Sarah's face.

"No we're not."

"I guess we could take two cars, but I don't like being separated."

"We're not going to have to do that either."

Sarah is staring at a green and white city bus that's sitting abandoned at the edge of the large parking lot.

Chris sees what she's looking at. "You're kidding."

"Why not? I've driven big stuff before. It's not that hard. Gas, brake, steering wheel. Plenty of trunk space."

"You're nuts."

"I'm brilliant."

Sarah walks over to the bus and pushes the folding door open. She hops in the driver's seat and smiles at Chris. "You coming sir?"

As Chris climbs aboard bus 125, Sarah discovers that the keys are still in the ignition. With a grin, she turns the key and the engine rumbles to life. "Lucky thing it stalled out and didn't burn all its gas idling!"

"Look, somebody left flowers on the dashboard." He points to a small bouquet of dried flowers still wrapped in plastic. "Must have been Fred's date night."

"I think he's going to be late." She releases the clutch and the bus lurches forward. "Shit!"

"Careful!" Chris says unhelpfully.

"It's OK. I've just got to get a handle of the transmission."

Sarah makes a wide turn and circles the bus into the shopping center. She is pleased and relieved to see a sprawling grocery store and a Rite Aid in the same complex as the Home Depot. Chris is pleased and relieved to see a Gamestop sandwiched between them.

In front of Home Depot a large white SUV sits parked in the handicapped spot. Before Chris can react, Sarah guns the engine and the bus surges forward. All twelve cylinders roaring, the bus picks up speed much faster than he imagined the large vehicle could accelerate. His eyes widen when he sees what she is aiming for. They crash into the side of the Lexus LX sending it careening out of the way. The back window of the SUV explodes and safety glass showers the pavement. The front axle snaps and two of the wheels are crushed under the car, destroying the flamboyant custom rims. It's silly. And *loud*.

"What the hell!?" Chris says, half startled, half

angry.

"It didn't have a handicap sticker. It's just rude."

Chris looks at her sternly, preparing to lecture her for being rash and impulsive, but after a beat, they both burst out laughing.

"I think this is our stop." Sarah says trying to catch her breath.

"That was stupid. Kind of fun. But stupid. Come on wife, let's go shopping."

***

Five blocks away, two former citizens of Detroit that now could best be described as zombies turn their heads towards the sound of the crash. They both pause for a second as if they were startled by the noise and after a moment of hesitation, start walking in the direction of Home Depot.

***

"Good. I'm glad there's a Rite Aid over there. Let's hit that first. We need as much medicine as we can get. Antibiotics, bandages, painkillers, anything we can find." Sarah starts to scribble a shopping list onto her hand with a ballpoint pen.

"Are you planning on getting injured?"

"I'm planning for what we can't plan."

They grab a shopping cart from the parking lot and head into the drug store. It's warm inside despite the fall chill. The air is thick and stale from being trapped for two months. Chris heads for the bandages and first-aid supplies and Sarah heads to the pharmacy counter.

"They have some air-casts here. Should I grab them?"

Sarah pops her head up over the counter. "Yeah. Grab everything. Get more condoms... no TV, no internet... we use a lot of them."

"Okey dokey."

Sarah shines her flashlight at the endless bottles of pills. Each of them has a long medical name that she doesn't recognize. She starts to feel frustrated and embarrassed. *How do I not know the actual names of any antibiotics? Fuck.* She wishes her iPhone worked so she could look it up.

She goes back to the counter and finds a dog-eared notebook filled with reference charts underneath a dried-up plant. It's covered with a thick layer of dust and probably hasn't been used since the pharmacists could look things up online, but it's exactly what she needs. She's happy to see it has a list of drugs broken down by type.

She murmurs to herself. "OK. Probably don't need opioids or boner pills... yet. Ah! Antibiotics!"

Armed with the reference guide, she grabs a couple of baskets and cleans out the pharmacy of anything she can identify the use of even if she can't imagine needing it. Better safe than sorry.

*

The Home Depot turned out to be fairly easy to

navigate. The emergency lights had long since run out of battery life, but they had flashlights to see by. And after finding the camping aisle, they had bright lanterns. They load two 10,000 watt generators onto a rolling palette and add a crate of heavy-duty extension cords. They stack another palette with power-tools and building supplies including a large selection of caulk, weather stripping and commercial plastic sheeting. And naturally they get every roll of duct tape in the entire warehouse.

The grocery store is not as easy or as pleasant. The smell coming from the Kroger is overpowering. All of the refrigerated cases of meat, vegetables and dairy have been enthusiastically rotting creating a mixture of awful smells that Chris can still taste even after plugging his nose. Still, they have a job to do and they fill up cart after cart with any food that looks like it hasn't spoiled and hundreds of gallons of bottled water and other beverages.

An hour and a half later, Chris and Sarah have loaded the bus with thirty-five shopping carts of supplies. Sarah creates high stacks of cereal, cake mix, coffee, pasta and jerky on top of cases of water, soda and juice. There are towers of cans and jars buttressed by enormous rows of toilet paper.

Chris rolls up with another shopping cart filled to the brim.

"What you got there?" Sarah calls out, not looking at him.

"Uh... Let's call it arts and entertainment?"

Chris loads a box of video games for his Xbox, six

cases of wine and liquor and a stack of pornography two feet high.

Sarah giggles but tries to put on a stern face. "Booze and porn?"

"It's a long winter!"

Sarah rolls her eyes while strategically covering several cases of craft beer and a stack of romance novels.

"What else do we need? I got all the batteries at Kroger, were there any more at the Gamestop?"

Chris does not respond.

"Chris?"

He speaks in a quiet monotone. Not panicked, but deadly serious. "We need to go."

"Why? Clouds?"

"No. A Fred. Look."

On the far side of the parking lot, a male zombie lumbers slowly in their direction. Chris is shocked to see how much the body has deteriorated. It is a truly horrible sight.

"Shit. Is he coming towards us?"

Sarah looks over his shoulder. "This is not a time to be curious. This is a time to get the fuck out of here."

"Right."

They throw the last cases of food onto the back seat of the bus and close the emergency door.

"Keep your eyes on Fred. He's getting closer."

"I see him."

Sarah climbs into the driver's seat and Chris stands in the bus's doorway looking warily at Fred. He hesitates for a second.

"He's a long way from the herd. I wonder if he was

trapped and finally escaped to head to the lot? It sure took him a long time to free himself."

"I don't know. He's headed in the wrong direction. He's headed for us. Get in. Let's get out of here."

The corpse closes in on the bus, now only about one hundred feet away. Chris makes an involuntary 'huh?' noise when Fred walks directly into a light post. The zombie staggers for a bit then continues in on their direction.

"I think he's blind."

Sarah starts the engine. She checks the gauges trying to figure out how much fuel they have. "What?"

"We should have thought of this already. Their eyes are rolled up, so of course they can't see. He's navigating by sound. As long as we stay-"

A hand closes on Chris' shoulder and pulls him backwards off the bus and out of Sarah's view. The sound of his scream sends blood rushing through her head so fast it makes the world seem like it's in slow motion.

The universe is instantly quieter as if everything was muted except for the sound of Chris calling out. She's up and out of her seat in less than a second. She grabs the baseball bat they stashed next to the door and runs out of the bus so fast she almost over-balances and falls. Almost. She catches herself and turns to face Chris who has been knocked to the ground and is pinned by three zombies.

"Chris!!"

Sarah's brain is in emergency slow-motion mode so she has time to remember how annoyed she is by the long list of movies in which women are depicted as weak and ineffectual when swinging a bat. She always thought of the image of Shelley Duvall weakly holding the middle of her bat and pathetically swiping it back and forth trying to ward off a maniacal Jack Nicholson. The subtle sexism pissed Sarah off. It was as if a woman would automatically be too overcome by her vagina emotions to plant her feet, turn her hips and swing.

Now watching her husband in danger, she begins to understand the panic that creeps up the back of your neck and makes your hands numb and your feet seem to be stuck in quicksand. But Sarah does what her father taught her to do before her first middle school softball game. "*Take a deep breath. Bend your knees a bit. Grip the bat firmly but don't squeeze it to death. Turn your hips and swing through your core not just with your arms. Commit your entire body's energy into the fluid motion of the bat. It's about transfer of energy, not just how hard you can swing.*"

Sarah swings at the first zombie's head with a ferocious but laser-focused intensity. She is startled, horrified even, but deep down in her animal brain, immensely satisfied when the head doesn't just get knocked back, it explodes. The dried brittle skin and tissue fly off in every direction. The scull cracks into several pieces, detaches completely from its body and hits the side of the bus with a loud clang, spraying brain matter like a Jackson Pollack painting. The body is knocked back into the second zombie causing it to fall as well.

Chris seizes the opportunity and log-rolls to his left,

knocking the third zombie down like a bowling pin. Panic coursing through his body, he leaps to his feet with the speed and agility that he had as a child before the growth spurt of puberty made him stiff, heavy and clumsy.

"Sarah! Look out!"

Fred, forgotten in all of the excitement, has advanced on them, now only a few feet away from Sarah's back. He raises his arms to grab her, but Chris moves too quickly. He shoves Sarah back into the doorway of the bus, ducks under Fred's arms and pushes him back into the two zombies who were getting up. Fred falls backwards into a tangled pile of limbs. It would be funny if their lives were not in danger. They looked like they were playing a drunken zombie version of naked Twister.

"CHRIS! Get in!"

From around the back of the bus come another half dozen Fred and Gingers. Chris hops in and Sarah uses the lever next to the driver's seat to slam the folding door closed. She starts the engine as the attackers start to clump behind the glass.

"Go! Go!" Chris puts his weight against the door, attempting to prevent the zombies from pushing it open.

Sarah slams her foot down on the gas pedal and the bus lurches forward, knocking several bodies down to get sucked under the tires and be crushed. She pays no mind to this as she drives out of the shopping center at a breakneck speed. Chris can hear the tires start to whistle and feel the bus rock on its shocks as Sarah accelerates into the corner. They clip several parked cars and can hear scraping metal and glass breaking.

"Sarah! Slow down! We're OK!"

"OK. OK. Fuck! Fuck! Are you hurt?"

"I'm fine."

Sarah sneaks a look at her husband. He is bleeding down the side of his right arm. Blood has started to collect on the band of his Timex before dripping onto the floor.

"You're bleeding!"

Chris looks down and notices the blood for the first time. "Shit. I think he clawed me."

"He didn't bite you did he!?"

"What difference does that make? This isn't 'Day of the Dead.'" Chris is speaking with more bravado than he feels.

"How the fuck do you know? The parasite lives in liquid. His spit, his blood."

"He didn't bite me."

Sarah relaxes, but only slightly. The street in front of them is blocked by a Toyota Prius that had been abandoned in the middle of the road. They would have been able to work their way around it in the van, but the sheer size of the bus makes it impossible to avoid. Fortunately, the massive weight of the large vehicle easily knocks the car out of the way.

"There must have been at least ten of them. Fuck."

"Sarah, you saved my life." Chris speaks with a genuine reverence. "You were totally badass."

"No worries. I got ya boo." She blows off his compliment, but can't contain a smirk as she changes the subject. "So, why did they leave the circle?"

"I think they were hungry."

"What?"

"They were emaciated. If they stayed at the circle, they probably haven't eaten for over a month."

"But why now? They weren't interested in food before."

"Zombie dancing is hungry work."

Sarah ignores the joke and focuses on the road. "How did they know where we were?"

"Noise. They heard us hit the SUV. They came to investigate."

Another car blocks the intersection. "Hold on to something!" Having no other choice, Sarah grimaces and smashes her way through that one too. "We're making a shit-ton of noise right now. We're going to lead them straight back to the library."

"We better slow down. Try not to hit anything."

"What the fuck do you think I'm trying to do!? I don't see a lot of other options."

Chris frowns. "I know. Let's at least try to avoid making any more noise than we have to."

They creep their way through traffic, doing their best to do so quietly, but they know that the engine of the bus sounds like a jumbo jet in the relative silence of the powerless city. They eventually arrive at their block to discover zombies everywhere. They're milling around the street and in front of the library. The closer ones look up at the sound of their engine.

"Holy shit. Ten, eleven... two more over there." Sarah's heart sinks. "We'll never get to unload."

"Circle around the block. Let's see if we can get a sense of what we're dealing with."

The bus creeps down the street squeezing between a Toyota Camry and a UPS Truck. They hear a crunching noise as they run over a discarded pair of glasses. Two Gingers and a Fred look up from their meandering down the sidewalk. Grimly counting, Chris and Sarah spot several more walking down the alley that runs alongside the parking garage that connects to the library. Eventually Chris nods. He has a plan.

"We just need a distraction."

"Distraction? It's going to take us at least an hour to get everything off of the bus. What's going to buy us that amount of time? We'll be exposed."

"Not if we can get into the garage."

"With a bus??"

"It will be tight, but I think it might be possible."

Sarah eyes the entrance to the parking garage warily. "Even if we could, what would be the point? We still can't unload."

"Trust me. I have a plan. But first we need to divert them away from the entrance. Ideas?"

"Yeah, actually I do. They respond to sound right? They're curious or hungry?"

Sarah explains her idea to Chris.

Three minutes later, they make their move. A block and a half away, there is a row of cars that look like they were abandoned while waiting for the stoplight. Quietly, Chris hops off of the bus and walks between them looking into the car windows. He realizes how silly it is to be ducking down as if he were James Bond when he remembers the zombies are blind.

He finds what he is looking for when he comes across a late model Ford Mustang parked on a meter next to a White Castle. As quietly as he can, he slowly opens the door and picks the keys up from where they had been abandoned on the floor-mat. Double-checking that the keychain has a remote lock/unlock device, he closes the door and presses the lock button. The Mustang's tail lights flash, acknowledging that the car is secure.

While Chris works on his task, Sarah slowly pulls up to the entrance of the parking garage. She's lined up the bus to get as straight a shot in as possible. She has her doubts about the height of the ceiling, but it looks like she might be able to squeeze in if she is willing to scrape some paint. She is.

The noise created by the bus's movement has drawn a handful of curious Fred and Gingers who are pawing at the windows. Their hands and faces hit the glass with a series of muffled thuds. Sarah double-checks that the doors are locked and silently prays to a God she does not really believe in, that her crazy plan will work.

After nodding to Sarah from down the street, Chris takes a deep breath and gives the Mustang a swift kick.

The car alarm starts to wail, the hazard lights flash rhythmically and Chris starts to run towards the garage. Much like the engine of the bus, the car alarm seems deafening in the silence of the street. The siren bounces off the buildings and echoes in strange loops as the shriek makes its way through downtown.

The zombies investigating the bus immediately start working their way towards the Mustang, completely ignoring Chris as he races back to the bus and hops on.

He is relieved to be back with her. "Neat trick. How'd you think of that?"

"The Walking Dead. Little did they know they were making educational TV. Should have been on PBS."

"Are you sure you can do this?"

"We're about to find out." Sarah presses on the gas pedal and the bus starts moving towards the entrance to the garage. She was right in thinking they would scrape some paint. In fact they rip the 'Clearance: 8 Feet 8 Inches' sign right off the ceiling as she breaks through the wooden traffic gate and makes the first turn into the parking area.

"Yikes. How much taller than eight-feet-eight do you think we are?" Chris says nervously.

"Probably at least a foot. But remember the posted clearance has to account for hanging lights and wires and cameras. We'll probably redecorate the ceiling a bit, but I think we'll fit."

They do. And through an almost miraculous feat of driving, aided by the fact that the garage is almost empty because nobody wanted to park in this neighborhood after dark, Sarah is able to get the bus not only into the garage, but up to the third floor where Chris tells her to stop.

"Wow," Chris says, stretching his neck. When he hears it cracking and popping, he realizes how much tension he is carrying. He lets a breath out with a hiss.

"Nice driving babe. I'm impressed."

"After driving my dad's harvesters, I can parallel park a fucking ocean liner."

"OK. Let's see if there's a way to block the entrance so they can't get in."

Carefully exiting the bus, Chris picks up his hockey stick and Sarah grabs her bat. They slowly start walking their way down the slanted concrete of the garage floor. They move together almost back to back, constantly on the lookout for movement.

"Why did you want me to get up to the third floor? You're not thinking of transferring the supplies from the roof are you?"

"Nope. We'd be way too exposed to the weather. Besides, we'd never be able to get the generators through the trap door. But we can't use our front door anymore with them out there."

"Obviously. So we're kinda fucked."

"Don't sweat it. I've got a better idea. We're going to-"

"Shh!"

Chris raises his stick and looks around for trouble. "What is it?"

"I hear something. Over there. That car."

They peer around the corner and see a green station wagon parked up against the far wall. The driver's side door has been left open and a set of women's clothing haphazardly litters the cement floor in front of it. A muffled sound escapes from inside the car. They can't quite see it, but some instinctual voice in the back of their heads tells them there is the tiniest hint of movement in the back seat.

Sarah's heart is racing. She knows they got lucky fighting the Fred and Gingers off at Home Depot. Every instinct in her body is screaming at her to slowly and quietly back away from the car. She puts her fingers over her lips and gives a 'Let's get out of here and keep moving' nod to Chris.

Chris shakes his head and whispers "No. We have to know if the garage is clear."

Reluctantly they creep towards the back of the car. There is a film of dust covering the back window. It's not the normal dirt and pollen that blankets everything in the country; it's that grey grimy film that coats every surface in large cities. The kind of grime that turns black when you try to clean it with a wet paper towel. It's the kind of thing that city dwellers deal with every single day but try not to think about too much.

The muffled noise continues. It sounds like something small is shifting around in the back seat. Sarah sees what it is first, recoiling then wiping a section of the window clean with her sleeve. She needs to get a better look, even if she desperately doesn't want to.

"Jesus. God no. Please."

Chris, who has remained a step behind to keep lookout, prepares for a fight. "What is it?!"

"Fuck." The word comes out in a mixture of revulsion and profound sadness. She stumbles away and vomits onto the floor spattering the crumpled blouse the driver must have been wearing. Chris reluctantly looks through the window himself and understands why.

The shell of a baby is still in the car seat. It's gaunt, bony and dehydrated. Its face looks unreal, like it is an animatronic baby made of silicone from some cheesy horror movie. Its skin is cracked and coming apart as if the silicone had dried and started breaking down. But this is not a prop. It is real and it is still moving. The baby blindly looks around with only the whites of its eyes. Its arms and legs are still continuing to twitch and spasm.

Chris somberly closes the driver's side door and puts his hand on Sarah's shoulder. "Let's keep moving. We can't help it. It can't hurt us."

They continue morosely walking down to the ground floor and to the exit. Chris points at the industrial rolling security gate hanging above the attendant's booth. "This is why it's good that nothing stays open 24 hours in Detroit. If we can close this, we can secure the entire garage!"

He tentatively pokes his head out to check the street. He can hear the car alarm wailing in the distance, but doesn't see any Fred and Gingers. He starts jabbing at the top of the gate with his hockey stick, attempting to get it to roll down. He tries to hook the end of his stick into the handle and pull it down with brute strength. This does not go well.

"Help me." He says, not looking back at Sarah.

The gate starts to roll down smoothly. Chris turns around, pleased with himself. Sarah is standing in the attendant's booth turning a key as a small motor lowers the gate.

"But there's no power?" Chris is confused.

"You think that security gates don't have battery backups? In this neighborhood?"

"Where did you get the key?"

Sarah holds up a pair of blue uniformed trousers she found on the floor.

"Ralph always wanted me to get in his pants."

"Dreams come true apparently."

Sarah gets back to business. "It's getting dark. I think we should get inside until morning. We can deal with the supplies tomorrow."

"Agreed."

"Now, how are we going to get back into the house? We sure can't use the front door."

"The roof. Follow me."

They walk back up though the parking garage, doing another thorough sweep of the cars, but nobody is there except the baby. When they arrive at the bus, Chris grabs a pair of bolt cutters and they continue to the top level of the garage.

There's only one car on the top floor and it looks like it has been there for a while, probably stolen and abandoned. But, the fourth floor connects with the roof of the library. Whoever built the garage topped the fence separating the two with razor wire to discourage anybody from roof-hopping. Undeterred, Chris cuts through the chain-link with the bolt cutters and they climb through and onto the roof of the library.

"OK, let's kill that damned alarm." Chris walks to the edge and looks down at the street below. His heart skips a beat when he sees that the Mustang has been swarmed by zombies. There are a lot of them, a startling, intimidating amount. Hundreds of naked ex-humans dully paw at the car. They've broken through the windshield and it is starting to sag on its shocks. Chris and Sarah give each other a look. Alone, a single zombie can't break through much of anything, but the destructive power of a large group of them is alarming.

Sarah arrives next to him. "Oh fuck." She takes a deep breath. "How can there be so many?"

"Apparently they can't see, but their hearing is great."

"We have a *big* problem."

"Yup." Chris aims the remote key at the Mustang and presses the unlock button. The car beeps its acknowledgment and the alarm stops.

CHAPTER 10

Later that night, Sarah and Chris sit at the table in the main room eating Cup of Soup. Sarah eats chicken and pea flavor though Chris thinks the idea of eating dehydrated chicken bits is not only disgusting, but practically begging for stomach problems that evening. Chris eats cheddar cheese flavor. Sarah has a very similar feeling about his selection, but they are both grateful to have a hot meal made possible by the camping stove they got on their trip. A gas lantern lights their faces but it is too weak to illuminate the entirety of the large room, leaving the space feeling somewhat gloomy. They are uncharacteristically quiet.

***

When Chris was eight, his father lost his job. Not

long after, he started to notice changes in his environment. The house, which used to be almost obsessively neat and tidy, slowly became messy and chaotic. His father started to leave bottles everywhere. Beer bottles lived in little nests next to the recliner. Empty wine bottles collected on the kitchen counter. Chris started discovering half-empty containers in the strangest places. It was almost like an Easter egg hunt. After discovering bottles with a happy-looking pirate on the label under the sink, in the couch cushions and even in his own sock drawer, he decided it wasn't an Easter egg hunt, but a search for pirate booty. It was kind of fun. But when he tried the brown liquid inside it, he discovered it was definitely not treasure.

Chris used to be really excited when his dad was home. His old job had kept him out of the house a lot and it was a treat to get to spend time on the weekends or on the rare evening when he got home before bedtime. Now that his father was home all the time because of something called 'cutbacks,' it wasn't as much fun anymore. He thought of his father in three distinct modes; Silly Daddy, Sleepy Daddy, and Mad Daddy. Silly Daddy was really fun. He would laugh at things that Chris didn't understand and make jokes that were confusing and sometimes naughty, but at least he seemed happy. At least he laughed a lot. But inevitably, Silly Daddy would transform into Clumsy Daddy, then become Sleepy or Mad Daddy.

Mad Daddy was terrifying. He didn't scream and yell or throw things, he just got cold and mean.

One summer day while he was playing in the yard, Chris was beset with the kind of random inspiration *only understood by children and he decided to climb the large fir tree next to his sandbox. He wasn't sure why he wanted to do it, he just wondered if he could. He pushed through the outer shell of stabby pine needles and discovered a mysterious world inside. The needles didn't go all the way to the trunk. Instead the branches inside were mostly clear and he could climb them fairly easily. It was dark and spooky in this secret tunnel up the tree, but adventure called. He'd only climbed a few feet when he discovered that he had gotten himself covered with pine pitch. It was on his hands and in his hair. It was sticky and stubborn, but at least it smelled nice. He continued up branch after branch, slowly working his way up the tree. He could not see the world outside his secret cave because he was protected by a thick wall of pine needles.*

Chris was in his own magical land where no one would ever find him. He felt truly content for the first time in a while. There were no scary guys from the mall here. His father didn't even know where he was. Nobody could see him. He could stay here safe and sound until he decided to re-emerge into the world. It was a liberating feeling. For some reason he felt like he could breathe deeper up here in his secret hideout. Perhaps it was just all the pine scented fresh air trapped inside the tree, or perhaps it was the solitude, but he felt calm and refreshed. It felt different than what he was used to. A very adult moment of clarity crept into his consciousness. I don't ever feel safe. I think people are supposed to feel safe. *He didn't analyze the thought, it just occurred to him.*

It was at that moment that he looked down and saw

that he was now twenty feet off the ground. He hadn't been thinking about the fact that he was going up *the tree, he was thinking about it as if he were going* into *the tree. To Chris it looked like he was a thousand miles in the air. His stomach dropped and the terror began. Ignoring the sticky pitch, he clung to the trunk of the tree with both arms as if his life depended on it.*

It took him ten minutes to gain the courage to try to climb down. He didn't even think of calling out and asking for help. He knew he was on his own. His feet suddenly felt clumsy and dead. He felt disconnected from his body, like he was operating his arms and legs by pulling puppet strings. He searched for the branches with his feet because he was too afraid to look down. A drop of sweat dripped off the tip of his nose and plummeted all the way to the ground. It felt like it took an hour to hit the carpet of reddish-brown dried pine needles at the base of the tree.

Inevitably Chris stepped on a branch that was too small to support his weight and heard a sickening crack. In an instant he felt himself starting to tumble down. He thought he was in free fall, but he actually mostly slid his way down the trunk. As he was knocked back and forth by the branches, he felt like a Plinko chip from his mom's favorite show, 'The Price is Right.' He cut his hand trying to grab onto a branch and knocked his knees into his chin when he hit the ground. But when he finally came to rest, he was more surprised than wounded. That is until he noticed a wet feeling on his forehead. He didn't even remember hitting his head. But when he reached his hand up to his brow, it came back slick with dark red blood. He sat there stunned for a moment. Then, abruptly, he was overwhelmed by his own sobbing. He was sore, he was sticky, he was bleeding, but mostly he was just horrified that something like this could happen.

When he ran back into the house, he found his father sitting in the recliner watching the Lions lose to the Vikings. Tears had streaked tracks through the pine pitch on Chris' cheeks and snot was trailing down his face and onto his shirt. Blood was still dripping down his forehead and onto the carpet.

"What the hell happened to you?" His father's voice wasn't slurring yet, but it already had a leaden thickness to it.

Chris choked out the story through his sobs. His father stared at him impassively, not moving from his spot on the recliner. When he was finished, his father didn't get up and give him a hug. Nor did he help him clean himself or treat the wound. Instead, he looked Chris straight in the eye and spoke in an icy monotone.

"Well, Chief, let me give you some advice. Learn it now and you won't end up a fucking failure like me." He lets out a short bitter laugh. "Your experiences in life are the result of your choices. You do stupid things and bad shit happens to you. If you make all the right decisions, then you can have whatever you want." He paused and stared at the boy for a moment. "Is this getting through?"

Chris nodded. He didn't understand, but he didn't know what else to do.

"You did something stupid right? Something you shouldn't have done?"

"I guess so. But it was an accident."

"*Bullshit. You didn't have an accident, you fucked up! So now you're paying the price. That's how the world works kid. Darwin was right. If you aren't smart enough or strong enough to control your life, you get what you deserve. And around and around we go.*" He raised his beer as if clinking cans with some invisible friend then took a long swig and cackled again.

"*But... but it wasn't my fault.*"

There was a dry crackling bitterness in his voice, as if angry dust would puff out of his mouth at any moment. "*Not your fault!? There's no such fucking thing. You're not a cripple or a moron.*" He looked at Chris and saw the fear in his son's eyes. The part of his father that was still sober caught himself and softened a bit. "*Look, Chris, come here for a second.*"

Reluctantly, Chris stepped closer. Still holding onto the beer, his father put his hands on Chris' shoulders and leaned in. Chris could feel the condensation from the beer bottle starting to seep through his shirt. His father's face was covered with a thin film of dried sweat. His eyes were bloodshot and tired and Chris could sense that they were fighting to maintain focus. His skin had taken on a greyish yellow tinge like it hadn't been in the sun for a long time. Chris smelled a sweet and sour odor on his father's breath. It smelled like the pirate drink under the smell of what his father called 'Millertime.' Under that was the stench of his father's B.O. The dizzying combination of smells turned his stomach.

"*Listen up Chris. You are so special. I hold you accountable for your actions because you are smarter than most little kids. Fuck, you're smarter than most adults. You've got to accept that and accept the responsibility that it comes with. The world is just math. All of our hopes and dreams and feelings all boil down to making the right calculations. Do the math right and you'll never fail. If you do fail it's because you didn't think through the consequences and you got what you deserved. I don't want to hear any excuses or any complaining. There is no such thing as a victim. Take your medicine like a man. You get me?"*

Chris did not.

"OK. Go clean yourself up."

When Chris went into the kitchen to look for Band-Aids, his mother was there working on dinner.

"Don't forget to wash your hands for dinner Chrissy. We're having meatloaf and scalloped potatoes. Just the way you like them." She didn't look up from her cooking to see the state Chris was in. She didn't seem to notice. She didn't seem to notice much of anything in those days.

***

"You've got to let me look at your cut again."

It's still dark and gloomy in the room, so Sarah grabs a flashlight to examine Chris' shoulder more carefully.

"I'm fine. You've checked it five times already."

"Look. In the 'real world' you can be idiot-tough-guy-man, but this is the zombie apocalypse world. I'm not going to fuck around with a wound. We've got to keep cleaning it. Take off your shirt."

"Sarah, I'm fine."

"I'll be the judge of that!" she says with more anger

than she intends. "Take off your shirt."

"OK. I will, but remember. I'm not Mikey. This is a different-"

"Don't you dare! You can't just use him every time you think I'm overreacting. That's a really shitty thing to do."

"I'm not-"

"Yes you are. You've been finding ten thousand different ways to subtly tell me I'm being overprotective."

He gives her a slightly condescending look and it sends her fury over the top.

"Stop looking at me like that! Like I'm overreacting like a crazy person!" She's shouting now.

"Nobody said you were crazy. I'm just saying that I've got this. I can take care of myself. It's not your responsibility."

"The fuck it isn't! I'm your wife!"

"No, I'm just saying that it's my job to take care of myself. I don't need you to figure out what to-"

"Chris! We work together. We need to help each other. You don't know everything and neither do I."

"I'm responsible for myself."

"That's moronic. We're responsible for each other. Tell your father to go fuck himself."

"Leave my father out of... It's got nothing to do with..." Chris now feels his own anger building. He wants to fight. He wants to tell her to fuck off, but right before he does, a tiny little voice in the back of his head whispers 'she's right buddy.' Deflated, he slowly shuts his mouth and just nods. Without looking her in the eye, he begins taking off his shirt. Underneath a strip of gauze is an eight-inch gash running down his shoulder.

"Look, I know you can't stand somebody taking care of you and I know it's annoying, but we need to clean it again. I think you should take some more antibiotics just to be safe."

"I dunno. We should save the antibiotics for emergencies."

"Emergencies! Like what? The end of the world?"

Chris closes his mouth and waits her out.

She considers shouting some more, but her own little voice catches her and she takes a deep breath before continuing. "I'm sorry. But we cleaned out an entire drug store. We have enough medication for two lifetimes."

Sarah takes their first aid kit out and starts to clean, disinfect, and re-dress the wound. Chris winces when Sarah pours iodine on the cut, but does not make a sound. There is a long beat of silence. They imagined they would be celebrating tonight after getting back with so many supplies, but the experience has left them both melancholy.

***

Chris always assumed he would have kids. He was startled when on his first real date with Sarah, she matter-of-factly announced that she would never have children.

They were having dinner at a brick-oven pizza place

down the block from Sarah's tiny studio apartment. They had just placed their orders, her sausage and basil and his pesto with truffle oil, when she set down her glass of wine and gave him the speech she gave to all of her first dates.

"Chris, you seem like a really nice guy. And I think you're cute and possibly datable. But, you should know right away that I don't want to have kids. Ever."

"Uh..."

"No, it's OK. I know I'm being weird, but we're adults and I don't want to waste your time. If you're dead set on having kids, it's totally cool and I won't be mad at all if you get up and leave this instant."

"Um... well I'm kind of excited about my pizza."

Sarah looked at him warily, checking for signs of panic. He looked a bit surprised but seemed to be still present. In fact she thought he might be bemused.

"Do you say that to the all the boys on your first dates?"

"Don't make fun of me. I'm trying to be fair."

"I'm not making fun of you. I think you might be putting the cart ahead of the horse, but it's honorable at least. And to be honest, I'm flattered that you think of me as a guy who might care, that you think I might be concerned with something more than just getting in your pants."

Sarah smiled and took a deep breath. She was relieved. She was used to two responses from this speech. Either the guy is horrified and judges her, thinking that she is a cold bitch who hates kids, or the guy is thrilled and thinks she's saying that she's a commitment-free slut.

"So...?"

"So I don't know. I always assumed I would have kids someday. But I like you. I don't have any idea yet if it's a deal-breaker for me in the long run. Or if there even is a long run. It's a first date right?" They both laughed nervously. "But I guess it's not a deal-breaker for me right now."

"Great."

There was a beat of awkward silence. Neither of them knew what to say next.

"So, I guess it's kind of sexist for me to be curious why you don't want to have kids? I mean, why would I assume that you would?"

"No, I think it's a fair question. I mean, I assumed you would too. See, kids are such an enormous responsibility. I don't just mean the huge amount of time and money it takes. It's not about fear of commitment or anything." She took a sip of wine. Chris let her formulate her thought. She rarely got this far in her previous attempts at explaining so she needed a moment. "It's about the responsibility of taking care of someone: to keep a child safe, to keep it happy. I mean, there are so many ways to fuck up someone's life. So many opportunities to fail a child. To do something horrible, even by accident. I know I'd screw up. I don't want that kind of pressure."

"I don't think anybody expects parents to be perfect. The very fact that you admit being fallible would make you a better parent than many."

"I'm not worried about being fallible. I'm not talking about forgetting to pick them up after soccer practice or sending them to their room unfairly. I'm

234

talking about big stuff. Safety. Do you have any idea how easy it is to kill a kid? You look the wrong way and BAM, it gets run over by a car, or falls off the balcony, or drinks poison or gets abducted by some predator. Then it's maimed or dead. And you've brought something into the world and filled its life with misery and pain."

Sarah's eyes filled up with tears. She didn't cry in front of him, but she slammed her napkin down more forcefully than she intended, got up and went to the restroom. When she returned a few minutes later, she was red-faced from embarrassment.

"Are you OK?"

"I'm so sorry. That was so embarrassing. I swear I'm not crazy."

"I shouldn't have asked. Obviously this means a great deal to you. It's none of my business."

"My little brother Mikey... he..." She felt her eyes start to well up again, but she was not going to let herself cry. She was angry at herself, ashamed at her lack of control. She stopped speaking and reached for her glass again.

Chris extended his arm and put his hand over hers, both holding on to her wine-glass for a moment.

"It's OK. You can tell me about it later. Or not at all."

A tear escaped her eye and hit the cloth napkin in front of her.

"Eek. I'm a guy's worst nightmare. The crazy girl who cries on the first date."

Chris looked at her seriously. "Yeah, but you have great boobs."

Sarah couldn't contain a grin. Chris smiled and released her hand. "Look, the pizza's here. Let's eat."

***

His wound cleaned and dressed again, Chris decides to break the silence. "So why did the circle break up? Why are they trying to eat us now after ignoring us for two months?"

"Your guess is as good as mine."

"I was hoping you had more bug trivia that would explain it." Chris gives Sarah a sad grin that looks more like a grimace.

She grimaces back. "Yikes. If I'm the source of our scientific wisdom, we're truly fucked."

"Well, I guess we can guess? Most parasites infect stuff because they want to eat right? They're creating a food source for themselves."

"Or their offspring. Some wasps lay eggs directly into living spiders or caterpillars and when they hatch, they explode right out of the poor thing."

"Ugh. And then the babies eat them?"

"Nope. The larvae mind-control the host to serve as a protector until they mature."

"That's freaking weird."

"Mikey loved telling that story."

"I'll bet. But we assume that eventually the host gets eaten?"

"Not always. Sometimes the unlucky bastards get eaten alive, from the inside. But other ones just starve to death because they don't have enough brain left to remember to eat. Of course there's the other category of parasites that just hangs out and eats what their host eats. Like a tapeworm."

"Oh right. Duh. So, what do we think's happening here? Did this parasite just run out of whatever they were eating in the bodies and need more? So they're making the bodies get them more food?"

"Maybe. It doesn't really matter does it?" Sarah has lost her scientific curiosity. To her it feels like intellectual vanity. They have no idea what's happening and they're deluding themselves pretending that a musician and a former architect could ever be capable of figuring it out. Right now, all that matters is survival.

"Before we just had to worry about water, now we've got... zombies everywhere."

"Lucky us."

He takes a deep breath and his words come out as almost a sigh. "So what do we do?"

"We have to build much stronger barricades. We have to find fuel. We have to get the supplies off the bus."

Chris can tell that Sarah wants to move on to more practical considerations, but he can't shake the nagging questions that have been eating at the back of his consciousness for a while now. The breakup of the circle seems to have amplified them. "I don't mean right now. Or tomorrow. I mean like forever. What do we *do*? What kind of life can we have? We still haven't found anyone else alive. Are we alone?"

Sarah looks into his eyes. They seem to have avoided

this conversation until now. "We can't possibly be the only survivors. Besides, the government could be working on a solution."

"I don't think there is a government anymore. I don't even think there is a society anymore. What if we truly are the last? What do we do? Just try to survive? What's the point? What's the endgame?"

"Well-"

Chris jumps back in. "I don't want to just exist. There has to be a future."

Sarah doesn't exactly know how to respond. She's not even sure how she feels. She has avoided thinking about it because the topic is crushing.

"What about..." He knows this is a dangerous topic, but he can't seem to contain himself. "...having a baby? If our species is going to survive we're going to-"

Sarah responds sharply. Her anger surprises even her. "We're not having baby. As far as we know, it's just us. Even if we popped out a dozen kids, it's not enough to repopulate humanity. If this is everywhere, then our species is going to die out either way. And you and I are going to die. Maybe tomorrow or maybe in fifty years, but either way, we're going to die. Do you want to leave a child *alone* in this fucking hell?"

Chris blinks. Her ferocity startles him, but her logic is sound. After a beat, he sighs again. "No. You're right."

Sarah closes her eyes for a moment and speaks more quietly, more slowly. "I'm sorry. I didn't mean to snap, I'm just- I don't know. Why *are* we still alive?"

Chris pauses and waits for Sarah to look at him

again. "You're the reason I'm alive."

Sarah stares back at her husband, disarmed. To her, his sweetness always feels a little heartbreaking. Sometimes his optimism and open heart made him seem the tiniest bit naïve. Like he didn't really know how cold and dark the world really was. On the other hand, it was this unbreakable capacity to find reasons for joy, for hope and for love that made her marry him. Somewhere along the line she had lost that part of herself.

For a long time she thought there was something she knew that he didn't. After all their years of marriage, she thinks perhaps it's the other way around. That he knows something she doesn't. She smiles. "I bet you say that to all the girls when society is destroyed by naked dancing zombies."

He ignores her attempt to deflect sentiment. "Shut up. Listen. That was true long before all this."

"Come here you."

She pulls him into an embrace. He nestles his head between her breasts. The gesture isn't sexual or desperate. They are just close, together.

*

The following morning the street in front of the library is still swarmed with the dead. The car alarm had drawn hundreds of them from blocks away. Now, even in the absence of more noise, they continue to mill about. They're hungry, but without some sort of external stimulus to draw them away, they have little reason to move on. A few of them wander away at the sound of a far-off dog barking, or sensing some trash blowing down the street, but they're leaving in a maddeningly slow trickle, not a stream.

Chris and Sarah stand on the roof watching them.

He puts his hands in his pockets. It's chilly today. He can feel winter at their heels. "They'll eventually disperse, but it could be days or even weeks before its safe enough to venture out again."

"Which we need to do soon because our fancy new generator is worthless without fuel."

"Yeah. Now that we've isolated the garage, we get gas from the cars safely, but obviously it wouldn't be nearly enough. We should figure out how much we're going to need."

She nods. "Way ahead of you. I already did the math. The generator burns about fourteen gallons a day if we run it 24/7. Even if we ration it, we might get what, a month out of the cars? We shouldn't use them unless there's an emergency. Right now we need to think bigger. A lot bigger."

"Are you going to be coy or are you going to tell me your idea?"

Sarah smiles at him. "A tanker truck."

"A tanker truck? Where on earth do we get one of those?"

"I don't know. There must be one somewhere. We can check around the gas stations, the highway maybe. Somebody had to be refueling the day it happened. If we look hard enough, we'll find one. It will be fun. We can plan a truck heist."

"Oceans Apocalypse?"

"Exactly."

Chris kicks his boot, thinking. "I really don't like the idea of being out there exposed for an indeterminate amount of time looking for something in an indeterminate location."

"I'm not sure we have any other choice."

"I guess. I can't think of anything else. Gas stations have fuel, but the pumps don't have power and we'd have no way of transporting it."

They look down at the walking corpses milling about below. Sarah nods. The decision has been made, but they both know they can't leave until the crowd disperses.

Sarah turns away from the street and looks at the hole Chris cut in the fence separating their roof from the parking garage. "So in the meantime, we've got to unload the bus. We can't get in from the street and the generator will never fit through the trapdoor on the roof. What are we going to do?"

Chris grins. Now he's being coy. He picks the sledge-hammer from the stack of tools he pulled out of the bus. "*I* have a brilliant plan for that."

*

When the library was designed, there was supposed to be a small, staff-only, flight of stairs connecting the head librarian's office down to the administrative area on the ground floor. Like so many of the other plans, they were never built. Eventually someone came along and bricked up the doorway that was supposed to lead to them. Chris points to the outline of the door. The bricks had been painted, but they still stand out against the otherwise plastered wall.

"Ever wondered what's on the other side of these bricks?"

"Girls suck at spatial reasoning."

"You're an architect!"

"I'm great with blueprints."

Chris smiles. "OK, help me with this."

Together they use duct tape to affix several layers of blankets and towels over the brick. When they finish, Chris grins like a naughty little boy and swings his sledge hammer into the wall as hard as he can. The blankets and towels serve as a muffle of sorts and soon bits of brick and dust start falling at their feet. It takes ten minutes of exhausting—and louder than they hoped—pounding before Chris pulls the muffle back to reveal a large hole in the brick wall exposing another wall of grey cinderblock.

"Huzzah. You've found cinderblock."

Chris wipes some sweat from his brow and turns back to his wife. "Yeah, but what's *behind* the cinderblock?"

He puts the blankets back down and continues breaking through. After another five minutes of smashing, he pulls the blanket back and there is a small hole in the cinderblock. A shaft of dim light shines through onto his face.

"Take a look."

Sarah looks through the hole. She sees a white

surface with green letters painted on it. She turns back, gleefully.

"DDOT. Our bus! We'll connect with the garage!"

"Yep! We just quadrupled our square footage."

*

Two hours later, they have created a crude but effective passageway between the office and the third floor of the parking garage. They stack box after box of food, water and supplies, creating a pantry in the office. In one corner, they have cases of canned soup, beans and vegetables next to hundreds of pounds of pasta, flour, sugar and rice. There are large containers of olive oil, canola oil and every sauce they could find. There are stacks and stacks of cookies, crackers, coffee and many boxes of candy. Next to the food sit several pallets of water, soda, juice and pretty much anything sealed and liquid.

In the far corner of the room is a veritable drug store of medications, first aid supplies and toiletries—including a comically large stack of toilet paper. Next to that sits all sorts of tools, hardware, batteries and candles. And of course there was the fun corner filled with cases of wine, beer, liquor, books, games, DVDs and of course, a prodigious stack of pornography.

Sarah surveys the room. "Pretty good haul. I think we should be fine through the winter."

"As long as we get enough fuel."

"Right. In the meantime, how are we going to get the generator inside? I don't think our new entrance is big enough."

"It's not. We're going to run a cable in through the hole. We don't want to be breathing the exhaust anyway. The garage is perfect for ventilation."

Sarah nods.

"Let's go set it up, shall we?"

"Set it up, sure. But remember, until we have a real fuel source we shouldn't run it unless we're in an emergency."

They go back into the parking garage and together lift the generator out of the bus. Chris stares at the instructions while Sarah goes to the side of the garage and looks down at the street.

"Oh shit." Sarah says gravely.

Chris joins her at the edge.

"Look at all of them. There's even more than before!"

There are now at least two hundred zombies down below. Several of them are pushing on the garage's gate. They heard the pounding and are now trying to get at the source of the noise.

"Oh my god. They can't get in can they?"

"I don't think so, but if many more come, all bets are off."

"I guess the blankets weren't enough."

"Damn. We've got to be so quiet."

Sarah frowns for a second. "That and we need to turn this library into a fortress."

*

The next morning Sarah sits on the floor going over the library's blueprints again. She draws several ideas with a Sharpie while Chris carries some of the tools down from the office. When Chris has collected all of the supplies, he stands over her shoulder for instructions.

"OK, let's review. Basement: Flooded, but no outside access. Ground floor: Bedroom, bathroom and kitchen. We'll have to board up all of the windows and the front door. If they get in, they'll start here. Second floor: Main library level. It's only accessible from the stairs off the kitchen. It's a convenient bottleneck, easier to defend. Third floor: Balcony level and office. Good news is there are no stairs to the balcony. The ladder should be easy to get rid of in an attack. All of our food and water is up there and we have an emergency exit into the garage. That's our last retreat point. Obviously the garage is our only door in or out now."

"OK. Makes sense to me."

"Now, we have fifteen two by fours and ten sheets of plywood left over from renovations. We'll use them to board up the ground floor windows and buttress the front door." Sarah brushes her hair back from her eyes unconsciously marking her forehead with the Sharpie.

"I'll start moving the wood downstairs."

"Great, I'll join you. Now do you understand this design? The strongest shape is a triangle. We nail the door shut, but then we buttress it with two triangular braces. Nail them right into the floor and into the door itself. It will take a pretty impressive amount of force to break through."

"You got it professor. Although, it's hard to take you seriously when you've tagged your forehead."

"Huh?"

"Never mind. OK, then what?"

"Next we nail the windows shut and back them with plywood and angled braces."

Chris nods. He only sort of gets what she's going for, but trusts her design. Sarah instinctually understands the exponential strength you get from good geometry. He was an 'A' student in English and art, but he gave up on math class when he knew he was going to a music school that didn't care about his academic record.

They set to the task of measuring and cutting the lumber. They brought home a menagerie of power tools from Home Depot, but they don't have the power to run them yet and even if they did, they couldn't risk the noise. So they are left with no choice but to cut the wood with hand saws. It's difficult, tiring work and they are soon covered in blisters and drop countless beads of sweat onto the little piles of dust they leave all over the floor, but Sarah's plan starts to come to fruition. The doors are now nailed shut and braced and plywood has been put up over all of the windows. The ground floor is now completely dark, only illuminated by their lanterns. It looks gloomy, like a tomb, but it feels secure.

Chris salutes his wife. "OK. That should keep them out pretty well!"

Sarah looks up at him from the floor. "That's only

the first line of protection. I'm designing our defense like a medieval castle. If they want us, they're going to have to get through several layers of obstacles. We can retreat through the house as each level gets breached."

"Oh yikes. Are we planning to get overrun?"

"Survivors prepare for the worst-case scenario. You really want to be improvising when they get through the windows?"

"No, I guess you're right. What's the next level?"

"Level two is the second floor. Since there's only one flight of stairs up to the library we know they have to go up them to get us."

"So we booby trap the stairs 'Home Alone' style?"

"Nope. We take them out entirely. They're wooden. We can just cut them out and replace them with a rope ladder that we could pull up if there's trouble."

"Like a tree fort!"

"Yeah, no zombies allowed."

Chris shakes his head, she never ceases to surprise him with her ingenuity, "You're a genius."

She hands him the saw and walks him over to the stairs. "Yes I am. But an idea is useless until it gets put into action. Start sawing."

"Are you sure we need to do this? This is going to be a pain in the ass when I want a snack in the middle of the night."

"Well at least you won't *be* the snack. Besides I know about the Oreos you have stashed under your side of the bed."

"Hmm... hard to argue with that logic." He stares

mournfully at his hands which have already cracked and blistered from the repetitive sawing, but he knows she's right. "Alright. Let's do this."

Two hours later, there are no stairs. Chris stands in the spot where they used to be and looks up at the—now empty—doorway above his head. "Yeah, that's a decent obstacle. Must be ten feet."

"Nine feet two inches. We'll need to be disciplined not to leave anything on the floor that could be used to help climb up."

"So is there another line of defense?"

"Of course, but that one's easy. It's already built. The balcony level."

"Right. Duh. So we're fortified? Should we get some crossbows and boiling oil?"

Sarah laughs. "No, no. Only suicidal idiots would try and fight an overwhelming force. Anybody who has any sense of self-preservation knows survival is mostly about retreating."

"You know this from all of your vast knowledge of medieval warfare?"

"I played Dungeons and Dragons for a bit."

"Seriously?"

"It was college. I was experimenting."

"Eek. Anyway, I guess now we need to go find the tanker truck."

Sarah nods. "Yeah, as soon as the Fred and Gingers disperse enough for us to sneak out. At the rate they're leaving, we're stuck in here for at least another day or two."

"Jesus. It's getting colder all the time. We're playing

a dangerous game with the snow."

"You got a better idea?"

"Nope."

***

"Those aren't the notes."

Chris flinches, startled. He had been so wrapped up in the music that he didn't hear his father come up behind him. He turns around to see his father swaying unsteadily on his feet. It was already 2:00 in the afternoon, Chris assumed he would have been asleep by then.

"I know Dad. I'm improvising. I'm playing for fun."

"If you're going to play, play it right. I don't want to hear any wrong notes."

"They're not wrong Dad. They're just different. I hear different music when I get excited or when I'm sad or whatever."

"The hell they are. Look at that page. It doesn't say play whatever new age nonsense you're feeling, it's specific. You kids these days are so arrogant. You think that every little thing that you think or feel is valid *and* important.*" His voice rises in pitch as his annoyance builds. "Guess what? Your little thoughts are not important. Your feelings are not important. What you* do *is important. Do your job."*

Chris can feel his temper rising, but knows better than to say anything. He was ten now, and his father had made it very clear that ten was old enough to learn to shut his mouth. His father snatches the music off the piano and roughly pushes it an inch away from Chris' face.

"Play it right, or not at all."

Chris never really understood why his father felt so strongly about how he played. He didn't even like music. He certainly couldn't read music and probably had no idea what the piece was supposed to sound like, but somehow he could always tell when Chris started improvising and it made him irate. Chris felt boxed in and controlled and years later he realized how hypocritical his father had been. His father had so little control over himself, his drinking, his anger, and even his continence when the drinking got really bad, but he somehow had the wherewithal to keep tabs on every note Chris played.

His father's glaring gaze did not make him quit the piano. In fact, before he turned eleven, he was performing with the Detroit Youth Orchestra. He was remarkably technically proficient. In fact, he was almost technically perfect, never missing a note. He was like a machine.

Chris liked the piano because—especially in a classical setting—it was a solitary instrument. When he performed in the youth orchestra, almost every other section was doubled, tripled or part of a sea of violins or army of trumpets. There was no chorus of keyboards. It was only him, by himself. He had complete autonomy over the eighty-eight keys, total control over the success or failure of the music played on them. It was only a matter of being good enough and working hard enough to hit each of the keys at exactly the right time in exactly the right combination with the exactly correct tempo, volume and articulation. Success was thrilling. He was the master of the black and white universe. Failure was obvious and humiliating.

Chris' teachers had always been impressed with his precision. He picked up the music faster than anyone they had ever seen. He worked harder than any other student from the time he first touched the keys. But his first teacher, Martha Trotsman, who doubled as his third grade science teacher, always had a nagging feeling that something was off in his playing. She never mentioned it, perhaps because she was so excited to have a student that actually practiced, but she wondered if she was missing something in her teaching.

When Chris was twelve, he started taking lessons from a well-known teacher at the Interlochen summer music camp. It was he who was the first to diagnose the limitation that would keep Chris from being any more than a moderate success as a musician.

Professor Granden, a plump older man with kind eyes, sat Chris down in the faculty room after the Michigan Youth Piano Competition. Chris sat rigidly. He was attempting to look as adult as possible, trying to hide his disappointment and anxiety. He was already starting to sport the acne that would plague most of his teenage-hood, but he still looked very much like a boy.

"Chris, do you know why you came in second place?"

"No I don't. I played everything right."

Chris looked down at his feet. He felt small sitting on the overstuffed couch. He'd never been in a faculty room before and he felt out of place. He wondered if he'd done something wrong and was going to get yelled at. Instead, Professor Granden handed him a mug of hot chocolate and sat down in the chair next to him.

"Yes you did. Exactly right."

"And Kyle messed up in the fourth movement. Why did he win?"

"Well that's a bit complicated. Let me ask you another question. What do you feel when you play?"

"Feel? I guess I'm trying to concentrate. I'm trying to make sure I get my fingering right."

"Is concentration a feeling?"

"Uh... well..." Chris wondered if this was some sort of a trap. He took a sip of his hot chocolate to buy time.

"It's OK. This isn't a quiz. When you play Mendelssohn, what do you feel? Happy? Sad? Excited?"

"I guess I feel a little nervous. I want to play it right."

"And that is perfectly understandable. Commendable even. But your playing is missing your feelings, your emotions, your passion for the music. We could hear how much you wanted to play the right notes, but we couldn't hear why you wanted to play the music. This is why you came in second."

"I'm sorry."

"No, no. You haven't done anything wrong. Chris, you play with your head and you play with your hands. And you're brilliant at both. In that way, you're more talented than anyone I've ever taught. But you need to learn how to play with your heart *too."*

Now Chris really felt like he was being trapped. This had to be some sort of trick, he was confused and scared. *"How am I supposed to do that? Play louder? Or faster? I play what the music says. What else do you want from me?"*

"No, it's not about that. It's more intangible."

Chris didn't know what that meant, but he wasn't about to let on and get tricked again. He just nodded.

Professor Granden could tell that Chris was lost and didn't quite know how to help him. He sighed, took off his glasses and looked at him sadly. "Chris do you enjoy playing piano?"

"I don't understand. What difference does that make? Is this a punishment?"

The older man was now getting flustered too. He had touched on something in Chris that was much bigger than piano and he didn't know how to back-pedal. "No... Chris, calm down. Nobody is mad at you. I'm trying to help you get better-"

"Am I not good enough? Are you kicking me out!?"

"No! Of course I'm not."

Chris was now red-faced and shouting. His ears had started to buzz with the feeling of betrayal. "I played it right! I did it perfect! Leave me alone!!"

He stormed out of the room before the tears began. He was desperate to get out of this horrible den that smelled like leather, cigars and old people. On his way out, he accidentally bumped into the end-table causing his mug of hot chocolate to topple off and crash to the floor. He did not stop, he could not stop, but he choked out a watery "Sorry!" as he half-walked, half-ran down the hallway.

Chris had no choice but to go back to his mother. She'd be waiting in the car. He would sit down in the back seat with his face beet-red and streaked with tears, but he already knew she would be blissfully unaware of his suffering. She checked the rear-view mirror carefully for traffic before she pulled out of her parking spot, but she did not see the look on Chris' face.

"That was such a lovely recital hall Chrissy."

Chris did not respond. He sat in silence, staring straight ahead, agonizing over the truly important question of the day;

'How am I going to tell Dad that I lost?'

*

When Chris started high school, something remarkable happened. In his second day at Middlefield High, he got completely lost searching for his third period math room. He knew the class was on the ground floor, but somehow found himself in the deserted basement. He opened door after door and just found maintenance and storage rooms. He was about to give up and ask for help, something his father would have been furious about, when he opened a green door into the school's boiler room. His heart skipped a beat. Tucked behind the large industrial boiler was an old upright piano. It was covered with dust and there was a stack of gym mats over half of the keys, but it seemed to call out to Chris.

'Nobody knows I'm here. I'm a secret. Just for you...'

Forgetting all about math class, Chris closed the door behind him and started to uncover the keys, setting the mats to the side and brushing off as much of the dust as he could. The boiler behind him radiated heat and made regular loud clanging noises, but Chris was only aware of the piano. He looked over his shoulder double-checking that he was alone and pressed a random key. An out-of-tune 'A flat' warbled out. The piano was old and in rough shape and it hadn't been that great a piano to start with—Chris didn't even recognize the brand—but this piano was special. This piano had been tucked away in a place where nobody thought of it, and more importantly, nobody could hear *it.*

He sat down on the creaking bench and put his hands on the keys. He was almost afraid to play anything, not because he would be heard, but because he wouldn't be. He could play anything *he wanted. He could play it* however *he wanted. The sense of freedom sent a chill down his spine.*

"Wow."

It was in that basement, cutting a class for the first time in his life, that Chris re-discovered his love of music. He played his secret piano every chance he got. He bought his own tuning tools and gradually and lovingly restored the piano to working order. He had to fix several broken keys and replace the felt pads with materials he 'borrowed' from art class, but soon the piano sung like it had never sung before. He improvised, he composed new melodies, adding jazz chords to Mozart and Brahms. He turned a Chopin melody into the basis of a 50's rock and roll tune. It was too hot in the room, it was noisy and dusty and he lived in fear of being caught by the janitor looking for a broom, but this tiny room and its ancient piano became Chris' sanctuary, and in this secret place, he was happy.

***

The next morning Sarah wakes slowly. She's curled up in bed under a pile of blankets listening to the beautiful music coming from the piano upstairs. Ever since they started dating, Sarah has enjoyed waking up to Chris playing. There was something soothing about starting her day to the mathematical precision of his music. Chris tried to explain that classical music follows intricate rules of keys, chord progressions and voice-leading. The melodies and counter-melodies dance together in beautiful and creative ways, but always within the delicate but rigid structure of western tonality. Leading tones resolve, harmonies flow in parallel thirds and sixths, but never parallel fourths or fifths. The dominant chord always leads back to the tonic, unless it deceptively continues the progression with a minor six chord.

Sarah listened intently, but still doesn't actually understand any of these rules. She doesn't care, she can instinctually feel the math being worked out in the interconnected landscape of melody and harmony. She has always been soothed by structures coming together in artistic ways. That's why she was drawn to architecture. In her half-conscious mind she's imagining complex but perfectly symmetrical shapes being formed by the music. That is until her eyes fly open in panic.

"Chris! Shit! Stop!" She jumps out of her bed and calls out to Chris.

Chris sits at the piano working his way through a Schubert sonata. "What? Why?"

"The noise!"

Sarah races into the kitchen and begins to climb the rope ladder up to the library.

"Huh?"

"They'll hear us!"

Chris' heart sinks. Feeling incredibly stupid, he flushes with embarrassment. "Fuck. I wasn't thinking."

Sarah does not respond. The gravity of the situation hits her before it dawns on him. Now that he has stopped playing, she slows down. She walks towards him gently.

"Oh damn." Chris speaks almost inaudibly. He stares down at his hands and slowly flexes his fingers. These are the fingers that have been his conduit to his passion, his identity. An identity that didn't come from the fingerprints at the tips of those fingers, but what they could create on piano keys.

He is battered by a crushing wave of sadness. He has devoted his life to music, to the piano, and he always had the nagging sense that there was something unfinished, that he was still waiting to emerge as the musician he could be. Even after the world crumbled around him, he felt the need to keep working, the desire to conquer his limitations and meet his potential. He can still feel the tiniest reverberations of the strings through his foot which remains on the sustain pedal. Slowly, as if reluctant to let go of someone he may never see again, he takes his hands off the keys and his foot off the pedal. Felt pads go down over the strings ceasing their vibration. He knows that he may never be able to make those strings vibrate again. The sound of the piano could draw them. They could be overrun and killed. It is no longer safe to play music.

He surveys the long glossy black body of the Steinway grand. For the first time, he notices that it looks a lot like a coffin. They both have hinged lids at the top of a long highly polished wood surface. Inside sits something that used to be alive and something he used to love.

Chris takes a deep breath in and then out.

"Chris?"

He does not respond. He continues to stare at the keyboard.

"Maybe someday we could get an electronic piano you can use with headphones? When we have power? Maybe in the summer?"

Chris slowly and silently closes the lid over the keyboard and walks out of the room.

A half hour passes before he returns. Sarah does not ask him where he has been or what he is feeling. Years of marriage taught her that he will want to talk about it, but now is not the time.

Chris looks at her with clear eyes. "Let's go check on our friends out there. We need to find that fuel."

*

The next day brings an oppressively steady rain. It doesn't ever come down hard, but the misty precipitation is persistent. The amount of rain doesn't matter to Chris and Sarah. A mist or a downpour will kill you just as easily. They are left having to deal with a curiously conflicting mixture of feelings. They feel a great pressure and anxiety about their dangerous trip to find fuel. They must do it. They must do it before the snow comes. But, they are trapped by the rain. They are trapped with nowhere to go and nothing much to do. So they sit in a state of anxious boredom. Chris imagines soldiers on the eve of battle must have felt something like this sensation. Whether it was primitive clans planning an attack on the neighboring village or GIs waiting to storm the beaches of Normandy, he envisions them spending sleepless nights in their tents or on their ships, nervously twiddling their thumbs knowing that by this time the next evening, some or all of them will likely be dead.

*

"So, how's it looking out there?" Sarah looks up from the raincoat she is mending with duct tape to see Chris climbing down the ladder from the office. The rain stopped in the night and although thick grey clouds still loomed overhead, Chris felt safe enough to check on the crowd of Fred and Gingers.

"Looks promising. There's only about ten of them down there that I could count. I think we can probably give it a try tomorrow. Weather permitting of course."

"Good. Clock is ticking."

"So I searched all the cars that were open for anything we could use."

"Find anything interesting?"

"I found this." He pulls a revolver out of his pocket.

"A gun? Are you nuts?"

"You're the one who wanted weaponry."

Sarah looks at him incredulously. "That was before! Now a gunshot could bring the entire population of the city down on us!"

"I know, but as a last resort or something?"

Her voice has an icy hardness to it. "Put it back. Get rid of it. Nothing good can come from that thing."

Chris puts the gun back in his pocket and starts to walk away. Sarah puts her hand on his shoulder and stops him.

"I'm sorry. I just-" She hesitates, searching for words. "Any scenario where we would use that is just too..."

"I don't want to think about it either. But..." He can tell this is not the time for this discussion so he changes the subject. "Let's try and get to sleep as soon as possible, we should head out at dawn."

Chris starts to turn away, but Sarah stops him again. She pulls him face to face, her eyes brimming with tears. They don't talk much about the danger they face or the distinct possibility that something could go wrong. Seriously wrong. They don't mention that they may not make it back from one of their trips. Or worse, that only one of them might make it back. There's no reason to point out that the most likely use for the gun is not to shoot zombies. She almost says this but from the look on his face, he clearly knows too. She decides to go with a simple "I love you Chris."

Chris puts his hands on her cheeks and kisses her on each eye.

PART III
THE DEAD

CHAPTER 11

A bright cold sun rises over the city. Although Chris and Sarah think it is November 14th, it's actually November 16th. Without the routine of a work week, without appointments, or a TV schedule, without Redwings games to keep track of or bills to pay, each individual day on the calendar becomes easier to miss. Sarah forgot to cross off a couple days on their calendar and never noticed. Not that it matters.

The city is supernaturally quiet. A cold wind blowing off the lake sends fallen leaves flipping and twirling down the dusty streets. A block away, the empty lot that had once served as the meeting ground of nearly the entire population of Detroit, the epicenter of the bizarre spectacle, the great circle that was the polar north of the end of humanity, is abandoned yet again.

The smell rising off the lot, were there anybody

there to smell it, is overpowering. A rotting stench of death radiates in a thick cloud for almost a mile. In the mixture of mud, trash and concrete lie the remains of tens of thousands of bodies that were trampled by the circle. No longer distinguishable as individual people, what is left is just a rotting mixture of flesh and dirt that will soon be frozen into the form of an enormous 'O' in the center of the city. It's as if the earth itself opened its mouth in a horrible silent scream.

In and around the lot, the ground looks as if it had been blanketed with several inches of dark black snow. But it isn't snow. The thick dark carpeting is made up of the bodies of over a billion flies that had died during the first frost of the winter. As they dry and become lighter, they start to blow in the wind and form crunchy drifts throughout downtown.

All through the empty shell of Detroit, the dead continue to silently and aimlessly roam down every street and alley. But, some of them seem to be subtly running out of steam, moving just a tiny bit more slowly than before. Still they are everywhere. And they continue to fill the streets in staggering numbers.

***

"Come on! We have to keep moving!"

Sarah's heart raced, not just from the hike but from a growling fear gnawing at the back of her consciousness. Mikey was slowing down. He was looking weaker, like a toy whose batteries were running out.

"I'm sleepy." Mikey seemed to be breathing too fast,

too shallowly. "My whole leg hurts."

"Let me see."

Sarah didn't really want to see. She knew there was nothing she could do except to get him to a doctor as soon as possible. But she knew that she had to look. She felt that she would not be acting like a responsible adult if she wasn't willing to see.

The wound had continued to fester. It had a greenish yellow tinge to the redness spreading out from the cut. What truly spooked her were the red streaks that emanated away from the gash. Dark lines radiated up his leg like lightning. She didn't know that this meant the infection was spreading or about the imminent danger of sepsis, or frankly what sepsis was, but she knew this was bad. Really bad.

She put her hand on his forehead again. His fever seemed to have gotten even worse. She could see him sweating despite the early fall chill. He was burning up. Not knowing why, but working on instinct, Sarah checked his pulse. His heartbeat was a blur. It was beating faster than she thought was even possible.

"Sarah?" Mikey's eyes seemed to have glazed over. *"What are we doing out in the woods?"*

Panic set in. She dropped her backpack and picked Mikey up piggy-back style. He was heavy, but her fear made him seem as light as a rag doll. She got about a quarter of a mile before Mikey lost consciousness and his arms dropped to his sides. He could no longer hold on to her.

Sarah screamed for help until her voice was raw. Nobody heard her. Tears streamed down her face as she picked him up and threw him over her shoulder like *she had seen firemen carry people on TV. He was intensely heavy now. He was completely limp and felt like he was filled with lead. She knew what limp weight was called but didn't want to think about it. But of course, the name kept creeping into her mind: dead weight.*

The pathway which had seemed so bright and friendly, so beautiful and natural when they walked down it six days ago now seemed horrible. She felt alone and isolated, even claustrophobic. The trees and bushes seemed to be closing in on her. They seemed to be menacing, laughing at her, trying to claw at her arms and trip up her feet. Why did I go out here where nobody could help us? What the fuck was I thinking? What the fuck were Mom and Dad thinking?! I'm not ready for this. What have I done!? Oh Mikey, I'm sorry! *Eventually all of her thoughts disappeared into a single-minded determination to get them out of the woods. She had to get him out of the fucking wilderness. She had to get him to help. To a hospital. To an adult.*

About a mile away from the edge of the woods, his body convulsed and she felt a spreading wet sensation down her back. He had vomited without regaining consciousness.

She carried him for three miles before she emerged at the entrance of the nature preserve. When she saw the first glint of sunlight shining off her car's windshield, she almost collapsed with relief and exhaustion. But she reminded herself that out of the woods, did not mean 'out of the woods'.

She put the unconscious Mikey in her car and drove down the narrow winding dirt road searching for civilization. She didn't know where the hospital was. She didn't have a cellphone, so she had no way to call for help. After a mile of frantic driving she saw a house and swerved into its driveway, her tires skidding a short rain of pebbles into the yard. After what seemed like an hour of shouting and pounding on the paint-flecked door of the weathered cottage, an old woman emerged. She had been sleeping and Sarah had to explain what was happening three times before the woman called an ambulance. Sarah was left with nothing to do but sit on the porch with Mikey's head in her lap. She stroked his hair slowly while sobbing harder than she thought possible. Feeling completely helpless, she frantically prayed for the sound of sirens.

"Ma'am?"

Somewhere in the haze of her desperate fear she had lost time. She had just laid Mikey down and immediately there was an EMT standing in front of her. Her mind was clouded, confused.

"Mikey's sick. He needs help." Her voice came out in a flat monotone. She felt such urgency, but her body seemed to be incapable of conveying it.

The EMT was a tall Indian man in his mid-forties. He looked down at Sarah with sad eyes. He was moving towards her deliberately.

She was confused by his calm demeanor. "What are you waiting for? Hurry!"

"Of course Ma'm. I'm going to do everything I can."

The EMT frowned grimly and knelt down to check Mikey's pulse. He looked back at the second EMT who was pulling a stretcher out of the rig.

"What's your name?"

"Huh?"

"Your name."

She felt as if she had disconnected from the world. It took her a moment to remember her name. "Sarah."

"OK Sarah. My name is Sajeev. How long have you been waiting for us?"

"I don't know."

The old woman who owned the house spoke from behind her. Sarah had forgotten she was there.

"We've been waiting about forty-five minutes. Took a while to find us out in the boonies huh?"

"Yes Ma'am."

Sarah shook her head. "What are you talking about? We just sat down."

Sajeev put his hand on her wrist, checking her pulse and shined a flashlight in her eyes. "Sarah, do you feel lightheaded at all?"

"What? Who cares? What the fuck are you doing? Take care of Mikey!"

The second EMT, who looked all of nineteen, arrived with the stretcher and looked nervously to Sajeev for guidance. Sajeev knelt down and took Sarah's hand.

"Sarah. I'm terribly sorry. Mikey's been dead for at least an hour."

***

Chris and Sarah stand on the roof of the library between the two water towers. They have dispensed with most of their weather gear. With the sun shining, they decided that the Fred and Gingers are the bigger threat and lighter clothes would allow them more mobility. Chris carries two backpacks with emergency supplies including food and water, tarps, tools and of course, duct tape.

Sarah completes her circle checking the sky in every direction, "Today's the day. No clouds."

"Alright. Let's do it."

Chris hands a backpack to Sarah. "I kinda wish we had gone to a sporting goods store and picked up some hockey equipment or something. Armor."

"We had no idea the Fred and Gingers were going to get bitey. Besides we lose any direct fight with more than one or two of them. If we survive, we survive on speed and stealth."

With the front door nailed shut and not wanting to risk opening the garage's security gate, Chris swings his leg over the edge of the roof and lowers himself onto the library's fire escape. He helps Sarah over the ledge and they work their way down to the street level. To their left is the corpse of a middle aged woman shuffling slowly down the sidewalk. A stomach churning smell exudes from her grayish skin as if she were rotting as she walked. With an uneasy glance between them, Chris and Sarah walk away as quietly as they can and duck down an alley.

"OK. Let's find a car. A hybrid would make less noise wouldn't it? I wonder how long their batteries hold a charge."

Chris is looking further down the alley. "I have an even better idea. Quieter."

He points to a bicycle stand where an abandoned

nest of bikes have been chained up. Some of them look like they have been there for years, covered in rust and missing wheels and seats, but several of them still look workable. He takes out his pair of bolt cutters from his backpack.

"Really?"

"You said speed and stealth." He starts to cut through the locks. "Besides it will be a lot easier to maneuver through traffic."

"I don't know Chris. It leaves us really exposed."

"We're assuming they're blind right? So they must operate by sound. This is the quietest way to go. Besides, our M1 battle tank gets terrible gas mileage."

"Fine, fine. Let's go."

He selects a large grey ten-speed with a basket attached to its handlebars. "Hi-Yo Silver," he whispers to himself.

"What's that?"

"Nothing. Something from a book I read once."

Sarah hops on a smaller red mountain bike. After confirming that the bikes were in working order, they begin to pedal through the streets, weaving between piles of clothes and abandoned cars with their eyes on a constant search for a tanker truck. They hop on and off the sidewalk avoiding drifts of fallen leaves, trash and a prodigious amount of flies. They pass zombie after zombie, sometimes solitary and sometimes in small clumps. An occasional Fred or Ginger will hear the whistle of the tires on the pavement and turn in their direction, but by the time they start moving, Chris and Sarah disappear behind a car or around the corner.

They slowly bike a grid through the city for hours, but the search is fruitless.

Slightly before 3:00, they stop in front of the enormous edifice of Ford Field and lean their bikes up on a bench. "Anybody scalping Lions tickets?"

Sarah drinks from a bottle of orange Gatorade. "Probably get a decent discount. The Lions haven't won a single game this season."

"So what else is new?"

She looks at her watch nervously.

"It's already afternoon. Sun starts going down at about five. We probably only have a few more hours to find a tanker in time to get back safely."

"Yeah, we should keep moving. Here, eat. We'll need energy." He tosses her a Power Bar and she chews on it reluctantly. She's not hungry, the anxiety has destroyed her appetite, but she knows that he's right.

Returning to the search, they pedal down Brush Street between Ford Field and Comerica Park and come across a rare sight in post-zombie Detroit. A car accident. When the water went bad, most drivers found themselves stuck in traffic, so even if their cars were in motion when they were infected after taking a sip of coffee or sticking their head into the rain to investigate why traffic had stopped, they weren't traveling at a high rate of speed. There were little fender-benders everywhere, but the SUV they see overturned on the intersection of Brush and Madison looks like it crashed doing at least seventy miles an hour. Most of the windows had blown out after it had rolled over several times, before coming to rest upside-down against a guard rail. The SUV's roof has collapsed in the front. A cracked light pole that had fallen across the road looks like it had been the original point of impact.

"Yikes." Sarah looks at the wreck through her binoculars from about a hundred yards away.

"Weird. They must have been going really fast when the virus hit. It doesn't make sense."

"I'm not sure that's when it happened."

"What do you mean?"

"Doesn't it look fresher to you? No dust all over it. No blowing trash collected in the corners."

"What are you saying?"

Sarah doesn't want to say what she's thinking right away. She wants to be sure. She walks a little closer before she continues. "I'm saying I think this happened recently. In the last couple of days. Maybe even more recently. They must have been survivors. Like us."

"Holy shit!"

Chris starts to bike rapidly towards the wreck. Sarah calls after him.

"Slowly. Careful."

When he gets within fifty feet, Chris stops pedaling altogether. He glides slowly. The only sound is the 'tick tick tick' of the bike's wheels slowing down. When Sarah catches up, she lets out a sickened gasp.

"Fuck."

"Jesus."

Spreading out in several directions from the car are large smears of blood. Half chewed bones are discarded randomly around the vehicle. The occupants have been eaten alive. There are no bodies to speak of. There are only remnants. The crunchy bits. A skull—too hard to break up and swallow—sits next to the broken side mirror dangling from its wiring. A ribcage lies next to the guard rail. Its front is torn open and emptied of organs, but what remains of its spine is still partially contained by a torn black leather jacket. The small size of the jacket is the only remaining clue that its owner had probably been female.

They stare in silence for a moment.

Sarah speaks quietly. "The blood is still tacky."

"Last 24 hours? Less maybe?"

"Mrrrrr..."

Chris and Sarah jump back from the sound coming from inside the car.

"Mrrrr...?"

Sarah recovers from being startled before he does. "Oh my God! Did somebody survive?" She starts to bend down to look into the car.

"Be careful!"

She gets on her hands and knees and shines a flashlight into the overturned SUV.

"Hello?"

She crawls in deeper and reaches in through a window.

"Meeeeerrrrroooo..."

"Oh!" Her voice softens into a coo. "Hi there little thing."

Chris wishes desperately that Sarah would be more careful, but he stands his ground ready for anything.

"What is it? A child? Alive?!"

Sarah looks back over her shoulder with a wide smile. "Not quite. Take this." She hands him the flashlight and reaches in as far as her arm can stretch. Finally her fingertip reaches its target and she pulls a small pet carrier out of the passenger side window. Inside the cage is a black and white long-haired kitten. It's scared, confused and meowing mournfully but very much alive and seemingly unhurt.

Chris stares at her dumbfounded. "A cat?"

"Kitten."

"If these people were alive, why in God's name would they be wasting resources on a fucking pet?"

"We're keeping it."

"What?!"

Sarah's decision surprises her too, but something inside her head clicks, accessing the part of her brain that had shut down when all hell broke loose. The nagging voice that demands that she do more than just subsist performing tasks and achieving practical successes returns. It's the voice that redefined her very idea of success, the pesky desire that told her to quit her lucrative job as an architect to try and make a life as an artist.

She looks off into the distance. "You asked me what we were going to do. What the point was."

"Right?"

"So far, everything we've done, we've done to survive. We've been running on instinct and adrenaline and a powerful will to stay alive."

Chris nods and looks to the horizon, partially to avoid looking at the grim sight in front of him.

"What is the point of existing—in surviving—if we don't *live*?" she continues.

All of the feelings she's been holding back while existing in long-term 'emergency mode' come rushing out. She's never felt as clear, as certain of what she wanted.

There are so many things they haven't talked about. Even after two months, they haven't really discussed the loss of all of their family and friends. They'd broached the topic offhand or obliquely. They made countless jokes, but they'd never really faced the reality head on—the distinct possibility that they had been forced to witness the end of everything they've ever cared about. They'd seen the demise of so many things that used to create the tapestry of their lives. There would be no more awkward Thanksgiving dinners with her parents. They will never get another Christmas card from an old high school acquaintance and wonder how they got their address. They'll never go see a new movie. There will never be another Superbowl. Another election. In fact, even the *ideas* they used to feel so passionately about are gone. Equality, justice and freedom are now all purely academic concepts. So many of the things they thought were important no longer matter. Everything is gone except each other.

Sarah turns and looks Chris right in eyes. "We're going to try and find a way to be *happy*. To make sure that there's still love in this shitty wasteland...tenderness...care. I dunno. Maybe we can't repopulate the planet or start a new society. Maybe we can't bring anything else into this world. But we can love what is here, we can love each other... and we can love Charlie."

"You named it."

"Yes."

"What if it's a girl?"

"Its name is Charlie."

Chris looks back at his wife. She's wearing cargo pants and a torn sweatshirt. She hasn't washed her hair in weeks and she smells a bit. But she's never looked more beautiful to him in his life.

He nods and picks up the cat carrier. "Are you sure we can't get a fish or something that doesn't have claws and shit in a box?"

She grins at him as he puts the pet carrier in the basket. After Sarah mounts her bike, they continue on in silence.

*

At four thirty in the afternoon, the sun is already starting to sag in the sky. Chris and Sarah bike along the side of I-75, the freeway that cuts a path right through downtown like an artery.

Chris finally breaks the silence. "It's good to know that there are other survivors. Or *were* other survivors."

"Yeah. It's great news actually. Although it's a little discouraging that if we fuck up like they did, we'll be reduced to smears on the pavement."

"Yeah. That's not ideal."

"But Charlie will be fine apparently."

"Apparently. He must have stayed quiet. Our Charlie is a survivor."

They bike across the John R Street overpass and look down into the Fisher Freeway's six lanes of submerged highway. When this section freeway was built in 1959, they chose to run it under the street level, creating a giant trough through midtown.

It's in that trough that Sarah finally spots pay dirt.

"Wait! There!"

Below them on the giant highway sits a large tanker truck with Exxon/Mobil stenciled on the side. The low sun glinting off its rounded silver tank is a welcome sight, a profound relief to both of them. What is not a relief is the fact that hundreds of zombies have wandered into the natural funnel created by the sunken expressway and gotten themselves trapped between its high walls. They fill the roadway, milling about in large clumps bumping into cars and each other.

"Well, we found a tanker. How are we going to get to it?"

Sarah doesn't have an answer for that one. "There's way too many of them. We can't just walk in there."

"We could do the car alarm trick again."

"I don't think so. They're too many. Even if we divert these ones, they'll be replaced by hundreds more. It would take hours and God knows how many we'd draw. Look at the freeway, they're down there for miles."

"Shit. You're right."

Chris surveys their options. The tanker is about

twenty feet away from the overpass which hangs sixteen feet above the highway. A panel van is stopped behind the tanker and directly below where Chris and Sarah are standing.

Chris points to the roof of the van. "We don't walk. We jump."

"You're not serious."

"If we can get on top of the van, we can jump from that to the back of the tanker. Just like Super Mario."

"I don't know. That's crazy."

"Look. The sun is going down. We don't have much time. We could come back later if we're lucky enough to have another clear day before the snow, but the freeway is collecting those bastards like a fruit fly trap. There's only going to be more of them, not less. We were out all day and didn't see other tankers. Winter could hit us tomorrow. We're desperate. This is our best option."

Sarah hates this idea. But he's right. "Yeah. I guess. Jesus, this is nuts."

"Yup."

Without hesitating, because he knows if he thinks about it too much, he will lose his nerve, Chris swings his leg over the railing. He reaches one foot onto the lip of the overpass' outer edge, and holding the railing with his hands he swings his other leg over. He turns himself around so he is facing the van, his arms behind him clinging to the railing.

Sarah lets out an unconscious groan.

"Ok. Fuck it."

"Chris, maybe we should-"

When Chris jumps, he does not look like Tom Cruise in some glossy action movie. His leap is awkward and sloppy. His arms flail and he tips forward at an unfortunate angle causing him to land on his torso, not his feet, hitting the roof of the van with the agility of a phonebook. The impact makes a terrifically loud booming noise as he dents the metal with his shoulder. The wind is knocked out of him so severely he feels like all of the oxygen in his lungs was suddenly deleted. The drowning sensation is accompanied by flashes of light in his peripheral vision. He wonders if the feeling of slipping is from being knocked silly before he realizes he is indeed sliding off the side of the van into the outstretched arms of the zombies already drawn by the noise.

"CHRIS!"

He flails his arms out wildly and catches hold of the van's roof rack. With the strength that only comes from true terror, he is able to flip his legs back onto the roof and right himself. He lies on the top of the van staring straight up at the sky for a long moment while he catches his breath.

"Chris!"

Chris sits back up. Dazed, he does a quick inventory of his limbs, and finding them all still attached, gets to his feet.

"I'm fine. I'm fine. You've got to jump!"

"Oh man. What are we doing?"

Sarah reaches down and picks up the cat carrier and prepares to toss it to Chris.

"Oh right. The fucking cat."

She throws the carrier containing the now severely pissed off Charlie to Chris. He catches it and sets it down at his feet.

"Come on! I'll catch you."

Sarah takes a deep breath and jumps, landing with slightly more agility that he did—on her feet at least. She lets out a short gasp on impact but is otherwise quiet. Chris grabs her and stabilizes her before she slips.

"You OK?"

"I'm fine."

They look down to see that the van is now completely swarmed with Fred and Gingers. Hundreds of hands now claw the sides, trying to get at their feet, creating a distinct and nauseating rocking motion as the combined force of their hands start to tip the van this way and that. Sarah looks as though she has lost focus. With a blank expression on her face, she stares down at the sea of bloody hands and desiccated eyes.

Chris gives her a panicked shake. "We have to move! OK!? You go first."

She is starting to look more than a little sick. But she takes another deep breath, drops onto the hood of the van and makes a giant leap towards the ladder on the back of the tanker. With a grunt, she grabs hold and scrambles up and onto the roof.

Sensing the motion and hearing Sarah's feet, the zombies start to swarm the front of the van. One starts climbing onto the hood.

As soon as she gets on top of the tanker, Chris tosses her the cat carrier. She fumbles and it starts to slide off the rounded edge of the tank, but in a desperate reach, she just manages to catch it with her finger.

Charlie continues to express displeasure with his treatment. The tiny kitten snarls and hisses from inside the cage with the fury of a much larger creature.

Chris starts frantically attempting to kick the zombies off the hood so he can make the jump.

"Chris!"

He put his foot on the chest of the closest Fred and pushes it back. The zombie falls into the horde, knocking them backwards. Seizing his momentary opportunity, Chris drops down onto the hood of the van and without stopping his motion, he leaps towards the tanker. Dozens of arms flail at his feet while he is in the air. A large bloody hand grabs onto his ankle slowing his momentum. Chris hits the side of the ladder, bounces off, and falls to the pavement, into a sea of flesh.

Sarah shrieks. "Nooooooo!!!"

Chris slams into the ground with a thud. He wonders why it is so dark for a moment then realizes the sheer mass of limbs, faces and hands grabbing at him from all directions have blocked out the setting sun. He kicks violently trying to free up space, but it's no use. In the background he can hear Sarah screaming, but the sound is muffled by the dense mass of bodies clawing at him. Several zombies drop to their knees and he is face to monstrous face with five former residents of Detroit. The smell is putrid. They are covered with blood, mucus, dirt and human feces. Their skin, when seen from up close, seems to have dried to the point of having the consistency of beef jerky. Human jerky.

Several of their eyes have cracked from dehydration and popped, leaving remnants that look like broken soft eggshells dangling out of their skulls. The flies had laid countless eggs and maggots had begun to grow into the wounds that covered the Fred and Gingers. Chris is filled with revulsion when a pile of maggots drops out of an eye-socket and falls onto his face.

In his panic-fueled mind, he notices that they don't seem to be breathing. He doesn't hear any of the moans and guttural noises that he remembers from the zombie movies he watched as a kid. These bodies no longer seem to be running on oxygen. In fact he gets the distinct impression that they are just meat suits for whatever else is now in charge.

Mouths snap at him, inches from his face. The horrifying sound of teeth dryly clapping together sends a shiver up his spine. It's a violent sound. They are biting so aggressively that several teeth break and he is showered with dusty bits of molars and incisors.

Chris can feel weight starting to press on him. Instantly he's eight years old again. He's back in the tree. The branches are trapping him in a dark claustrophobic cocoon. He knows he's in danger; he's climbed too high without realizing it. He wants to cling to the sticky trunk and wait for rescue, but knows he must keep moving. The walls enclosing him are not made up of nice-smelling pine needles, they are literally trying to grab him and tear him apart. Nobody can save him now. He can only save himself.

He needs to move or die. With all the effort his adrenalized body can muster he rolls hard to the left.

He trips up the first row of bodies and keeps rolling over the fallen corpses until he is parallel with the truck. Three bodies block his only route of escape—under the tank. When he gets to his feet, he thinks of the old coach of the Denver Broncos, Mike Shanahan, who instructed his offensive line to use cut blocks. The huge men would literally dive at the knees of their opponents to open up space for Terrell Davis to run through. It was dirty, but it was effective. He does a cut block of his own, diving at the knees of the two zombies in his way and is slightly satisfied and slightly horrified to hear all of their weakened tendons snap apart like old string. The knees buckle backwards, folding them over in a heap. Chris rolls over their mangled bodies and into the relative shelter beneath the tanker.

He looks for daylight and finds it on the far side of the rig. He rolls out and up to his feet. With most of the zombies on the far side of the tanker, he is briefly in the clear but the ladder on the back of the tank is completely swarmed. Sarah's back is to him as she screams wordlessly into the horde. She could not see through the bodies and had not seen him roll under the truck.

As Chris climbs one of the huge wheels and reaches for the railing on top of the tank, he sees Sarah planning to jump off the other side to rescue him. She doesn't say anything, but he can read her body language and he sees her make the decision. He's so out of breath the world is swimming, but he's able to choke out sound.

"SARAH!! No!"

Sarah turns around to see his hand poke up to grab the rail. She drops to her knees to help him up.

"Chris!! Fuck. Jesus. Fuck!"

Chris pulls his torso up and she helps him swing his legs over and onto the roof. He collapses at her feet, panting in exhaustion.

Abruptly dropping to her knees, she frantically checks his body for injuries. "Where are you hurt!?"

Chris is so exhausted he can barely speak, but he's able to choke out, "I'm OK. I'm OK."

Ignoring him, Sarah turns him over and continues checking for blood, bone or other injury. Chris eventually catches his breath enough to speak normally.

"I'm OK. We have to keep moving."

Sarah looks up to see that all the commotion has attracted another flood of Fred and Gingers. Hundreds stream down the freeway from both directions. Sarah thinks it looks like someone just opened the gates at Woodstock and every Fred and Ginger in the world is rushing to get seats close to the stage. *Grateful Dead indeed.*

The sun is starting to set over the skyline. They can feel it rapidly getting darker and the impending darkness sets off an ancient instinctual alarm that reminds them that humans used to be prey. The onrushers are throwing long shadows on the road in front of them as they charge the truck. The glare from the low sun makes it hard for Chris and Sarah to see the danger converging, but they have no trouble hearing the impacts as one after another zombie runs into the tanker.

The dead are swarming. They start to climb. They're climbing the rig. They're climbing each other.

Chris and Sarah scramble down the tank and onto the roof of the cab. It's obvious that they won't be able to get in through the doors. The zombies block both sides and are packed three-deep.

"The sunroof." Sarah pulls a hammer out of her bag.

Sarah raises the hammer and brings it down onto the window as hard as she can. The glass seems unimpressed by her attack and the hammer bounces off. She tries again. A third time. Chris reaches to try himself, but she lets out a scream of frustration and shatters the safety glass into the cab below. She jumps in through the sunroof feet first, noticeably wincing when she lands. She locks both of the doors while Chris tosses the cat carrier in and falls into the seat beside her.

They are safe. For a moment at least.

"Woah."

Sarah grimaces. "Well that went exactly to plan right?"

"Exactly. Are the keys in the ignition?"

Sarah checks. Her heart drops. "No! Shit."

"You've got to be kidding me! Fuck! Try the shade? That's where they always are in movies."

"And it never makes sense."

"They have to be here. We're in the middle of the highway. A Fred wouldn't have taken the keys with him."

"Yeah, but he might just have easily dropped them outside. If that happened, we're fucked."

"Don't you think I know that?!"

They frantically search the cab, digging through the pair of pants the driver abandoned and pawing through the trash that litters the floor. They are immensely relieved when Sarah ducks her head down and finds the keychain at her feet under an old McDonald's wrapper.

"Thank God."

Sarah pops her head up with a sigh of relief that is immediately choked out when she sees a horrible face on the other side of the window. She is face-to-face with a middle-aged woman. The only that separates them is a thin pane of glass, and death.

The face used to belong to Kathryn McKitrich, a gym teacher at the Heavenly Mercy Catholic High School. She had loved her job teaching the basics of basketball, football and floor hockey to disinterested hormone-poisoned teenagers. It was a simple but satisfying life for Kathryn. She wasn't a nun. She wasn't even Catholic but the job provided a steady salary and benefits for her and her wife Terri. She used to be self-conscious about being such a stereotype: the lesbian gym teacher. But Terri always told her not to be bothered by it. She said if she loved her job that's all that mattered and if anybody gave her shit about being a stereotype, fuck 'em. Kathryn spent twenty years wearing the shorts and holding the whistle. Ironically the Catholics never really bothered her about being a lesbian either. She heard horror stories about gay teachers being fired in Philadelphia and in the south, but at her school at least they pretty much minded their own business. Her boss pretended not to notice that Terri was a woman when she was listed as her spouse on insurance forms. Kathryn assumed this was because her boss, a nun, probably also preferred the company of women and chose life as a nun in a time when it was much more difficult to live openly, or even secretly, with someone of the same gender. It broke Kathryn's heart a little bit, but she wasn't one to question somebody else's decisions if they were happy. Apparently, her boss was.

Kathryn's body had lost an eye somewhere in the circle. The socket had filled with a dark mixture of dirty blood and pus. Her scalp had cracked and started to peel back at the intersection of her forehead and her greying hair. The exposed skull that peeks out from the ever-widening slit in her skin is bright white. As she wipes her face over the glass, the slit opens further, exposing a nest of maggots which gets mashed into the glass. Her jaw snaps open and shut rapidly as she attempts to bite through the window. Her broken teeth make a chilling dry scraping sound on the glass.

Sarah screams and drops the keys. What used to be Kathryn, the dedicated gym teacher stereotype, starts to pound on the glass. It makes a terrifyingly loud noise.

Sarah is now screaming her words without realizing it. "Fuck!!"

Chris grabs her shoulder. "Sarah. Stop. Breathe. You

have to calm down."

"Fuck!"

She retrieves the keys but her hands are shaking too badly to get the key into the ignition.

"SARAH! Stop. Close your eyes. Count down from ten. Do it!"

The pounding on the glass is starting to intensify as more and more hands join in. Many of them are horribly mangled. They have dislocated fingers going in strange directions. Some have missing fingers. Some have missing hands.

"OK. Ten, nine, eight, seven,"

"Keep breathing."

"Six, five, four, three, two, one."

She opens her eyes. She is still frightened but not panicked.

Chris continues. "Move quickly, but with purpose. Put the keys in the ignition. Start the engine."

Sarah starts to think more clearly. Her hands have stopped shaking as badly. "Nice trick. You learn that in one of your secret boy meetings about fighter jets and guns?"

"I saw it on an episode of Lost."

"Ah. Of course. What I wouldn't do for a nonsensical Polar Bear about now."

She puts the key in the ignition and turns it. The motor makes a series of groans and clicks, but the engine does not start.

Chris grimaces for a second then tries to appear calm. He hopes she doesn't see his fear. This is not good.

This time Sarah is the calm one. "It's a Diesel. When it's cold you have to warm up the fuel injectors." She flips a switch and a small light on the dash illuminates. She waits for ten seconds then tries again. The engine roars to life. She puts the truck in first gear and slams on the gas.

The engine roars, but the wheels do not turn.

Chris tries to speak calmly, trying to avoid scaring her again. "What's wrong now? Are you in gear?"

"Yes!" A cosmically intense frustration boils almost instantaneously, making her want to smash something with her bare hands. This isn't fair. None of this is fair. "Shit!"

"Try again." Chris is now having a harder time appearing calm. His mind races for new options. The pounding on the glass continues to intensify. The sound of fingernails, teeth and exposed bone scraping the outside of his window starts to gnaw at the edges of his sanity.

Click... click... click... SLAM!... click... scrape... clack... SLAM!

Sarah puts the truck in gear and presses the gas pedal more slowly. The wheels still do not turn.

"Is there a parking brake?" Chris asks.

"Yeah, right there. But it's not on. Why can't we fucking move!?"

Sarah closes her eyes and takes a deep breath. She feels like somewhere in the cloudy recesses of her mind, there is an answer. She imagines herself pushing through the clouds and rifling through file cabinets that store her life's memories. She doesn't imagine pulling out a piece of paper or anything quite so cinematic; rather the information seems to interrupt her imagination. She opens her eyes with an unlikely grin.

"Wait! You're sort of right. Something this big has got to have air brakes! You have to build up the air pressure in the brake lines before they will release."

She finds the switch for the air compressor and flips it on. The compressor's tiny engine starts to hum and the cab is filled with a hissing noise as the pressure begins to build.

"Look at the gauge. It has to build up to 90 PSI before we can go."

The windows are now completely covered with zombies. They've climbed onto the hood and are fighting to get through the windshield. The glow of the setting sun is almost blocked out by the cluster of Fred and Gingers. Tiny shafts of light peek through the bodies as they shift and swarm, exposing random little flashes of a beautiful sunset. Chris is grateful to be behind glass, but he wonders how long before they break the windshield or discover that the sunroof is wide open.

"How much longer is this going to take?" He asks with a great deal more urgency than he'd intended to convey.

"We're up to forty PSI. Soon."

The hissing gets louder and louder. It sounds like a jet engine warming up from a distance. The pounding and scraping on the glass continues.

Click... click... THUMP... scrape... scree... SLAM!...

Chris discovers that yes, it is possible to be more afraid than he was five minutes ago.

The pressure takes less than ninety seconds to build up, but it feels like a lifetime, especially when a crack appears in Sarah's window.

The gage hits 90 PSI and there is a satisfying beep.

"Yes! What do you say we get the fuck out of here?!"

Sarah depresses the clutch, shifts into first gear and hits the gas. The engine roars, but the tires are barely turning. The truck is completely swamped in flesh, slowing their momentum. But eventually the 380 horsepower engine is too much for the Fred and Gingers to hold back.

The first few zombies get knocked down and are crushed under the enormous tires. Whatever fluids remain in the bodies leak out as they are pulverized and it causes the tanker to lose traction. The tires start to slip and spin giving Sarah the sensation that they are trying to plow through a snow drift. She knows the feeling well. First you get slowed by pushing through the snow, and then you have to deal with the loss of traction it causes. It does nothing to improve Sarah's frustration. But as she switches to second gear, the other wheels find traction and compensate. As the truck picks up speed, it begins to plow a pathway through the naked horde. The truck crushes dozens of zombies, causing the ground to become even more saturated with entrails and human debris. The wheels continue to spin and slide down the highway. Sarah remembers her father's advice for driving in snow.

'*Spinning your tires just makes it worse Sarah.*' She lets off the gas a bit and tries to slow the wheels to get better footing. It's good advice and they eventually pick up enough speed to get some stability.

"Jesus!"

The tanker finally hits fifteen miles an hour, leaving a wake of spatter and twisted bodies behind them.

"Look out!" Chris points at the line of abandoned cars blocking their pathway. They are seconds from crashing into a dusty Toyota Camry.

"Uh, what do you want me to do?! We can't go around. We're going to have to go through!"

The wheels are now firmly in contact with the pavement as Sarah accelerates. They slam into the Camry, flipping it up on its side and smashing it into a Jeep. Glass flies everywhere. The sound from the impact booms its way down the trench and is followed by a series of teeth-clenching metal scraping noises as the tanker struggles to push cars out of its path.

The enormous engine roars as they plow their way down the freeway. Several former citizens of Detroit are trapped between cars and cut in half. After narrowly avoiding a black Escalade, they finally hit a patch of open road and are able to drive in the clear for a bit. Sarah throws the rig into fourth gear and accelerates.

"Why are you speeding up?!"

"We've got to get through that line of cars at the exit."

Chris sees what she is headed for. The off-ramp leading up and to the right is blocked by a line of cars.

Sarah continues. "We need as much momentum as we can get. We're going to have to push through them uphill!"

"Right. But keep in mind we're carrying nine thousand gallons of gasoline. We're a rolling bomb."

Sarah frowns. "Yeah. And there I was thinking we were running out of things that were about to kill us."

They hit the exit ramp going nearly fifty miles per hour. The first car they hit, a Honda Accord, is thrown airborne by the enormous force of the tanker. It flips up into the air, flies off the ramp and slams back down onto the highway below. It rolls once and scrapes along the concrete wall for nearly twenty yards before finally coming to rest. The tanker careens forward squeezing itself between the railing and the row of vehicles that had been attempting to get off Fisher at exit 50. It clips the side of a delivery van and runs into an unfortunate curious Fred who explodes like a bug on the enormous grill. Various body parts fly up and into the windshield causing both Chris and Sarah to unconsciously groan unspellable noises of horror.

They reach the top of the exit ramp and believe they are home free, or at least off the freeway, before Sarah runs into the curb trying to take the corner too sharply. The cab bounces into the air and starts to tip at a sickening angle.

"Oh fuck!"

Chris' momentary sensation of weightlessness causes an instantaneous bout of stomach-clenching nausea. He watches Sarah hover above him as the cab debates whether or not to flip over.

The weight of the tank behind the cab combined with a well-welded hitch is the only thing that prevents Chris and Sarah from death that evening. The hitch holds and the cab bounces back down heavily.

Sarah never loses control of the wheel and continues down the street, but she can taste a coppery liquid filling her mouth. She realizes she must have bitten her tongue pretty badly slamming back down and spits the blood out at her feet. The image of the red splat on her shoes combined with the bitter metallic taste chews at her consciousness. Her peripheral vision starts dimming as she knocks into a parked Volkswagen turning down Woodward Ave.

"Sarah?"

She can hear someone trying to talk to her. It's faint. *Perhaps a dream? Or just a memory?*

"Sarah!!" Chris puts his arm on her shoulder and gives her a strong shake.

She begins to feel the unnerving sensation that the murky world she thought wasn't real, is very real indeed.

"Sarah brake! Brakes!!"

She can see a building approaching. Something about it seems too real to be a figment of her imagination and she realizes that she is still driving and they are about to run into a fast food restaurant. She slams on the air brakes. The pedal shudders under her foot as the cab around her begins to shake. The brakes make an inconceivably loud noise, like a combination of an air horn and a metallic scream. They miss running into a sign for the Golden Arches by only a few feet.

"Sarah what's wrong? Did you pass out!?"

She is still groggy but she fights through the fog. "I'm ok. I just greyed out for a bit. Sorry."

The tanker sits idling loudly face to face with a smiling red and yellow plastic clown. They can see Fred and Gingers starting to stumble around the corner investigating the noise.

"We have to keep moving. It's almost dark. Are you OK to drive?"

Sarah swallows her nausea and grimly nods. She spits another mouthful of blood at her feet. Now driving at a less reckless speed, she navigates the rig through the neighborhood and arrives on the side street next to their parking garage. She kills the engine immediately, knowing each second of noise draws more zombies. They look out the windows and see that, once again, they are completely surrounded. There are not nearly as many there as were funneled into the highway, but enough that they are definitely not safe to exit the truck. A few of them bump into the tanker, but since it stopped making noise, they seem to have a hard time identifying its meaty center.

"There's too many to try and out-run. We'll have to wait for them to disperse. I guess we're spending the night in the cab."

Sarah looks nervously at the broken sunroof above their heads. Chris nods and pulls a roll of duct tape and a tarp out of his emergency bag. He spreads the tarp over the hole and tapes it down.

"Good enough for now. Not like we have any

choice." He surveys the interior of the cab. Opening a curtain behind their seats, he discovers a small sleeping area with a twin mattress. It is littered with more candy and fast food wrappers. Chris grimaces when he discovers a large Gatorade bottle filled with what is clearly urine. Several pictures are taped to the walls that have obviously been torn out of dirty magazines. Chris beckons to Sarah. "We've got the honeymoon suite tonight."

When Sarah looks back at him, Chris notices she looks pretty white. *Maybe she's just overwhelmed?*

"I have something to tell you." She says simply.

"What's that?

"I broke my ankle. When I jumped onto the van."

"What!? You didn't tell me! How did you drive? How could you possibly have-?"

Sarah interrupts him with a grim smile. "I'm going to pass out now. See you in a bit."

She does indeed pass out. Chris pulls her onto the mattress, trying to ignore the occasional suspicious stain on the fabric. He lies her down as gently as possible and looks over her ankle. It is already purple and has swollen up to twice its regular size. He tears up an old sheet he found tucked between the mattress and the wall and attempts to find something to serve as a splint for her ankle. He eventually finds the source of the dirty pictures in a stack of well-worn porn magazines under the mattress. He rolls a couple of them around her ankle and ties them down as tightly as he can with strips of fabric and duct tape. He then takes their two backpacks and uses them to elevate her ankle. He wishes he could give her some pain medicine. They have Advil in their emergency bags, but Sarah does not stir. So he just holds her hand and listens to her breathing.

In ten minutes he has no choice but to sit feeling helpless, exhausted and immensely frustrated by the fact that there is nothing else he can do to help his wife.

"Meeeerrrrow?"

A quiet mewling is floating out from the cat carrier. He opens the cage and Charlie emerges looking about as shell-shocked as Chris and Sarah. He offers the kitten some water from his bottle and Charlie drinks greedily. Chris finds himself immensely grateful for the company as he watches the last of the light disappear behind the grey line of buildings. Soon, the exhausted man and the traumatized kitten sit together in complete darkness. They listen to the zombies shuffle and bump into the cab now and then. It's cold. Their body heat does help warm up the cab a little bit, but the late fall night brings temperatures down to the mid-thirties.

With nothing else to do, Chris has plenty of time to ponder the cold. One of the secrets that homeless people and animals know is that thirty degrees when you are walking down the street to get a Pumpkin Spice latte, or going for a yuppie fall jog is a completely different temperature than thirty degrees when you are stuck outdoors permanently. It's a different experience when ten minutes in the cold turns into ten hours. It begins to seep into all parts of your body, radiating from every object. The cold begins to take on its own characteristics, as if it were a thing not a temperature. It feels stiff and sore, like a bruise.

Chris wraps Sarah in both of their jackets and the two ratty blankets that were on top of the mattress. He sits lookout from the driver's seat shivering with his hands in his armpits.

Chris does not believe in God. Religion has never even been a part of his life and he's never felt the absence of a deity. He's not a secret believer who pretends to espouse atheism out of some sort of intellectual vanity, but then prays when feeling desperate. He truly has no one to ask for help.

But he does realize that for this night at least, he dearly wishes there were something more powerful than himself to look out for them. To look out for her.

But Chris knows that wishing will not make it so.

CHAPTER 12

It's a beautiful morning in Detroit. There is a cold crispness to the air but the sun is shining brightly. Weather like this would normally brighten the moods of the people waking up to it, bright sunlight being such a rarity for this part of the country, especially in this time of the year. It's the type of morning that could make you think that the Lions might actually have a shot against the Packers this Sunday, or that there is a chance Uncle Pete might just be able to contain himself from saying something racist when the turkey arrives at Thanksgiving dinner. But this morning there is nobody in the city that is even aware of the unseasonably cheery weather.

Chris tried to keep watch through the night, but exhaustion eventually took over and he has fallen asleep. He's slumped against the passenger side door with his head resting on the window. Charlie huddles in a ball of fur on his chest.

Sarah is awakened by a sunbeam glaring onto her face and sleepily rubs her eyes. When she tries to turn over, she is rudely reminded of her broken ankle by the shot of red pain that runs up her leg and seems to radiate all the way to the tips of her fingers. She swears under her breath and looks over at Chris.

She tries to muffle her scream behind her hands.

The anguished sound she makes sends Charlie bolting off to the relative safety under the passenger seat. Chris sits up with a start.

Ignoring the agony in her foot, Sarah scrambles away from Chris in terror. Chris frantically looks around for the danger before he realizes it's him she is afraid of.

She stares intensely into his eyes for a moment and is finally able to speak. "Chris!? Is that you? Are you OK?"

"Yeah. Of course. What are you talking about?!"

She points behind him at the window. On the inside of the glass, where he had been leaning his head, the window has fogged up with condensation. Beads of water drip slowly down the glass. There is a spot where his forehead rubbed a section of the water clean.

And yet Chris is very much aware of himself and very much not a zombie.

"Why? Why didn't it infect you?"

"I don't know!"

He stares at the glass for a while and wipes the wetness off his forehead with the sleeve of his shirt.

"Wait. It's not from the outside. It's from inside. From my breath."

Sarah lets out a weak sigh of relief and is silent for a moment.

"How is your ankle?"

"Hurts like a motherfucker."

"You should take some Advil."

"Yeah, I should take a lot more than that, but not until we get inside."

Chris looks out the window to see how many Fred and Gingers are still around. There are a few of them shuffling down the block and one walking down the alley next to the tanker.

He nods. "Not too bad. We should be OK if we're quiet. But how are we going to get in if you can't climb up the fire escape?"

"We don't have to climb. I have the key to the garage's emergency exit."

"What?! You had that the whole time? Why didn't we go out that way in the first place?"

"Well I'd rather not advertise to the Fred and Gingers that we're ever in the garage. Who knows, they might remember where the noise came from. Besides, you were so excited about playing Indiana Jones." Her paragraph is punctuated by a coughing spell.

"Are you OK? You look a little feverish."

"I'm fine. Let's focus on getting inside."

Chris begins to packs up their gear. As he puts a reluctant Charlie back in his cage, they plan their escape. After a few minutes, they open the passenger side door as slowly and quietly as they can. Chris goes first and then helps Sarah down. She winces with each step, unable to put weight on her ankle.

As quietly as possible, but without hesitation, they work their way around the front of the rig and look down the alley toward the garage's side door. Sarah leans heavily on Chris, holding the cage in her other hand.

Slowly walking down the alley between them and the door is what used to be a thin black woman. She must have been truly beautiful before but now she is shrunken and hollow. The skin on the bottoms of her feet have worn down to the point where they can hear the 'click... click... click' of her fibula bone hitting the pavement as she walks in no particular direction.

Propping Sarah up, Chris takes a baseball out of his pocket and holds it in his right hand. He looks at Sarah to confirm she knows the plan. When she nods, he tosses the baseball over the Ginger's head, well past the door. The ball bounces off the pavement and runs into a couple of metal trashcans at the end of the alley. The body that used to be inhabited by Kirsten ("Not Kristen!"), an aspiring model who dreamt of moving to New York City and modeling clothes on Project Runway, turns and begins moving in the direction of the noise.

Chris and Sarah move in behind her towards the door. They're making more sound than they would like to, but they mutually and instinctually decide that speed is more important than stealth at the moment. Sarah has the key out by the time they reach the door and long before Kirsten, not Kristen, turns around, they are safely in their parking garage.

"Wait here. Let me find something we can use as a crutch." Chris helps her down to the floor and leans her up against the cement wall.

He dashes up the ramp looking into the cars he knows are unlocked. Last week, while searching the cars looking for supplies, he marked those he was able to get into with spray paint. He wasn't about to try breaking into any locked vehicle for fear of setting off the car, but there were a handful of folks who, inexplicably, left their cars unlocked or had been exposed in the garage and dropped their keys. He opens doors and goes through various backseats before he discovers exactly what he needs on the roof of a Subaru Outback he had first disregarded because it was locked. Atop the roof sits a ski rack with two sets of downhill skis and, more importantly for Chris' purposes, two sets of ski poles. Chris takes a set of poles down and duct tapes the bottom of them together tightly. Then he spreads the tops about eight inches apart and uses duct tape to create two handles. He puts one handle in the middle for her hand and another higher one for her armpit. His work is crude, but the design is sound. Her weight will pull the poles in tight on her shoulder and give her enough support to get inside at least. He returns to Sarah and presents his invention.

"Well done MacGyver."

"Thanks. Let's get inside Tiny Tim."

With his help, Sarah is able to get back to her feet and upright. They slowly start limping their way through the garage. About halfway up the second floor, she stops him.

"Are you OK? Is the pain too bad? I can try and carry you."

"No, no. I'm fine. Just wait a minute. Listen."

"To what?"

"The baby. I don't hear it."

They quietly move closer to the car that the baby is trapped in. Listening carefully, they hold their breaths—but there is no sound. Chris instinctively steps between the car and Sarah.

"Could it have escaped?"

"I don't think so."

They cautiously walk up to the car and look in the window. The baby is motionless.

"I think it's dead."

"It was dead a long time ago. But I think you're right. It looks dead dead."

They both can feel the intangible presence of death, that pit of your stomach instinct that tells you the thing you are looking at is not asleep. That the electrical impulses that cause brain activity, as limited as it may have been in this case, have ceased.

Chris carefully opens the door and they stare at the baby for a moment before he dares borrow Sarah's crutch and gently poke at it. What they see initially horrifies them. Then it fills them with a recently unfamiliar feeling: hope.

When the pole touches the baby's arm, it starts to crumble before their eyes, as if it had been mummified for a thousand years. Dust puffs out as several dried chunks of skin fall off and disintegrate like old plaster. It is no longer even a body, just a dried husk. And it is, completely, dead.

"How could it have dried out so much? Shouldn't it take years to look like this?"

Sarah thinks for a second. "Maybe the parasite or whatever consumed all the water?"

Chris shakes his head. "Eek. It makes my skin crawl. It's so disturbing."

Sarah takes a short intake of breath. Her eyes flash with excitement. Her expression is almost rapturous. "No it's not! Holy shit! Don't you know what this means?"

"What?"

Her smile is wide. After all the fear and exhaustion that Chris has felt, her smile is healing even if he doesn't understand why she is smiling yet. She takes him by the shoulders. "They're going to die! They're going to starve to death! Or dry up! Or whatever. But these fuckers are going to die."

Chris is stunned. Then he lets out an unconscious yelp. He hesitates for a moment and says the slightly obvious but sobering truth.

"We just have to make it long enough..."

"Right. But if this one died already, the adults don't have long!"

Chris looks into her eyes. They are tired, bloodshot and obviously still in a great deal of pain, but they look as happy as he has seen them since this all began.

"Holy shit. We're going to survive."

*

Sarah lies on the couch reading a novel. Her injured ankle is elevated and splinted as well as a well-intentioned but distinctly amateur husband can accomplish. The dirty magazines have been replaced with the air cast that Chris picked up at the drug store. He returns from the upstairs office store room with a bottle of pills.

"OK. Are you sure these are the right antibiotics?"

"Yeah. Those are the ones. I doubled checked the book."

"I wish I knew better how to tell if your ankle is set properly."

Sarah gives him a comforting grin. "It is. Remember, this is the third time I've broken this bastard. It feels alright. Hurts like hell. But alright."

"Keep drinking the water. You don't want to get dehydrated."

"I know. But we don't have an unlimited supply. We barely have enough to get through the winter."

"We'll worry about that later. Now I have to find a way to keep you warm. You look like you're freezing."

Sarah pulls the blankets up to her chin. "I'm fine."

Chris sits down beside her on the couch and puts his hand on her forehead. "Bullshit. You're shivering. I'm pretty sure you're running a fever. Are you sure you don't want the big kid pain meds?"

"Nah, I'm fine."

"Ok, but take the ibuprofen to keep the swelling down."

"Yes nurse."

"Now, it's time we got ourselves out of the Stone Age. The generator is just about ready to go. I think it's time to get it some fuel."

After the incredibly difficult and dangerous job of acquiring the tanker, the final task of hooking up the generator seems simple by comparison. He heads through the passageway onto the third floor of the garage. Chris takes three ten-gallon gas cans out of the bus and sets them next to the generator. Then, he carries a fifty foot hose to the open side of the garage and drops one end of it down to the street, on top of the tanker. On the other end of the hose, he attaches a foot pump.

Because Chris had remembered to swipe the tanker manual from the cab, he knew it was useless to attempt to connect his garden hose to the industrial nozzles on the bottom of the tank. So his plan was to open one of the smaller access holes on the top of the tanker and put the hose into the tank directly. If he secured it carefully, he could leave the hose hooked up to the tanker and pump gas all the way up into the garage as the winter went along.

Chris walks down the three levels and emerges out the side door. He carefully surveys the alley for Fred and Gingers. With the coast clear, he quickly walks to the tanker and climbs the ladder. The end of his hose lies across the truck where he had dropped it. His best access point is at the vapor vent located on the top back of the tank. When he opens the vent, he can smell the sickly sweet smell of gasoline. Much to his relief, his hose fits into the pipe and he feeds in six or seven feet until he hears it make a watery clank on the bottom of the reservoir.

Chris then uses silicone caulk to fill the extra space between the inside of the vent and the hose to make it water-tight and covers the whole thing with plastic sheeting and duct tape.

A small part of him is disappointed that Sarah isn't there to see his act of manliness. He always felt that he could never quite live up to the manly image of her father. His father-in-law was a large man who had been hardened by decades of farm work. His body seemed to creak and pop with every movement. He used to complain that his joints were tired from all of the repetitive lifting and hauling, but to Chris it always seemed like the complaint was also partially a boast and partially a judgment of those who hadn't done as much physical work in their life.

The main thing that always made Chris feel insecure around his father-in-law was the differences in their hands. Her father's hands were huge. They were callused and scarred from years of toiling outdoors. His left pinky stuck out at a slightly odd angle from a break that never healed correctly. They were gnarled and ugly but incredibly strong and Chris' hands seemed small and delicate in comparison. As a pianist, his hands were his life, so he took very meticulous care of them. He kept them protected from the weather, moisturized them regularly and kept his nails neat and trimmed. When they shook hands, Chris felt weak. And even though he was annoyed at himself for such a sexist thought, it made him feel womanly.

Sarah's father never directly made mention of Chris' lack of farm-toughness, but he noticed that when her father took Sarah and her brothers out to the barn to show off the new tractor or to go out snowmobiling or fix their fences, Chris often didn't end up on the invite list. He didn't think his lack of inclusion was meant to be mean. They just figured he wouldn't be interested. In truth, he wasn't really interested, but he would have appreciated being included. Heading back into the garage and walking back up to the generator on the third level, he imagines his father-in-law giving him a quiet nod of approval.

As he starts working the foot pump, he has to restrain himself from cheering when gasoline starts pouring out of the hose and into his gas can. He fills each of the cans carefully and then fuels the generator. He hesitates before pressing the start button. On the box, the generator promised to be the quietest on the market but the prospect of it sounding like a lawnmower makes him nervous. He begins to think of various ideas to dampen the noise, but pushes the thought away, at least temporarily. Right now they need heat.

He presses the starter and the engine sputters for a second, then purrs to life. It's not silent, but at least it is consistent. He hopes the drone of the engine will eventually blend into the ambient noise and not draw too much attention.

He plugs a heavy duty extension cord into the bank of electrical sockets on the side of the generator and begins to un-spool the long orange cable. He goes through the makeshift door they installed to keep their passageway weather-tight, and carries the cord onto the upper ring of the library. He leans against the railing and looks triumphantly down at Sarah. She smiles back up at him.

"How'd it go mighty hunter? What have you killed and brought back to your wife's cave?"

He tosses the cord down to where she is laying on the couch. "Plug in your space heater and find out."

She does. The power light turns on brightly and she can feel the heating coils starting to cycle up. She gratefully applauds him as he slides down the ladder like a firefighter.

"You did it. You're a badass."

"We did it."

Chris plugs the cable into a power strip, reattaches the heater and plugs in a lamp. When he sits down next to her and switches on the light, they take a moment to silently bask in the cheery glow. The sixty watts thrown off by the bulb are a welcome return to normalcy and combined with the warmth being provided by the space heater, it's almost cozy.

Chris puts his arm around his wife. "Power! Now was that so hard?"

Sarah swats him playfully. "Not funny. You can be cute when my ankle is healed."

"Bah. So... how long is it appropriate to wait before I hook up my Xbox?"

CHAPTER 13

C*hris only played one truly great performance in his entire piano career. He played more technically perfect shows than he was able to count, but there was only one concert he truly played as well as he knew he could. After his meeting with Professor Granden when he was twelve, he knew that if he wanted to be successful, he would have to develop a love of playing. And, in his secret practice room in the basement of his high school, he did.*

The problem he was never able to solve was that despite this love of playing, he was never able to love performing. As soon as an audience was present, something in Chris' brain shut off his feelings. As if the spell created by the music that allowed him to access his emotions could only be in effect when he played in solitude. He felt trapped in a perverted version of Cinderella where the clock stuck midnight the minute someone was listening—even Sarah. Perhaps in the deep dark recesses of his mind, he knew that his relationship with music was just too private to share, that to be witnessed while he was emotionally entwined with his playing seemed voyeuristic and invasive.

The spell was broken only once. It was the concerto he performed on the night his father died.

It wasn't supposed to be a special performance. He was scheduled to play Edvard Grieg's Piano Concerto in A Minor with the Ann Arbor Symphony Orchestra. The theater was run down and the attendance would be sparse, but it was a gig and he and Sarah needed the money.

That evening while Chris was showering in their hotel room—before putting on the same old tux he wore the night he met Sarah—the phone in their room rang. They had only been married for two years and she still traveled with him to all of his concerts. He kept telling her there was no reason for her to sit through a concerto he had performed countless times, but she always insisted on going. She was putting on her earrings when the call came in. It was Chris' mother.

"Oh, Hi Rita! Chris is in the shower, do you want me to have him call you back when he gets out?"

"No, no. No need. I just wanted to get him a message."

Sarah didn't really want to be on the phone with Chris' mother without him there. She was a difficult person to talk to one-on-one. She always seemed slightly off, slightly distant. "Oh OK. Are you sure I can't get him? He just went in."

"No, it's fine. I just thought he should know that his

father died this afternoon."

Sarah was silent. She's wasn't sure how to respond. Rita had just announced that her husband had died in such a completely matter-of-fact manner, she might just have been reminding them to wear hats because it was going to be cold that day.

"Oh my God, Rita, I'm so sorry. I-... let me get Chris!"

"No, it's alright. He wasn't well. It's a good thing."

"I didn't even know he was ill? I'm... you must feel... Is there anything I can do?"

"No, no. Just tell Chris. I assume he'd want to know. I've got to run. Bye."

"But-"

Rita had hung up. Sarah stared at the receiver in her hand dumbfounded until she heard the shower stop.

"Who was that?" Chris called from the bathroom.

"Uh..." Sarah didn't know what to say. She debated whether it was a good idea to tell him now, right before a concert, or if she should wait. Is waiting dishonest or kind? What is the right thing to do here? What would he want? *Still undecided, she chose to stall for more time. "Nobody... it was the hotel calling to let us know that we can have a late checkout."*

"Oh sweet!"

The shower resumed.

Sarah sat down on the edge of the bed dumbly staring at the faded blankets. Chris' family always freaked her out a bit. They had very little contact with Chris and he didn't talk about them very much. She saw them at the occasional holiday and at their wedding of course, but their relationship always felt perfunctory.

It was obvious that Chris and his father hadn't been close, at least not since he was little. But it was equally obvious how powerful an influence his father had been on his life. Sarah couldn't always tell whether Chris was subconsciously trying to please or piss off his father, but his actions always seemed to use his father's opinions as a reference point.

She felt paralyzed.

Fuck! I have to tell him, but before or after the performance? Oh God, what the hell am I supposed to do here?

She couldn't seem to make a decision so she kept stalling and pretended that everything was normal. Chris, being remarkably intuitive about other people's emotions, even if he was fairly dense about his own feelings, could tell that something was wrong right away. When he got out of the shower he saw her still sitting on the bed staring at the wall. When she noticed him, she jumped a bit and started fixing her hair.

"What's going on? Are you OK?"

"Yeah, I'm fine. Sorry, I just spaced out there for a second."

"Is there something on your mind?"

"No! Not at all. We should get moving, we don't want to be late!"

"I'm not playing until after intermission."

"I don't want to miss the first half. I love Beethoven!"

She seemed to be talking very loudly without realizing it, over-selling her cheerfulness. Chris was disconcerted. She never kept secrets and he wanted to know what was bothering her so much. He asked a few more times, but she continued to deny that anything was amiss. They sat together in the back of the theater and watched the first half of the concert in silence.

An hour later, they stood backstage while the orchestra re-tuned. Chris pulled Sarah into the wings next to the wall of thick ropes that operated the theater's fly system.

"Seriously, what's wrong?"

"What makes you think there's something wrong?"

"You're acting weird. I know something is up."

She sighed. "Yeah, OK, there is. But I'll tell you after the concert OK? Intermission is almost over. You gotta go play!"

"Come on, tell me now or I'll be so distracted I won't be able to remember the music."

Sarah frowned. She knew she was trapped but she also knew that whatever the right decision was, it definitely was not telling him less than a minute before he went on.

Chris pressed the issue. "Oh shit! You're not pregnant are you?"

"No. No. I... uh..."

"Then what!?"

"Fuck. That was your mother on the phone. Your father died."

Chris froze. His face didn't change, it just stopped moving. "Oh. OK."

"Chris I'm so sorry. Are you alright?"

"Yeah, of course. I...uh..." The sound of the orchestra tuning finished. There was an expectant silence from

the stage. Chris nodded. "That's my cue. See you after the concert."

He walked onto the stage and sat at the piano to a smattering of applause. The conductor raised his baton and looked at Chris. Chris nodded again, the timpani rolled and he began to play.

From the very first notes, the iconic falling octaves used in so many movies, TV shows, and cheesy commercials, Chris felt completely different. Something about the music felt strange. He would best describe it as 'loose'. His fingers were hitting all the right keys at all the right times, but he felt like there was magically more space—more space in the room, more space between the keys. He even felt like there was more oxygen in the air. It was a completely indescribable sensation. He wasn't used to feeling anything but tight when he performed. Now he seemed to be feeling ten different emotions at once. He felt sadness, relief, freedom, joy and despair all at the same time. He was so overwhelmed by all of his emotions, he was losing track of the math of the music. He wasn't thinking about his fingering or the exact tempo markings, he was just reacting to the sound. He was somehow completely in charge of and completely at the mercy of what he was creating. He wasn't just exactly replicating what Grieg wrote more than a hundred years ago, he was expressing what he was feeling right in that moment.

That night, Chris was free. He was absolved of the expectations and restrictions he had felt his whole life and was free to feel and do whatever he wanted to. His father was dead. His father was no longer watching him, no longer telling him to 'play it right' through *rum-thickened lips.*

Chris noticed that he was grinning to himself. It was a surprise. He had always been teased by his friends for having such a serious face while he played, as if he were angry at the music. Chris knew he wasn't angry, he wasn't feeling much of anything, he was just concentrating. But that night, he was grinning. He was sad, but he also felt lighter than he had in his entire life. He caught himself quietly humming along to the melody.

Most of the people in attendance that night probably couldn't explain why the performance was so great, but something special was in the air and they all knew it. The audience members who may have been dragged there by a spouse—and expected to be bored silly—forgot all about checking their phones for fantasy football updates. There was no typical rustling of programs in the quiet sections. The audience barely even shifted in their seats.

Chris knew he may never be able to replicate a performance like that again. But all that mattered to him was that Sarah had been there to witness it.

If Sarah had one big secret in their marriage, it was the fact that she had not been there to hear him play that night. After watching him walk onto the stage, she went to go take her seat in the house. Unfortunately, because she was unfamiliar with the theater, she walked through a door that she thought would lead to the seats and actually ended up in the alley behind the building. Feeling incredibly dumb for not noticing that she had walked outdoors instead of into a theater, she turned around quickly to grab the door, but it had already closed and locked behind her. Sarah had been so distracted that she might as well have walked onto the moon. She swore loudly, then winced realizing that she needed to be quiet with the concert resuming. She ran down the alley and returned to the front doors. They were locked. Because Chris was playing after the intermission, they had already closed the box office and gone home.

"Fuuuuuuuuuuuck!"

She screamed in frustration and rattled the doors, it was no use. Nobody could hear her. She had no choice but to wait outside until the concert finished and sneak back in as the crowd left. Tears streaming down her face, she sat down on the sidewalk and berated herself for all of the mistakes she made that night that left her sitting on the dirty sidewalk while Chris played a concert seconds after finding out his father had died.

When she heard the surprisingly enthusiastic applause, she jumped up and waited for the first patron to exit. It took longer than she expected, usually some asshole leaves before the applause, but nobody did. She had no idea that the concert had been a transcendent experience for Chris, but she knew from the cheering that something important had happened. She had to restrain herself from punching the glass.

Eventually she got back into the theater and found Chris sitting on a folding chair backstage. He looked shell-shocked, but when he saw her he smiled one of the most radiant, bittersweet smiles she had ever seen.

"Sarah. I did it. I may never be able to do that again, but I'm so grateful that you were here with me."

Her heart broke for him and without hesitating, she

told the biggest lie of her life.

Chris didn't have a miraculous musical breakthrough and become a rich and famous pianist after that performance. The moment of Hallmark movie catharsis didn't last forever. In fact he has not yet performed with that much freedom and joy again. All of the feelings that were able to escape that night slowly but surely got bottled back up as he attended the funeral, helped his mother handle the estate and eventually went back to his normal life. Freedom is not an easy thing to accept or integrate. It took more courage than he had. But Chris was happy to know, that at least for a moment, that freedom did exist.

***

Chris does not set up the Xbox that night, but he does do something else they've been looking forward to doing for months: he charges Sarah's iPhone. There is no cellular service of course, but by sharing the earbuds, they can enjoy listening to music together. They start with 'Florence and the Machine', and then switch to the first movement of a Mozart piano concerto and alternate back and forth between her selections and his. Charlie sits on Sarah's lap batting at the wire.

Sarah scrolls through her music library for a moment and looks up to see tears leaking down Chris' face.

"What's wrong?"

"Nothing. I just realized that when those fuckers die out I get to play my piano again."

Sarah smiles and takes his hand in hers. He continues.

"I'm just happy I can even look at the piano again. I haven't been able to face it since... it was too painful. And right now I can't touch it, but I know I will be able to someday. Maybe soon, maybe not, but eventually. It's like finding out that a loved one you thought was lost at sea is still alive and on their way home."

"I guess even in the apocalypse, nothing is permanent."

"Other than death."

Sarah looks back down at the phone, her balloon not quite popped, but slightly deflated by the grim reminder. "Other than death."

Chris puts his arm around her and gives her a hug. He watches her search for her next selection and something catches his eye. "Wait? Is that date right?!"

The phone's display reads: 9:12 PM, November 29th.

Sarah shrugs. "I guess we lost a couple of days."

"Shit! It's your birthday! I almost forgot your birthday!"

"Because we thought today was the 25th. Besides, I think the days of birthday parties are done sweetheart."

Chris is already on his feet. "Nonsense! I have a surprise for you!"

"Is it more Advil?"

"Of course!" He tosses her the bottle. Then jumping into his infomercial voice, "But wait, there's more!"

Chris dashes through the library and heads down the rope ladder into their kitchen. He is gone for a moment, giving Sarah a second to appreciate his childlike enthusiasm for celebrating things. When they started dating, she hadn't paid any attention to her birthday in years. But on her first birthday after they were together, he arrived at her door holding a large chocolate cake with candles blazing. It both made her laugh and made her a bit melancholy. Ever since, he never failed to produce a cake for her on her birthday.

After a couple of minutes, Sarah spots the top of his head as he awkwardly climbs the ladder holding a bottle of wine under his arm and a plate in his teeth.

"Close your eyes!" He mumbles around the plate.

He reaches up and sets the plate on the library floor while he finishes climbing. On it is a set of five hostess cupcakes each sporting eight blazing birthday candles. He puts aside the wine and brings the plate towards her. He moves slowly so he doesn't accidentally blow out the candles.

"OK! Open your eyes!"

She laughs and claps her hands. "You've got to be kidding me."

"Happy 29th Birthday!"

"How many is that?"

Chris keeps moving toward her. He's very pleased with himself for remembering to sneakily grab birthday candles on their trip to Home Depot.

"I think it's the eleventh time we've celebrated it."

She grimaces. "Ah, so that's why there's almost more candle than cupcake."

"You're the hottest woman in the world. And always will be."

"I might be the only woman in the world."

"Technical victory is still victory!"

Having finally reached her, Chris leans down to give her a kiss. In doing so, he causes one of the top-heavy cupcakes to overbalance, tumble to the floor and roll under the couch.

"Oops!"

She laughs and shakes her head. "This might be the eleventh time you've dropped my cake too."

Chris bends down to retrieve the cupcake from under the couch. It rolls all the way to the back and comes to rest against the wall. The candle's flame starts to dance with some forgotten junk mail that still seems to live in every corner of their house despite the fact that mail is no longer being delivered.

"Oops! Candles!" Chris drops to his knees and attempts to reach it with his hand. The paper begins to crisp and darken from the heat of the flame.

"Shit! Put it out."

Chris desperately tries to reach it, but his arm is too short. The paper alights with a crackle and the fire starts to spread at an alarming rate.

"Fuck, I can't reach it! Hand me your crutch."

They can smell the acrid smoke coming from a Sears catalog. They only become truly alarmed when the curtain that drops down between the couch and the window begins to catch fire too.

"Forget the crutch, move the couch!" Sarah pushes herself up with her one good foot and hops around their coffee table to get out of the way. She picks up a blanket from the floor, ready to hand it to Chris.

He yanks the couch aside exposing the fire and releasing a cloud of thick black smoke that billows up from where the fire was attempting to burn the flame-resistant fabric. Sarah tosses him the blanket and he smothers the flame before it can spread. Once the mail is extinguished, he flips the couch and pats out the last small tendrils still trying to consume the bottom.

He coughs a couple of times and rubs his eyes. The smoke is still hanging around in a grimy haze, but the fire is out.

Sarah's heart is still racing. "Jesus. That was close."

"Right? Now that we have power, maybe we should give all the open flame a break."

"That sounds like a good idea because you sir, are a total spaz." She smiles at him affectionately. The excitement has not made her forget his kind gesture. "A very sweet total-"

BRRREEETT! BRRREEETT! BRRREEETT!!!

The shrieking noise startles them so much they don't speak for a second.

BRRREEETT! BRRREEETT! BRRREEETT!!!

The fire alarm is screeching bloody murder. This is not a home smoke detector. This is a heavy-duty commercial system. It is loud. Really loud. Strobe lights start flashing from the emergency fire boxes hung throughout the building. Chris and Sarah need to shout to be heard.

Chris stares dumbly at the flashing red box. "How could the alarms work? They don't have power!"

"Battery backup! Fire alarms can't stop working just because the power is off."

"I thought the batteries would have run out by now! Fuck, I should have thought-"

BRRREEETT! BRRREEETT! BRRREEETT!!!

"Does it matter now?! We have to turn it off! We're going to draw in every fucking one of them for miles!"

"You're right. The control box is in the basement. I'll go kill it!" Chris starts running towards the rope ladder leading downstairs.

"Wait! Stop! We have a much bigger problem."

"What could be a bigger problem than this?!"

BRRREEETT! BRRREEETT! BRRREEETT!!!

Sarah struggles to her feet. She grabs her make-shift crutch and starts to hobble towards him as fast as she can.

"The sprinklers! They turn on automatically after five minutes. And they use the water from the exposed tank! We'll be infected!"

The gravity of the situation finally hits Chris. He cuts her off. "OK. There must be some sort of way to shut them off."

"I'm sure there is but I have no idea how. I've never had a fucking sprinkler system!"

"There must be a valve on the roof. Let's go. Even if we can't shut it off, we'll at least be safe up there."

BRRREEETT! BRRREEETT! BRRREEETT!!!

"I can't climb fast enough! Besides we need to shut off the alarm too. Water or zombies. Either way we die."

"But-"

"I can go down a lot faster than I can go up. I'll try and deal with the alarm, you shut off the water. We have maybe three minutes left. Go!!!"

Chris runs up the ladder to the balcony and heads towards the trap door that leads to the roof. His heart is pounding and his ears are ringing from the shrieking alarm but his mind is laser-focused on the task at hand. *Stop the water. Save Sarah.* He is halfway up the second ladder to the trap door when he realizes it's going to be pitch-black on the roof and he needs a light. He lets go of the ladder and drops back down to the floor. He races back to the doorway that leads to the balcony. He silently thanks Sarah for having the forethought to insist that they leave a flashlight in every doorframe for emergencies.

BRRREEETT! BRRREEETT! BRRREEETT!!!

*

Sarah reaches the rope ladder leading down to the kitchen. Ignoring the searing pain in her ankle, she swings her bad foot over the edge and puts it on their homemade rung. It's dark in the hallway below but her vision is overwhelmed by the dizzying combination of flashing strobe lights and the stars she sees every time she puts weight on her broken ankle. Her stomach lurches but she knows she must keep moving. Or die.

BRRREEETT! BRRREEETT! BRRREEETT!!!

*

Out in the dark quiet streets of abandoned Detroit, the shrieking alarm cuts through the silence with the subtlety of a chainsaw. The strobe lights flash from the second and third floor windows of the library. It's like a beacon.

BRRREEETT! BRRREEETT! BRRREEETT!!! The sound ricochets through the city like a homing signal. In a radius of over a mile, countless Freds and Gingers turn their heads and look up. They hear the alarm. They can sense the flashes of light. They can't see it but they can feel it, like the light that gets turned on while someone is sleeping. They start walking towards the library.

*

Chris throws the trap door open and climbs out onto the roof. After spending what seems like twenty minutes, although it is less than ten seconds, frantically searching with his flashlight, he locates the old wooden water tower. He sweeps the beam of light back and forth looking for the pipe connecting the water tower to the sprinkler system. Of course all of it is buried under the tarps they put down and he has to tear through them with his bare hands. There is no time for gloves or weather gear. He has no choice but to ignore the fact that if there is a pocket of water trapped in the plastic, he's completely unprotected. Sweating despite the cold, he starts yanking them back. There must be a shutoff valve. There must be.

*

Sarah unconsciously cries out in pain as she steps off the ladder and runs toward the basement door. There is no time for crutches. There is no time for limping. She puts her full weight on her broken ankle with each step, hearing sickening crunching and grinding noises from the mess that her foot has become. She can feel shards of bone grating together but she snags the emergency flashlight from the kitchen and shines it at the door down to the basement. The batteries are almost dead, but she can see the bench they pushed in front of the door to remind them to never go down there.

"FUCK!" She throws the worthless flashlight aside and starts to push the bench out of the way. They intentionally barricaded themselves out of the basement when it became flooded with contaminated water. They did this as a safety measure. The fire alarm and sprinkler system were supposed to be safety measures. The irony of them being put in mortal peril by two layers of safety precautions is not lost on Sarah.

"Damn it! Why didn't we think of this?!"

*

Chris locates a pipe sticking down from the bottom of the water tower's wooden base. It's old, rusted and probably made out of lead. He frantically looks around for a valve, but there is none that he can see.

"Where is it?! Damn it!"

Shining his flashlight at anything that looks like it might stop the flow of water, he begins to follow the pipe along the roof.

*

Sarah throws the basement door open with a grunt. It's heavy and thick, obviously original, not a thin cheap modern door. It creaks and shudders on its unbalanced hinges.

BRRREEETT! BRRREEETT! BRRREEETT!!!

Sarah looks down the stairs and sees nothing but inky blackness. The strobe lights are making it impossible for her eyes to adjust and she knows she'll be blind down there. Flash. She is relieved to see that there is another strobing alarm box in the basement. With each dazzlingly bright flash of light, she sees images of the stairs leading down, the large red fire alarm control box, and the two feet of standing water covering the entire basement floor up and over the first two stairs. The strobe gives the illusion that she is actually looking at still photographs shown one at a time. Every second, the flash refreshes the image. She sees that she's going to have to reach out over the water to access the box. One slip, one toe in the water and she's dead.

BRRREEETT! BRRREEETT! BRRREEETT!!!

What she does not see is the object perched on top of the red box. Tucked and forgotten behind the wiring pipe by the fire code inspector two years ago, sits a large industrial flashlight covered in a thin layer of dust.

*

Outside the library, thousands of bodies move towards the noise with a singular purpose. Less than thirty seconds after the noise begins, the first few zombies start trying to break through the front of the building. They don't distinguish between doors and walls and windows. They can't tell the difference. They just want in. Blocks away, more and more turn down the streets and head towards the library. They don't all arrive at once, but they are coming.

*

"Shit!"

Sarah works her way down the stairs. Unnoticed tears trace their way down her face on tracks first laid by pain sweat. With great effort, she gets to the third step from the bottom. It's the last step not submerged in the scuzzy standing water. She is dizzy from the incessant flashing lights, the agony from her foot, and her own fear, but she holds tight to the railing and leans out over the water. *The fire box is right there, just focus, Sarah, focus!* She opens the access door revealing a glowing LCD panel that displays "FIRE DETECTED: TO CANCEL ALARM, PLEASE INPUT CODE."

"Code?! What fucking code?!"

*

Right before the pipe angles straight down and into the building, Chris sees what he's looking for: the shutoff valve. It looks rusted and corroded, like it has been sitting outside in the elements for decades. Chris is dismayed to see that it is a twisting knob like in a shower instead of a straight lever.

"Shit."

Thinking 'righty-tighty, lefty-loosey' he tries to turn the knob to the right. It does not budge. Eighty years of dirt, rust, corrosion and lack of maintenance has practically welded the valve open.

"GODDAMNIT!!"

*

BRRREEETT! BRRREEETT! BRRREEETT!!!

Sarah frantically mashes buttons looking for some way to subvert the fire department cancel code. She thinks there must be some sort of 'false alarm' button. It's no use. The box stubbornly waits for a code that a helpful fireman will never input. She knows she has less than a minute before the sprinklers turn on. There is no time.

"Goddamn it! Fuck you!!!"

She starts to smash the box with her fists. She puts her entire weight behind each thrust showing no regard for her hands. She is once again reminded of a lesson her father taught her. Not how to swing a bat, but how to throw a punch. *It's the same principal, kiddo. It's about transfer of energy. Plant your feet, turn your hips and put your entire bodyweight into your fist. Almost like you aren't punching with your arm, you're punching with your torso and your fist is just along for the ride.'*

The screen snaps. Buttons fly off and land in the water. She hears a suspicious crack from her pinky. Her hand starts to bleed.

*

The veins in Chris' neck bulge out from his effort to try to get the valve to turn. He's desperate to get more leverage, but his hands can only do so much.

"FUCKASSMOTHERFUCKER TURNYOUFUCKINGSHITFUCKER!!!"

He screams with frustration and considers trying to break the pipe. *It's lead so probably not that strong. Of course I would probably be showered in the water and killed, but maybe Sarah would be safe?*

Finally, after a knuckle-cracking surge of desperation, the valve starts to turn. Crunchy bits of rust fall from threads that are being used for the first time since the Depression. Once loosened, the valve turns quickly and Chris closes it as hard as he can.

He screams a wordless cry of triumph to the sky and falls onto his back.

*

More and more zombies start pushing on the walls

of the library. The first few have been joined by ten more. Within minutes, they are joined by a hundred. Mindlessly pushing. More coming. So many more coming.

*

Sarah's pinky finger is clearly broken, sticking out at a ninety degree angle. It's a sickening sight, but she has no awareness of it.

BRRREEETT! BRRREEETT! BRRREEETT!!!

She smashes her way through the keypad and LCD screen. There is a now a hole in the panel exposing the wiring and she doesn't understand why the alarm hasn't stopped yet. She reaches her hand into the hole and starts tearing out the wires themselves. Sparks start arcing out of the box and Sarah is hit with a series of small electrical shocks. Undeterred, she exposes the motherboard, a flat rectangular piece of circuitry covered with sockets and microchips. She knows this is the brain. She reaches back for one last hit and with all of her might smashes the motherboard into pieces.

Two things happen with that punch. One, the alarm finally ceases, though the strobe lights continue. Two, the flashlight on the top of the box finally slips off its perch and starts to tumble. It plummets down, pulled by the inexorable force of gravity, toward the flat dark body of water. It takes two flashes of the strobe light to tip, fall and make contact with the surface. Sarah sees them both, like two Polaroid pictures. In the first flash Sarah sees it just starting to tip and slide over the side. In the blackness, unseen by anyone, the flashlight has time to rotate two full revolutions on its axis. In the second flash of the strobe, she sees it hit the murky black water.

When the flashlight hits the surface, the impact is especially violent because the water had been so calm. It had sat undisturbed by currents or rain or wind. There were no fish or frogs moving around in its depths. It had been completely placid like cool dark glass.

The water splashes up and out, showering droplets in all directions. Sarah doesn't see the drop that hits her right arm. But she feels it.

*

Chris only allows himself to lie down for the length of a single breath to celebrate his victory before he scrambles to his feet to go help Sarah. He can hear the alarm screaming below him and has almost reached the trapdoor when it abruptly ceases. He pauses for a second waiting for the next scream. It doesn't come. His heart leaps.

"She did it. Yes!! Sarah! You did it! We did it!"

He charges down the trapdoor and into the office. He feels like his feet are barely touching the ground as he rounds the corner out of the office and onto the balcony. He slides down the ladder into the main library still shouting to Sarah and laughing with relief.

*

One hundred bodies pushing at the library walls are joined by two hundred more. With the entire perimeter of the building completely covered with the dead, those who can't reach it directly start climbing each other and pushing on the zombies in front of them. They are creating second, third and fourth rows of bodies all pushing together.

*

When Chris reaches the top of the rope ladder leading down into the kitchen, he falls to his knees looking down for Sarah.

"Sarah! You did it! I turned off the sprinklers! We're-"

Chris is not prepared for what he sees.

Sarah is standing in the kitchen looking back up at him. She is completely naked.

Sarah faces him, still, almost frozen. Her arms lay limply at her side. A slow trickle of blood leaks out of her right hand creating an expanding cluster of red droplets on the floor. She is only lit by the incessant strobe lights, but he can see that her face is completely expressionless.

All of the sound drops out of Chris' head. He can't hear the pounding on the walls. He can't hear Charlie's meowed protests of all of the commotion. He can't even hear his own words. "Oh my God."

Sarah stares back at him, fighting hard against the growing blackness in her head. She fights to speak. She fights for consciousness. Using the last of her desperate determination, she wills her mouth to move.

"Chris..."

The plywood barricades at the front door and windows start to shudder and buckle. But Chris hears only Sarah.

"Sarah!!!"

Her eyes seem to be losing focus and she looks unstable on her legs. He can see how hard she is fighting to stay in her body, but she's losing the battle.

The last word he hears comes out as a choked mumble, but Chris understands it.

"...love."

It is at this moment that the barricades fail. All of the wooden barriers blocking the doors and the windows simultaneously explode inward. In an instant Sarah disappears in an avalanche of zombies and a cloud of splinters and pieces of plywood.

Chris screams with an agony he did not think was possible.

"Noooooooooo!!"

He falls back on his heels, his hands dropping lifelessly to the floor beside him. She's gone. All of his hopes and dreams, plans and ambitions drain out of him. His very will to live is evaporating like mist.

"There are all sorts of dangers all around us... They can all hurt you. Kill you even. What happened today was that you did something stupid... Whatever happens after that is your fault..."

Chris watches with little interest as dust, glass and bits of plywood fly through their hallway and into the kitchen. He rather detachedly notes the feeling of simulated slow motion created by the strobes continuing to flash.

With the last shred of self preservation he feels, perhaps only because it was Sarah's last request, he pulls the rope ladder up just as the first wave of the dead crash through the wooden detritus littering what used to be *their* home.

He drops the end of the ladder at his side and watches as dozens of Fred and Gingers flood into the hallway where the stairs had been. They are trapped down there, unable to climb up to where Chris sits motionless.

He tries to push all thought out of his mind, but his father's voice keeps interjecting. *"You didn't have an accident, you fucked up! So now you're paying the price. That's how the world works kid. Darwin was right..."*

A moment passes. Perhaps ten minutes, perhaps only seconds. Chris has lost all sense of the passage of time. The first few layers of zombies have been crushed up against the wall like victims of a soccer riot. Under all of the intense pressure, the Fred and Gingers literally start to break apart. They're being smashed together and compressed while they continue desperately clawing at the wall. They have become incredibly dry and brittle. Limbs crack and snap like dry twigs underfoot. The body parts filter down to the floor. An arm here, a leg there, a skull or two fall to the dusty hardwood, creating a terrible pile of dried flesh and bone. Each Fred or Ginger that breaks apart is replaced by another, each standing a few inches higher than the last.

Chris remains frozen. As he watches, he absentmindedly thinks of the fable of the mouse that falls into a bucket of cream. Using exceptional determination, the mouse keeps swimming for so long he churns the cream into butter and is able to climb out of the bucket to safety. Chris lets out a dry giggle. He wonders if he is going insane.

Wave after wave of zombies crash into the wall below his feet. They continue slamming into the hallway and each other, cracking apart and falling to the floor. The mound rises just a bit higher with each body. Within an hour they have begun to form a makeshift ramp of themselves. Chris has not moved. He's not sure why he would move. *To what purpose?* He wonders why he's ever done anything.

The first hand to reach the top of the stairs brushes his shoe and attempts to grab hold of his foot. It used to be a female hand. It's the hand that belonged to a hardworking owner of a struggling craft ice cream shop.

The hand on his shoe breaks Chris out of his dissociative state and he stands up slowly. He wills his eyes to come into focus and looks down at the horrifying sight below him. Normal sound slowly returns and he can hear the horrible thrusting, crunching, cracking, scraping sounds of all of the Fred and Gingers trying to get at him.

He realizes he has nowhere to go but up. This had always been Sarah's plan, to keep retreating higher and higher. They might be able to climb over each other in the narrow space of the hallway, but they would never be able to do it in the expanse of the library.

But the plan was always to retreat *together*. Sarah's body is down there somewhere in the mosh pit of zombies on the ground floor. She is probably being trampled into something unrecognizable. *Of course Sarah is no longer Sarah. She is one of them now.* He doesn't want to think about it, but now that he is awake and in the world again, it's all he can think about. He is using their survival plan alone. The guilt eats at his insides like some sort of ravenous creature.

Still, he climbs the ladder up onto the library's balcony, breaks it off the railing and tosses it back down as what used to be Shirley climbs over the lip of the stairs and reaches the main library level.

He looks around for Charlie despite himself.

"Jesus. Why am I looking for a fucking cat?!"

Chris hates himself for trying to rescue an animal when he has already failed his wife, but a new voice in his head, perhaps Sarah's, whispers *'because you can still care. Because you can still love...'*

Charlie is nowhere to be found. Chris knows that he won't be found unless he wants to be, and he's probably dead anyway.

"Fuck it."

Chris goes through the passageway into the garage. Maybe if they are focusing on the front of the library, he can escape out that way. He runs to the open side and looks down. His plans are immediately dashed. The street is wall-to-wall flesh. He can't even see the pavement through the maze of Fred and Gingers. It's like Mardi Gras for zombies.

Knowing escape is completely impossible, he returns to the balcony of the library and watches as a hundred zombies claw around the room attempting to get up. The dead work their way around the space trampling all of their, now his, possessions. The TV falls with a crash. The space heaters are flattened. All the pictures of their wedding and their road trips across the country get knocked off the walls and ground into the floor. More and more charge into the room. They're blindly clawing at the walls and each other.

Chris winces when one of the piano legs gets kicked out. The Steinway crashes to the floor with a horrifying jangle. The noise only seems to increase the intensity of the zombie's thrashing. More and more attempt to pack themselves into the library.

Time passes. Chris doesn't know how long he sits there, nor does he care.

The Fred and Gingers continue roiling around, but they can't get up to the second level. They can't climb the walls and—because their furniture was in the center of the room, away from the balcony—climbing the couch, piano, or the table was useless too. They climb each other, but are not organized enough to reach the balcony twelve feet above their heads. The doorway up from the kitchen has become clogged with bodies. The attack has reached a stalemate.

Chris sits silently watching as his life literally crumbles around him.

"The world is just math. All of our hopes and dreams and feelings all boil down to making the right

calculations. Do the math right and you'll never fail. If you do fail it's because you didn't think through the consequences and you got what you deserved... There is no such thing as a victim."

He does not cry. He is too sad to cry, too sad to feel. He is numb. More time passes. Hours. Eventually, despite his pain, or perhaps because of it, he falls asleep, clinging to a picture of Sarah.

*

A hand closes on his arm. Chris jolts awake. He's confused.

What's going on? Why am I on the floor? Oh no. Please no... Then more practical thoughts barge their way into his consciousness. *Did they get in through the garage? The roof? Where?*

He twists his arm back and opens his eyes. He is face to face with a child. Or what used to be a child.

Somewhere behind the cold white eyes and the dry cracked skin caked in blood and grime used to live a boy who cracked himself up inventing the word 'boobucopia.' A nice boy who cared about football, comic books and Karen Tyson's bra strap, not necessarily in that order. A boy who knew what it felt like to feel threatened, cornered and trapped. But he somehow never turned that feeling into a desire to threaten anybody else. Now, the boy who used to be called Kevin no longer cares about such things. He is just hungry.

For a moment Chris just stares back at the creature

Kevin has become. He marvels at the fact that the small body could have survived this long in the horde. *How has he not trampled? He must be tough, or lucky. Lucky... right.*

Coming to his senses, Chris frantically kicks at the child zombie and it falls back down to the floor below. He realizes that the boy had somehow climbed one of the double-length curtains up to the balcony. He dashes around the perimeter of the room yanking them up.

There are still hundreds of bodies down there, but some seem to have been trampled and some have expired on their own. In the corner of the room, a Ginger that appears to have sagged down and died is spontaneously crumbling to dust.

With the curtains removed, Chris see a bit better. The light in the library has that grainy grey quality of the first break of dawn. Something about the idea that the sun will rise, that there will be another day, cracks a dam in his head. *If there is going to be a tomorrow, than this is real. What happened to Sarah is real. She's really gone. Gone forever.* Chris knows that he will have to face the dawn without her, alone.

The tears finally come and he sobs until he is truly exhausted. Until he is truly empty.

After an hour, he runs out of tears. He's just thirsty.

I need some water. Water...oh... After a split second of being distracted by practical thinking, everything comes flooding back. *Oh right... water killed Sarah.*

Chris remembers hearing someone describe grief as a process of forgetting and remembering over and over until the new reality becomes a permanent part of you, like a scar. *Who said that? Who cares?*

He expects to cry some more, but nothing comes out. Eventually, he stands up and walks into the office. He forces himself to pick up a bottle of water and sit down at his desk. When he tries to twist the cap open, his hands are shaking so much he drops it. Water pours out, creating an expanding puddle on the hardwood.

"Fuck!" He falls to his hands and knees, instinctually reaching for the bottle, but stops. *Why bother?*

Chris sits down on the floor behind his desk. From his seated position, he reaches into the drawer and removes the gun he promised Sarah he had thrown away. He leans his back against the desk and looks at the weapon while the rest of the water spills out.

"*But... but it wasn't my fault.*"

"*Not your fault!? There's no such fucking thing. You're not a cripple or a moron... There is no such thing as a victim. Take your medicine like a man.*"

He raises the gun to his temple. On second thought he puts the barrel in his mouth, aiming the gun slightly up like he has seen in the movies. He closes his eyes and takes a deep breath.

"Mrrrow?"

Chris opens his eyes. He does not remove the gun from his mouth nor does he take his finger off the trigger. Charlie is standing in the doorway leading back into the library. Chris wonders where he has been all this time. *In some secret hiding place that only cats know about?*

He tries to say "Go away" but the sound is muffled by the gun in his mouth. It sounds like "Gooo waaaa" to him. It's a silly noise. He is surprised when he can't contain a giggle.

"Goo waaa!" He repeats. His body starts to shake in the tentative place between a laugh and a sob. "Goo waa aarrrrreee!"

Charlie does not go away. Chris starts to laugh in earnest. *Fuck you Dad! You didn't account for feline intervention.* The cat walks up to him and nuzzles his elbow, brushing against the grip of the gun.

Chris stops laughing. The sadness returns, but he is defeated. He lowers the gun and sets it at his side. Charlie climbs into his lap and Chris starts to pet him slowly.

"Go away Charlie."

*

A day passes. Chris can't bring himself to even stand up, but he sits in the office with Charlie and forces himself to stay alive at least. He has no desire to keep doing the basic things to sustain life: eating, drinking, sleeping, breathing, but he knows that Sarah would have wanted him to. It's not enough to get him off the floor, but it's enough to make him keep taking in oxygen.

He doesn't bother to look down into the library to check on the Fred and Gingers, he can hear them stumbling around and bumping into each other. He wonders if it might be the tiniest bit quieter down there, but he doesn't care enough to really think about it.

*

On the second day, Chris wishes he had access to their bathroom. Something about feeling such a basic and banal desire brings the tears back and he spends much of the day alternating between silently and loudly sobbing. The Fred and Gingers are definitely less active. He goes to the railing and looks down to discover that more than a third of them have expired. The floor is covered with a strange granular substance. It drifts in little piles and dustings like sand kicked onto a boardwalk.

The rest of the bodies mill about blindly, walking

through their own remains as if they were going for a stroll on the beach. Chris figures, at some point, that sand might be all that is left of the human race. Dust to dust.

*

On the fourth day something truly horrible occurs to him. Even though Sarah got turned, and had probably been trampled by the horde, her body was fresh. It wasn't going to turn into dry residue or powder; it was still going to be flesh and bone. In time he may be able to dispose of the zombies with a broom and a dustpan, but Sarah's body was still going to be there. It was going to be mostly human, and even if it was just a bloody pile of tissue, it would still be her.

The instant he has the thought, he vomits up the pack of stale Oreo cookies he had eaten for breakfast.

"I don't know if I can do this Charlie."

The kitten doesn't respond. Charlie seems to have recovered from all of the commotion and has accepted the new reality with the ease of a simpler creature. He cheerily bats a bottle cap across the floor at Chris' feet.

*

On the fifth day, he begins to brainstorm ways to get the rest of them out of their (his) house. The zombies can't get to him, but he is trapped in the office. It's a stalemate and he is tired of waiting. When he investigates the street again, he sees a similar scene to what is playing out in the library on a much larger scale. Hundreds of zombies have fallen and died, while thousands more wade through their half-decomposed companions.

The solution ends up being simple: he needs another diversion. Grimly reminding himself that there are no bonus points for creativity, he decides to set off another car alarm. The noise will draw them out of the library and hopefully away from his block. The problem is he can't get out of the building to trigger the alarm.

Then, with a hint of embarrassment—because he doesn't want to remember why he had it out in the first place—he remembers the gun. *I can just shoot a car. That should set it off. I wonder how far a bullet can go?*

Chris knows nothing about guns and when he stands on the roof and selects an Audi parked a block and a half away, he's not sure what to do. *I know there's a safety on it somewhere... Probably this switch here?* When he flips the switch he thinks is the safety, the ammunition cartridge drops out of the grip and clatters at his feet.

"Shit!"

He jumps back as if it might bite him, but nothing happens. When he retrieves the cartridge and collects himself he is able to giggle at his own fear of the gun.

"Well at least I know it's loaded."

He eventually figures out how to reload the pistol and release the safety. He takes it in both hands and aims it at the car. He is well aware that he has almost no chance of hitting the car he is aiming at, but he hopes he will get close enough to hit one of the cars on the street. Any alarm will do. He winces and pulls the trigger.

It's loud, but he expected it to be deafening. He missed the Audi, but had at least fired the gun safely. Heartened, he takes aim and shoots again. It takes five shots, but eventually he hears the wail of a protesting alarm. He knows he won't be able to turn it off, but he is beyond caring. *They'll probably destroy it soon enough.*

When he returns to the library, the Fred and Gingers are already heading for the exit. They clumsily bump into the walls and each other in search of the noise, but they eventually start finding their way out. Chris hears thump after thump as one by one they fall into hallway.

*

On the sixth day, Chris wakes with a strong desire to clean himself up. He smells terrible and is covered with dust, sweat and tears. Snot from crying had formed a crust over his unshaven beard. For whatever reason, this morning he feels that it is time to start taking care of himself. He takes a bottle of water and washes as well as he can. Most of his clothes had been in their bedroom on the ground floor but he finds a fresh t-shirt that had been drying on the balcony when they were overrun.

He looks over the railing again to check on the Fred

and Gingers and finds them pretty much finished. They're mostly either gone or dead. One Fred is still alive, but has fallen down and slumped against the wall. The only motion Chris sees is his jaw dryly opening and closing and an occasional tired twitch. His legs have already begun breaking down, melting back into the earth, a sand castle slowly being eroded by the tide.

He is no longer a threat.

Chris realizes he doesn't have a way down to the library floor. The wooden ladder that used to be attached to the balcony sits a story below him in a pile of zombie dust. Then he remembers the curtains. If they held the weight of the boy zombie, then it might hold his. He yanks one of them down from the window and ties it to the railing. Steeling himself for what he is going to find, he tucks his trusty hockey stick under his arm, and awkwardly climbs down the thick fabric to the floor below.

He surveys the devastation in the room. Almost everything is destroyed—their furniture, their keepsakes. He can't bring himself to inspect the piano too closely.

The sound of the dusty remains under his feet sends a chill up his spine. It makes a crisp crunchy noise when he steps on it that reminds him more of dry arctic snow than beach sand. He dispatches the last Fred with the end of his stick, breaking through the skull as easily as if he were poking through a snowman.

"Ick."

He knows he has to muster the courage to look

down the empty stairway into the kitchen. He doesn't want to go anywhere near it, but he must face Sarah's remains. She deserves more than rotting in pieces on their kitchen floor. As he approaches the edge, he feels his stomach lurch, he really doesn't want to see this. He looks anyway.

To his surprise he doesn't see a huge pool of blood in the center of the room. He doesn't see her body anywhere. He wonders if she was trampled into so many pieces that she might not be recognizable. With a revolted sadness he thinks that maybe their dusty remains could have acted like the sawdust a janitor puts on puke in an elementary school.

"Oh Sarah. I'm sorry."

He tosses the rope ladder down and descends into the kitchen below. It would have been pitch black in there, but since the windows and doors had blown wide open, he can see well enough to search. With a shudder of disgust he wades through three feet of human snowdrifts that accumulated where the stairs would have been, and reluctantly continues searching for what remains of Sarah.

Thump.

Chris jumps backward in surprise. He hadn't realized that there were any zombies still down there. He whirls around holding his hockey stick in front of him. He doesn't see anything moving.

Thump.

It's coming from the basement. Behind the thick wooden door, something is moving. Chris runs through all of the possibilities in his mind. It could be a

Fred or Ginger that got pushed down there by the horde. The door could easily have been slammed shut in all of the chaos and trapped one of them in the basement.

Then another idea occurs to him. *Maybe Sarah's body ended up in there.* Could the zombie version of her have been trapped in the basement and now is trying to get to the circle? Chris is not sure if he can face seeing her like that, but what choice did he have?

Thump.

"Oh God. Sarah..." tears start falling again. This is the hardest thing he's ever imagined doing. With a sob, he opens the door. It creaks and shudders in his hands—which are already shaking—and he steels himself for the grim reality behind it.

The sound is almost inaudible. Out of the pitch darkness, comes a dry desperate whisper, more croaked than spoken.

"What... took you so long... husband?"

ABOUT THE AUTHOR

Keith Varney is a theater geek who grew up on a dirt road in Vermont who—after a detour at opera school—ended up in New York City writing—and occasionally performing in—musicals. He is a Star Trek nerd, a hockey nut (go Bruins!), fantasy football champion and walking contradiction. After becoming an award-winning writer of musical comedy, the next step was obviously an apocalyptic horror series. He has written Book, Music and Lyrics in various combinations for I GOT FIRED (Best American Musical - DIMF, Theater for the American Musical Award), ELWAY: THE MUSICAL, THE OTHER SEX, JOSHUA: THE MUSICAL, PIE EATER, BLOODY BLOODY ANGELA LANSBURY: MURDER SHE WROTE LIVE & SCOOBY DOOSICAL. He has also written songs for *Submissions Only*, *Hot Mess in Manhattan*, *See You Lighter*, *My Mother is a Sex Therapist* & *Dystopia Gardens*. As an actor he has performed professionally in musicals including *Les Miserables*, *The Producers*, *The Full Monty*, *Titanic* and *I Got Fired* (Best Actor in a Musical - DIMF). He has a degree in classical voice from the Eastman School of Music. He now lives in Astoria NY with his wife Jillian, who is a Broadway actress. "The Dead Circle" was his debut novel. For more information, please visit www.keithvarneywriter.com.

THE DEAD CIRCLE SERIES

The story continues in **Beneath The Snow** (The Dead Circle – Book 2). Available on now in Paperback and Digital Download.

Chris and Sarah's quest for survival continues in the aftermath of the fall of Detroit. Battered, alone and newly homeless, they must find a new place to live as winter overtakes the city. Contaminated snow covers everything. Touch it and die. But what lies beneath the snow might be even more dangerous...

If you liked the "The Dead Circle"—or even if you hated it—feel free to drop Keith a line at keithvarneywriter@gmail.com.

Made in the USA
Middletown, DE
18 September 2018